Yellow Moon Justice

This is an indie-authored, indie-published work.

Fiction under the pen name JoJo Riley
Yellow Moon Rising (Book One)
Yellow Moon Justice (Book Two)

Nonfiction under the pen name Pjo Riley
Atheist in Church – on heaven and other mysteries
Postcards from Planet Eldercare – the final frontier

Novel due in summer 2025
The Patron Saint of Lost Souls

More info at www.pjoriley.com
Cover design by Lynne Pierce

Special thanks to cultural consultants Danialle Rose, of the Cheyenne River Sioux, and Thomas Ghost Dog, of the Oglala Nation, for their invaluable insights into culture, history, and language; and for Thomas's permission for the use of his hometown of Manderson, South Dakota, nearby to which his grandfather William Ghost Dog sponsored the first rodeo held on Pine Ridge Reservation land.

My gratitude endures.

A Yellow Moon never forgets.
Raylene Little Moon

Pine Ridge Reservation, SD
1936

With the odors of her uncle's fire — scorched bone, cordwood, smoldering wool — in her nostrils and hair, Raylene Little Moon drove out of the bad lands, the *makhósica*, and south through the Pine Ridge Reservation. She carried the turtle doll's cash hidden away. Her cow pony rode securely in the van behind Raymond's truck, her truck now. Ray, her father's twin brother, had been her second *até*, her second father. She was still digesting what he had done and admitted to, and what he had said, but because he had talked in riddles at the end, she wasn't certain what could be believed and what could not.

Under skies at one moment blue, the next gray with clouds, she drove with her window half open to cool the heat of her burdened heart. For years, she had led a mostly solitary life, but still, she swallowed hard at the thought of being the last living member of her immediate family.

The dirt roads she and Ray had traveled north were now nearly impassable after two days of sporadic snowfall that turned creek beds into bridges of ice. Jouncing along, she formed the beginnings of a plan in which she uncovered the details surrounding her sister Annie's death in Kansas City.

She felt certain now that Ray had blamed his brother for Annie's death, but questions remained regarding who had arranged Annie's burial and exactly where she had been laid to rest. Discovering those names and details should, she hoped, bring a sense of peace about losing her only sister, if ever there could be peace. On the other hand, gaining this knowledge might do just the opposite. It might haunt her. She sent a message to the sky. *Annie, I will not give up until I find you.* First, though, she needed to deliver the hard news about Ray to Wilma Manheart.

The streets of Oglala were damp with lingering patches of snow, but the sky was clearing. This being October, the weather might change again within an hour. Raylene pulled to a stop across the paved road from Wilma's market. Even though on the prairie, death was as common as the cycle of seasons, bringing the news of Raymond's death to Wilma pained her a little. She sensed that he and she had been close.

She had just set one boot on the street when the market door opened and Wilma stepped out, hand on her heart and a stunned look on her face. Raylene crossed toward her as Wilma said, "I saw the truck and thought —. But it's you. That means Raymond is ..."

"Dead. I figured you should hear it from me."

Wilma dropped her hands. "Just like my dream." She looked left down the road then off to the right, as if somehow the landscape had changed. "Did he fight you?"

"I gave him no opportunity." Her uncle had claimed to have waited for her, but he had also called her by her mother's name, so perhaps his thoughts had already been reaching for the spirit world. What she did not say to Wilma was that Raymond had insisted on dying near the place that held the ashes of Raylene's mother.

Wilma squelched a shiver before standing straighter.

"I would like to buy supplies," said Raylene.

The woman turned and Raylene followed her into the market. Rough as its wind-scrubbed exterior looked, it was the only market serving the southwest quadrant of the reservation. It also held the town's postal window and therefore enjoyed the luxury of electricity for lights and cold cases and a telephone. Wilma crossed to warm her hands at the pot-bellied wood stove. She said, "Did he say my name?"

Raylene thought a moment. Comforting words seemed in order. "He wished for you to be alright." Wilma studied Raylene for any sign of fabrication but Raylene held steady under the woman's gaze until Wilma glanced away. Raylene turned toward the nearest shelves to give the woman a stitch of privacy.

"Will you go back to your job?" asked Wilma. She meant the H-bar-H, where Raylene worked as a ranch hand, and where the boss had fired her for needing time away to find Raymond, her father's killer.

Raylene selected cans of vegetables, a small sack of corn meal, and another of flour. "My sister's death remains a mystery," she said, crossing to the front counter. The next part was harder to admit: "Ray suggested that she died from drinking bad hooch in Thomas's saloon."

"Could that be true?"

"Perhaps. But Thomas was honorable, that's what I believe, so I am of two minds about it."

Wilma pulled an empty grain sack from behind the counter and began to pack it with Raylene's items, adding a tin of lard and a hunk of bacon.

Raylene caught Wilma's eye. "Did Ray ever tell you that *he* was my father?" The notion that her mother had married one twin brother while loving the other still brought confusion. Both had been a father to her, yet Thomas had officially been Father while Raymond had often acted as a father.

Wilma pursed her lips and swallowed hard. At last, she shook her head before spending more time than necessary penciling Raylene's purchases into the market ledger. Wilma knew more than she was saying, but did that even matter now that Raymond was no longer here to provide more details? Was it Raylene's folly to have listened to a dying uncle's mumblings, half desiring them to be true while unable to accept them at face value? It occurred to her that Wilma must have loved Ray to have kept his secrets.

Wilma said, "Oh. A letter came after you left. It's been sitting here." She moved to the general delivery slot behind the far end of the counter and returned with a crumpled envelope.

The letter's initials and return address were for Kansas City, Missouri but not for the undertaker's location. Raylene dropped the letter into her sack of purchases as if it held no import when in fact its arrival surprised her. For all the wrong reasons, she was acquainted with just one person who had those initials. Ordinarily, she addressed her own problems and made her own amends, but she was about to head for Kansas City where she would be an outsider, at a disadvantage. A Kansas City insider might help her gain access to those with answers about Annie's death and the letter was from just such a person.

Raylene's travel followed a south-easterly route and was slow-going, given the need to regularly exercise her piebald in open stretches of grassland. To keep predators at bay and ward off the prairie cold at night, she quartered Kota inside the horse van under blankets. She herself slept with all her clothes on inside her bedroll atop the truck's narrow front seat. At first, stars made pinpricks of background through the windshield, but eventually the view fogged with her breath so that the morning sun's appearance resembled light through gauze.

For each of four mornings and three nights, she lit a fire and cooked some simple food made from supplies left over from Ray and those she had purchased from Wilma. During driving hours, undulating country glided past — grasslands and farms, bony livestock, abandoned homesteads crumbling beneath the incessant wind, and burbling streams here and there. Every few hours, she unloaded Kota and walked him about to let him stretch his legs amid grasshoppers whirring up from the earth.

Late on the fourth day, she motored through healthier-looking fields on the outskirts of Kansas City, Kansas, diminutive sister to Kansas City, Missouri, which lay east of the Kansas River, itself a branch off the "Big Muddy" Missouri River. The Kansas side was smaller and sparser in its display of businesses that were necessary to country life. The Missouri side, with its extensive railyards and grand rail station, had grown the fastest.

Of the few stables operating on the Kansas side of the river, one was run by German-Polish brothers by the name of Brugmann, who spoke with thick accents and kept their property neat as a city park. The old man could be harsh, but Raylene trusted him. People who tended properly to domesticated animals were okay by her.

She pulled into the stable drive and proceeded to park on the dirt yard. A bearded man came out of the stable to greet her. "Hello, Heinz," she said, climbing down from the truck. "I have not seen you in some time." When he paused as if trying to match a name to her face, she said, "I am Raylene, daughter of Thomas Yellow Moon."

The man raised an eyebrow. "*Ja*. I remember you. It's been a few years." He looked down at his hands then back at her. "We heard about Thomas's death, and your sister. A shame."

"Raymond is gone now too."

He was silent a moment. "He had a way with horses, Raymond did."

Raylene changed the subject. "I brought my Kota to stable with you, if you will also put him on grass sometimes. And I would park this van out of your way while I am in town."

"Put it over there. Your pony must be expert with cattle by now."

"He is surefooted and smart." She did not add, *My last best friend.*

"I will meet him and see for myself."

She nodded. Heinz would assess Kota's coat and mane, his alertness to new surroundings, the gleam of intelligence in his eyes.

After arrangements were concluded and Kota delivered to a stable stall, Raylene pulled her rig around to a spot out of the stable's traffic patterns and unhitched the van, balancing its tongue atop a stack of bricks provided for the purpose. Then she drove to the nearest service station for fuel and a map of Kansas City, Missouri.

In the late afternoon she drove across the Kansas Avenue bridge to the eastern, Missouri, side of the city, proceeding until she reached a neighborhood of houses with yards full of trees. In the glow of early evening, gold and brown leaves skittered along the pavement and across the yellowing lawns. She parked and got out to stand before a house that by Oglala standards would be a mansion, but in this city was probably average. This particular house, painted a dusty blue with white storm shutters, appeared to silently watch Chestnut Avenue through half-drawn drapes that gave the house a shy look. By now, she had memorized the letter Wilma had handed over. This was its sender's address.

After a moment, Raylene advanced to the front porch and rang the bell, which sounded a distant chime. After a pause there came the sound of footsteps within and shadowy movement behind the leaded glass pane to left of the front door. When the door swung open, there stood the railroad detective who just weeks ago had tracked her to the Pine Ridge. Through the screen door, his reddish hair looked slightly disheveled. He leaned his left arm in its thick plaster cast against the doorframe as if for balance. He pushed his eyeglasses up with his other hand as recognition lit his face. "Miss Little Moon," said John Murphy, "this is a surprise."

Upon hearing the front door chime, Murphy had struggled to finish pulling his necktie free with a lack of grace that left it crumpled. For the last few weeks, his broken arm had impeded almost every activity he attempted, from bathing to dressing to driving. He had learned to scribble notes with his right hand while balancing his notebook on his cast, but the ambidexterity he had once practiced in childhood now proved less graceful as he wielded a toothbrush or parted his hair with his "wrong" hand.

This was the hour when the mechanic who had agreed to fetch his automobile for service was due. Awhile back, his coupe had suffered cosmetic damage during a journey on rough roads, and recently begun to drip oil. Nothing serious, he hoped. As the door chime faded away, he had swung through his bedroom doorway and strode to the front of the house, pulling his coupe's ignition key from his pants pocket.

Beyond the screen door, though, stood no mechanic, but a smallish shadowy shape backlit by the fading light of day. A moment passed as his brain processed the details he could make out: a western hat, canvas barn coat, leather-looking pants, the last person he expected to find on his doorstep — Annie Moon's younger sister, whom he'd last glimpsed in South Dakota. He worked to keep his pulse in check. There was much about this self-contained woman that intrigued and attracted him. The wicked-looking knife he'd known her to carry was probably concealed by her coat.

Raylene said, "I've come to ask for your help regarding my sister's death."

The last time Murphy had seen Raylene Little Moon, she was growing smaller in his rear-view mirror after having remedied a dire situation he'd been caught in. But things had changed for him, requiring him to decline her request.

When he didn't speak, she continued. "Your letter was some time reaching me." A page she carried fluttered a little in her hand.

Murphy's thoughts were racing about how he wished to see her in better light, to gauge if current reality compared with his memory of her face from their encounter in the undertaker's parlor. He took a half step to one side. "Will you come in?"

"Not unless you meant what you wrote. You offered help."

Murphy paused again. *Always best to think before speaking.* He knew which line from his letter had brought her here. "After reconsidering, I struck through that wording. I may have been mistaken to write you like I did. I was feeling ..."

"Relieved that your life had been spared and you escaped with only a broken arm? You followed me across Kansas and Nebraska to accuse my dead sister of possessing jewelry that was not hers."

"I had hoped you might know if she had hidden it or given it away."

"Your thoughts are for jewelry given by your boss as gifts and later wanted back, while my thoughts are for how my sister died and if any identifiable person was the cause. I came here thinking you might help me. I recall doing *you* a great favor."

Murphy felt his face go hot and was glad to be in shadow.

His recollection of her favor was as clear as his recurring dream of being back in the wind-scoured reservation saloon surrounded by angry men. He licked his lips and leaned against the doorjamb. The cast on his arm altered his gait and posture and now, after a day's work, he felt the tympani section in his lower back begin its beat of discomfort. "Miss Little Moon, I am no longer assured of my own employment after your compatriots stole my boss's cash, along with my own, adding to the expenses incurred and inflaming his ire. Mr. Campbell is still weighing matters and I am trying to remain on his good side."

When Raylene gazed through the shadows at him, he nearly faltered. She was in the right. But when she failed to speak, he added, "I sympathize, I do."

At last, she said, "Sympathy is of little help. Without assistance from someone with the knowledge and access I lack I will be forced to take an approach that might annoy some people."

He felt her words as a warning concurrent with his position on the wrong side of her request. Also, on the wrong side of what his boss wanted. He gave a small groan as a nerve in his back shot pain down his right leg. "Miss Yellow Moon, won't you please come in? Maybe we can come to an understanding."

"Your wife might not appreciate me in your home."

Murphy inhaled at the mention of his wife. "She is elsewhere for the foreseeable future."

"But you remain married."

Murphy nodded.

"Mr. Murphy, surely you can understand my need for answers. If you cannot grant me the assistance I need, I'll take my leave. The day grows short and I need to secure lodging."

"Hotels might not ..." He lifted his good hand then let it

drop.

"I'm sure you are right. Good night, Mr. Murphy."

"Good night," he said to the back of her. She was already descending his porch steps on her way to a dark truck parked opposite the house. The paper she carried was surely the letter he had pecked out on a borrowed typewriter in a Rapid City hotel because that way, no one in a Union Pacific office would catch him in the act of writing to a person of interest in an investigation, unofficial or not. After what she had done for him, he felt he owed her more of what he knew about her sister.

It was true that in his letter he had mentioned an inadequate police file. But that was before Campbell's wife had noticed a pendant necklace and pink-gold ring missing from her vast collection. Before the wife could fire their housekeeper, his boss wove a fantastical fabrication and now, with his boss's wife in danger of discovering Mr. Campbell's lie (and thus his involvement with Annie Moon), Murphy was under fire for his failure to find the missing jewels. He had been asked to unjam his boss's marital problems though he could hardly agree with his boss's indiscretions, which ran counter to his own practices. Helping his boss, though, would save his own job. Though Raylene Little Moon had not offered to assist further regarding the jewelry, Murphy sensed that *somehow* she could be of help to him.

October 22, 1936

Dear Catherine,

It has been too long since I last wrote. With my good arm in a cast, I now attempt typing, not my strong suit. We are in a warm spell, but your mountain location might already be under snow. Your Nurse Jeffries said the almanac portends an early Colorado winter.

My boss is in a rage lately, no thanks to the unfortunate events of late last month. He blames me, but honestly, the blame starts with him and a girl he must have met in a saloon. I've put that wrong as she bears no blame and is deceased now. The saloon part is conjecture. I don't know how they met.

Mr. Campbell is sufficiently angry with me about his stolen funds to now assign me the most meager cases. He ~~ciites~~ cites my injured arm as justification but I know there is more to it. Of course I did not intend what happened. I was there on his orders. When he decides that I am sufficiently inadequate, unfair as it might be, he will fire me.

In any event, between your father's legacy and our savings, you will be provided proper care no matter my circumstances. I sign off with best wishes from afar.

Your husband,
John

Two

As was his practice, Murphy entered the Union Pacific Railroad freight offices just after 7:00 a.m. He liked to check in before walking to a diner that served the surrounding neighborhood. When he dropped a letter in the outgoing mail basket, Georgia, one of the early morning secretaries looked up.

"A letter for your wife?" she asked. "That's sweet."

"I suspect she's beyond thinking my letters matter, and that's alright."

She smiled wryly. "Maybe they matter to you."

Words eluded Murphy whenever he tried to explain the sanitarium's description of his wife's decline into her own silent madness. Catherine had once been a vibrant debutante of Kansas City, a blonde beauty of Midwestern stock. Practical, but the type to thrive among dress shops and sugar cakes. She had never even voted and would not budge from her position that the business of politics was messy and unfit for genteel company. He had not disabused her of the notion that ladies didn't belong debating matters of governance and now he was glad that he had not tried to persuade her otherwise. Her memories, if she retained any at all, need not include arguments and debates for which she had had no appetite.

He did want Catherine safe and well cared for, but each time he recalled being told that she did not seem to recognize his name any longer, he felt a stab of sorrow for how in the last few years life had proved so unkind to her. The same hand of fate had left him without a wife's companionship. Inside, he knew that his continuing letters to her had become a mechanism for reinforcing in his own mind that he remained married and therefore remained dutiful. As far as the church was concerned, his marriage still stood — his father had always said, "Don't expect life to be fair" — and he hadn't the heart to seek a divorce. None of this kept him from admiring the women around him.

Georgia, for instance, with the slender figure of a moderate eater, and great legs beneath the plain, straight skirts she wore. As the weather cooled toward winter, all the women would shift to wearing heavier stockings, which could be carefully mended. Winter would bring out boots and longer skirts. Of course, almost any legs of the female persuasion, no matter their coverage, were better than none at all.

Gentle Georgia was rarely ruffled by Campbell or the peculiarities of those for whom she acted as secretary and assistant. She possessed a soft voice and a fiancé, which did not surprise Murphy one whit. Good looking with a respectable job, she would be a catch. A flare of guilt from his Catholic upbringing stemmed further thoughts about what such a catch might or might not consider romantic — *Stop that,* he told himself.

"I'll be back shortly," he said, so that if Campbell, the freight boss, arrived early, she could mention she'd already seen him come through. His reputation could stand some lubrication. "Want to come for coffee?" he asked, knowing she would not accept.

She shook her head. "I'll take a break at 10:00."

Another characteristic of Murphy's married-bachelor life: eating in restaurants for most daytime meals. He had employed the grown daughter of a church acquaintance for minor housekeeping and preparing soup for supper. She came three days a week and seemed to be practicing variations on soup, leaving him a pot of the stuff which he could heat on the stovetop without burning down the place. Under Catherine's influence, he had kept fairly regular hours at work so that they could dine together most evenings. Now though, work hours and mealtimes fed his need to keep busy before heading home to an empty house. He had even taken to stopping in at the office on weekends to see if the yard crews had noted troubles he could bring to his boss's attention.

Returning from breakfast at 7:45, he found a message on his desk to call the passenger terminal manager about a Pekinese gone missing on the overnight from Chicago. *Thank God,* he thought. That ought to be worth most of a day beyond the reach of Campbell's increasingly disagreeable temperament.

The missing Pekinese proved elusive. After interviewing its matronly owner at the downtown Crown Hotel and receiving a description of the dog, Murphy headed to stately Union Station to dictate a telegraph message — "Watch for Missing Dog!" — to the onboard crew of the train that had already proceeded on its way west. He then commandeered two baggage porters to send on a thorough search of the ornate passenger depot and its public amenities while he nosed around the ticket and operations offices, interrupting purchasing agents and operations clerks as he scanned for the flash of a rhinestone collar beneath desks and behind cabinets.

While the dog's owner was certain her "sweet baby" could have been dog-napped for ransom, Murphy thought it more likely that someone had committed an outright theft or else the pet had simply wandered off in search of good smells or some canine company. He had no photographic likeness to show around, but there couldn't be too many red-and-tan dust mops running loose around the U.P. railyards.

Eventually, the search team reconvened without having had any luck. Next came a trek to the cacophonous maintenance sheds, where metal was being pounded into submission. There, mechanics responded with mute shakes of their heads to his inquiry. Next, he trekked to the food service building with its humming refrigerators and haze of odors. There, Negro food workers deferred to their white bosses, who declared on behalf of all that the dog had not been seen. Murphy requisitioned a slice of beefsteak to dangle in the air as he tromped between buildings, querying switching workers and clean-up crews about the missing dog, to no avail. The search team broke for lunch at mid-afternoon, splitting up afterwards for the canvassing of the closest businesses and hotels. By late afternoon they remained empty-handed.

Murphy trudged back to the office to report in.

"Jesus Christ!" said Mr. Campbell. "I can't believe you can't find a fucking dog. How hard is it to find an animal that does not drive a carriage or a car, does not rent a hotel room, does not window shop for dresses or hats. Mrs. Worthridge is the goddamn second cousin of the Minneapolis operations manager. We cannot fail to find her damn dog."

Campbell punctuated his words with his fist upon his desk — *Bang Bang Bang* — and Murphy had no doubt that Campbell would like to punctuate Murphy's sweaty face with that fist. This wasn't really about the dog.

Murphy lifted his hands in surrender, his left arm flagging in its plaster cast. What he needed was a hot soak in the tub of his quiet house and a bowl of whatever soup Ruby had devised for him. Maybe he'd start that new Agatha Christie novel he'd bought the previous weekend but hadn't cracked open yet.

"We looked everywhere," he offered. "A couple of the porters helped us search. Not even a rib-eye steak worked."

"Maybe it's not hiding, but gone. That'll be rich. We've lost a stupid dog belonging to a stupid dog owner and we'll have to replace it somehow." Campbell yanked open a desk drawer and extracted a small silver flask that he swigged from, ignoring Murphy as he did so.

"We'll search again tomorrow," said Murphy. "I'll have the print shop make up some handbills to post around. Do you want a Lost Dog notice or a Reward notice?"

Campbell rubbed his forehead. "No telling what a replacement for a foo-foo-assed dog like that would cost. Find out and offer a lesser reward for its return. I can feel it. We're getting stuck with this one." He frowned at Murphy, who nodded and turned to go.

"And while you're at it," growled Campbell, "check all the pawn shops around these parts. Again. I've got to have that jewelry back soon."

As Murphy exited the boss's office, he nodded to the two afternoon secretaries, who had surely heard the exchange. He was fairly certain that no one was safe from Campbell's ire. If Campbell's wife wasn't happy, no one in proximity to him would be.

Retrieving his overcoat from the office he shared with a junior detective, he glanced at his inbox. A pink phone message slip lay atop correspondence awaiting his signature. He picked it up. There was no number for returning the call, but he recognized the looping hand of Georgia, she of the shapely legs who had left work in time to meet her fiancé for a Friday evening rendezvous. *Lucky you*, he thought silently.

The message bore few words — the date, the time, and *Miss Raylene called and will call again.*

Mrs. Gunther looked up as Raylene appeared at the bottom of the boarding house stairs. "How was your sleep?" she asked. Raylene nodded. "The hot bath helped."

"As I said yesterday, I'm not sure I would have recognized you from your last visit. Your hair is ..."

"Chopped."

"An apt description. You look less like Annie this way."

"I was in a hurry and cut it myself." For the purpose of changing her appearance while tracking Raymond.

"It won't matter if you're not seeking a job. Otherwise ... here, let me get some eggs cooking."

Raylene sipped coffee while watching Mrs. Gunther move from boxy refrigerator to modern stove, city luxuries powered by reliable electricity that many rural folks did not yet enjoy. Today she would visit the public cemetery to see where her sister's body had come to rest, an arrangement made by some mystery person. It had not been Raylene, nor Ray (if she could believe him), and likely not Thomas, who was himself killed soon after. Almost everything about Annie's death and burial had happened too fast.

"Here you go," said Mrs. Gunther, setting a plate of fried eggs and toast before Raylene. "I'd sit with you, but I need to start the bread for supper. You don't mind, do you? I'd probably ask you a lot of questions. I guess I'm that way with all the girls."

Raylene, though, was lodging with Mrs. Gunther in order to ask her own questions. The house where Annie had boarded was on the Kansas side of the river and Thomas's saloon on the Missouri side, but she couldn't discount Mrs. Gunther knowing some important detail. She herself knew so little. She asked, "How many boarders do you usually have?"

The landlady answered as she pulled flour from one

cupboard and loaf pans from another. "Three is my limit, unless there's a pair who wants to share. Like sisters, or cousins. They might take just one room and share a bigger bed or we squeeze two smaller beds in. You came at the right time since Annie's room was paid through the end of October. It seemed only fair to hold her room and clothing, though I wasn't sure anyone would come for them."

Raylene had last night glanced through the cartons holding Annie's belongings. A couple of skirts and one dress. A jacket, a sweater, one pair of dressy shoes and some stockings. Pajamas, undergarments, ordinary items all, and certainly no valuable jewelry. In the pocket of the jacket, she'd found a thin copper necklace with a tiny turtle figure attached on a wire loop, the sort of shiny thing a girl might choose, though Annie had been twenty-seven. No girl. "Did anyone come to see you after Annie died?"

The woman paused at mixing her bread dough. "First a policeman, then an Indian man who said he was her father. Later, I saw the death notice of Thomas Yellow Moon, and that was her father, right? Yours too, I guess. Last was the railroad detective, which was strange. I mean, the police, yes. The family, yes. But a railroad man?"

"He was looking for jewelry."

"That's what he claimed. I have to say I wasn't sure about letting him look around, but he convinced me."

"But he didn't find jewelry."

"I told him I hadn't found any either and showed him the door."

Raylene smiled at that last part and tried to picture the U.P. detective inspecting Annie's belongings. He didn't seem the type to rifle through a woman's clothing, but perhaps that was part of the job, handling people's possessions. He certainly seemed determined. And of course, there was the photo he had once carried, now in her possession. The only photo in existence of her sister.

"I don't suppose you would know any bootleggers," said Raylene.

Mrs. Gunther looked sharply in Raylene's direction, a stricken look on her face. "Me? Goodness no! Why would you even suggest such a thing?"

"I mean no insult. I'm just — I need to find who is bootlegging around these parts."

Mrs. Gunther let out a breath. "Well. You may be certain that I don't have any acquaintance with such people, and I would walk away should I meet one."

Raylene carried her plate and cup to the sink. "I'll get going."

"Supper's at 5:30 but if you don't make it, I'll leave a plate in the oven."

Annie had died in the saloon her father managed. Their father. Or else an uncle, depending on whether Ray's last words were true. That was on the Missouri side of Kansas City, as was a large cemetery for common folk. Churches had small graveyards too. Raylene checked her city map then set out.

The oldest public cemetery, designated as such not long after the founding of the town of Kansas, Missouri, by those whose shared interests with neighboring Westport, was originally intended for the vast numbers of cholera dead. Since those years, that cemetery had filled rapidly, the neighbor-towns had merged, and the town of Kansas became Kansas City.

Raylene entered the undulating grounds not far from the sexton's cottage, through a section of eighty-year-old graves of the town's founders and those of soldiers who had fought on both sides of the Civil War. Markers made of granite had weathered the passage of time, but the oldest limestone and wooden markers had softened with age. After dying of consumption, Raylene's mother Helen might have been buried here in the company of others without affiliation to city fathers and residents who worshiped in churches — Pawnee and Kickapoo, Potawatomi and people of other tribes who had left designated reservations to look for work in the city. Also, migrants and the children and grandchildren of enslaved African people, all of them in one way or another dispossessed of their own lands. If allowed, there would be a section to one side for Chinese, who along with Irish workers had toiled building rail lines that connected the country. But Helen did not lie here because Raylene's father had carried Helen's ashes home and placed them beneath a cairn among the canyons of the *makhósica*.

Raylene moved methodically from the oldest graves to those of the 1910s and 20s, then to where an empty grave sat waiting its consignment. Two unmarked plots wore heaps of freshly-turned black dirt. Those were graves of the last few days, while her sister would lie among the dead of the last four weeks. She studied the newest rows, pausing to check each temporary marker. From the moment she had entered these quiet, grassy grounds, she felt a thread pulling at her, the pull growing stronger as she advanced toward an area with rough wooden crosses low to the ground. Her pulse quickened. *I am here. I am coming for you.*

When she came to stand before the plot that had beckoned her, she found it was not Annie's gravesite, but Thomas's. On the crude cross:

Thomas Yellow Moon
d. Sept. 1936

The grave belonged to Thomas, who had died following Annie. Recollections of the Conboie undertaker's parlor came to her. The fresh-cut box smelling of pine and Thomas laid out in a plain white shirt, excepting for a scar or two looking identical to his twin Ray. He had been a father to admire for his hunting skills and loyalty to her mother. He had taught her to ride, tan hides, and work leather. Though he was absent often, especially in their school years, she and Annie had felt his presence.

A few weeks ago, Raylene had arrived in Missouri from South Dakota to find Thomas already embalmed, so had left his body with the undertaker's assistant in order to search for Thomas's killer — her Uncle Raymond. She had located Raymond and exacted retribution, in the process receiving Ray's hazy claim about Thomas's role in Annie's death and which of them had been Raylene's true father. Had Ray been exaggerating? Perhaps. But even exaggerations contain some truth.

Now, she cast her gaze around the section of cemetery in which she stood and turned a slow circle to take in the gently rolling acreage that the city was beginning to subsume. The cemetery's trees seemed to rattle their red and yellow leaves in time to the breeze. If, as the undertaker had claimed, Annie had died two or three days before Thomas, her grave should be here among ordinary people, poor people, but there seemed to be no grave marked with her name. *Where is my sister?* Raylene started back toward the sexton's cottage. Surely there would be a record.

At the cottage, Raylene found a hunched and shrunken man, his face deeply weathered, his breath carrying the unmistakable odor of whiskey. She removed her hat, a western style that broke the sun. The man remained silent, so she let a few moments elapse then addressed him. "Sir, if you are the sexton here, I have come to locate my sister's grave."

The man grunted but said nothing else, so she continued. "Her name is Annie Moon. Will you check your records?"

He seemed to be studying her hair. At last, he spoke. "You a girl or a guy?"

Raylene knew that if she wanted cooperation, she should hold her tongue, but said, "What does that have to do with identifying a grave?"

Frowning, the man said, "I got no time for you. I got a body on the way."

Raylene glanced around as if checking the doorstep.

"Don't get smart with me. I got work to do."

Raylene tried to keep frustration from her voice. "I am only asking to locate the grave of Annie Moon, dead and buried sometime after the nineteenth or twentieth of September. I am not sure the exact day."

"She like you?"

"Do you mean Lakota? She is also part Crow. Like me."

The man frowned. "Did you look around?" He waved a gnarled hand in the direction Raylene had searched. "There's a Moon out there. I saw to his pine box myself."

Raylene doubted that the man could have missed her half-hour of wanderings among the dead under his care. "There were recently turned graves where I looked. I think I would have found it."

The man harrumphed and glanced everywhere but at Raylene, as if she were just another leaf drifted in upon the threshold. At last, understanding dawned and she reached into her pants pocket to extract a quarter. She had not expected to face extortion in the cemetery, but there it was. He looked blank until she handed over a second quarter. Once the coins were in his pocket, he turned toward a stack of ledgers on a desk in the far corner. Pulling the top one closer, he flipped through its pages. "After the twentieth?" he asked.

"And before the twenty-sixth."

"Did the coroner handle the body?"

"Conboie Undertaking."

The man flipped back and forth between pages so quickly that he could not have been reading them. "There's no record, means she's not here."

Raylene stood a moment, digesting his words. There must be a mistake. She had read the undertaker's letter multiple times and it gave Annie's death as the 20th. Even one day earlier or later would not have greatly shifted the week of her burial. "Could you have missed a record?"

Now the man turned his craggy face and speared her with an angry look. "I don't miss any records, not in twenty-five years."

Raylene held the sexton's gaze. Uncle Ray had always counseled that to outsmart opponents, she should know how their thoughts worked. This man was clearly an opponent, and easy to read, but she was not in competition with him. They were not after the same thing. Still, she advanced a step closer and held out her hand. "I will have my coins back."

"Don't know what you mean."

"If you have never missed a record, you knew there was only one Moon before you took my money."

The man drew himself up to his full height, such as it was, and balled his fists into sledgehammer shapes. "If you're callin' me a liar, you can take your red ass outta here before I throw it out."

She stood her ground and he stood his. She said, "I will not fight you. I did not come for that, but let my promise sit with you — a Yellow Moon cheated has a very long memory."

Exiting back through the cemetery gates, Raylene passed a black-skinned man wearing worn denim work clothes and dirt-caked boots. As if headed to work, he carried a spade and a ragged straw hat. She nodded in greeting. His response was the merest inclination of his head. Silently, she wished him well if he meant to work with the Union Cemetery sexton.

Across town, Murphy stepped into K.C. Jewelry and Loan, the oldest of the city's pawn shops, which also sold new jewelry. He was no stranger to this type of business, having regular occasion to search for items boosted from Union Pacific passengers and less often from the U.P. maintenance sheds. Occasionally such enquiries were fruitful, often they were not. Today, after arranging for the U.P. print shop to run up a batch of reward posters for the missing dog, he instructed one of the shop boys to paste them outside the passenger depot, throughout downtown, and along major arterial routes. Rather than wait for Monday, he had started rounds again through local shops where Mrs. Campbell's missing jewelry might reside. The jewels, of course, were not part of an official U.P. case, but of necessary import created by his boss's indiscretions.

He found himself once more wondering which of the office secretaries Campbell had made overtures toward. Any of them? All of them? Or did Campbell not go for pale approximations of Annie Moon with her dark waterfall of hair and dark eyes. Dark in other places, too, no doubt. Through his enquiries, he'd learned that Annie had been hardworking and gentle-natured. A drinker, but that could be said about a lot of Indians. Also Irish. Also whites. And come to think of it, the same could be said of his boss.

"Mr. Murphy," called the pawn shop owner from behind a glass-top counter, "is it pleasure or business today?"

"Mr. Levine, have I ever visited for pleasure?"

The shop owner grinned. "No, but I keep hoping you'll buy

something for your sweetheart."

"I have a wife."

Levine shrugged as if such a situation was none of his doing. "Well, it's Saturday, and I close early, so tell me what brings you in."

"I'm back looking for that same jewelry as earlier this month. I have drawings this time." Murphy extracted two sketches from his jacket pocket that he'd had made locally from additional photos his boss lent him. Decent depictions, if he did say so.

Levine said he had not seen the jewels, so Murphy took a turn around the cases and shelves as was his custom, always on the lookout for items previously reported to U.P. as stolen or lost. On the off chance that a fresh set of eyes might spot missing items, the police department also circulated a monthly list of "Reported Missing" items to pawn shops and detectives. Since the crash of '29, so many household goods and jewels had flooded hock shops that it wasn't unusual to spot gold watches previously given to commemorate retirements or even wedding rings. Grandma's brooches, wedding crystal, firearms, sometimes saddles and tack.

Before the crash and right as it started, Murphy had worked for his father's accountancy. Even after the crash began, accountants were busy, though as often with bankruptcy documents as anything. And of course, they served businesses that were always in the chips — druggists, movie theaters, burlesque shows and other enterprises where people for a time forgot their woes. In those days, a steady paycheck was better than gold, but in spite of that, he'd taken the leap to work for U.P.

Murphy had once located a sterling silver bowl gone missing from the governor's house that had ended up pawned. He was new to detective work then, so luck had surely played into it, but he did have a head for details. Naturally, Mr. Campbell had represented the department in taking credit for the find, but everyone knew it had been Murphy's keen eye.

After finishing his perusal of dust-free shelves and displays, Murphy pulled a folded handbill from his pocket and handed it to Levine. He said, "I know you don't take dogs in trade, but if you notice someone with this one, I'd sure like to know about it."

Levine glanced at the page and gave an amused smile. "If I put you onto it, I'll want that reward."

"It'll be yours, and gladly," said Murphy. Finding that floor-mop of a dog would help ease Campbell's mind and therefore his own. Doing so might help him keep his job. He bade farewell and returned to his coupe where he checked the pavement for any new oil leak. You never knew how much damage a long trip on gravel roads could do to your automobile. No new drips meant the mechanic had done a good job of taking care of his baby. Murphy smiled to himself. Thank God for small favors.

Raylene exited her truck onto the street holding Conboie & Sons undertaking business. After leaving Union Cemetery, she had returned to Mrs. Gunther's boarding house to peruse the Times, Kansas City's morning newspaper subscribed to by those on both sides of the river. Her reward was a notice for a service being held that afternoon at Conboie's, which had handled Annie's burial. Annie had not claimed a religion, but even so, native people would rest near where Thomas had been buried alongside indigents and miscellaneous unclaimed dead. She had seen Thomas's gravesite and knew exactly where Ray's bones rested in South Dakota. Now she wanted to sit by Annie's grave and speak to her.

Not long ago, Gerald Lambert of Conboie & Son had

evaded Raylene's direct questions about who had paid to bury her sister. If directness wouldn't work, perhaps she needed a roundabout approach.

That's how she found herself about to attend a service for a man traveling from California on the way to a Pennsylvania wedding, felled by a chicken bone during a restaurant meal. So said the morning Times's notice.

Swiftly, Raylene had donned Annie's navy skirt, white blouse, and dark jacket and pulled on Annie's best shoes after stuffing the toes with paper. The wrong-sized clothing billowed around her, but with her hair disguised by Mrs. Gunther's lace scarf and a paper fan in hand, she hoped to pass for an anonymous mourner. If an opportunity presented itself, she would confront Conboie or his assistant Lambert regarding Annie's burial record.

On Eleventh Street in the oldest part of town, memories of family members who had breathed their last in Kansas City rose up around her — her solemn mother whose sad eyes predicted the hardships that would befall her. Thomas, who embodied a warrior ethos, honor-bound to provide for his family but at odds with how the larger world disdained those values. With no son to raise, Thomas had taught Raylene to compete with the boys. Annie, though, had run with boys in a different way, taking to city life as if to a dream.

It felt strange to think of them as having died so far from their home country, but of course they were like so many who yearned for prosperity or peace or acceptance and thought it existed elsewhere. No different than settlers who had once driven oxen-powered wagons across prairies to reach what they thought would be the land of plenty. No different than explorers who plied stormy seas in pursuit of untold treasures. Seekers were everywhere and her people were no different.

As she reached the undertaker's entry, a woman of

indeterminate age in a dark dress opened the door ahead of her. Raylene followed, pulling her black lace head scarf lower like a veil. Inside the parlor, she noted suitcases stacked to one side and took a chair opposite the single woman sitting to the left. Though the shadowy parlor was pleasantly cool, she opened Mrs. Gunther's fan to hide behind.

Four adults, one with a tow-headed child by the hand, were gathered at the front around an open, silver-gray casket with ornate chrome and brass adornments. From across time, the voice of Conboie's assistant, Mr. Lambert, came to her again — "Family members quite often prefer something more memorable." He had meant a fancy casket with silk lining like the one these mourners stood over, their voices carrying throughout the quiet parlor: "Poor Uncle," and "Now he'll never ..." One of the more mature voices intoned, "He would be mortified to think we would hold up the wedding by missing our train." "Or miss the wedding altogether," came a reply. Murmuring and muffled sobs ensued.

Through the gap between veil and fan, Raylene observed Mr. Lambert, dressed in a black suit, observing the gathering from one side, hands clasped as if in prayer or contemplation of heavenly matters. In her experience, he was *All Business*. At his signal, a hidden organ began to play a solemn version of I Have a Father in the Promised Land, leading the mourners to take seats at the front.

After two more hymns, one of them containing the words "Shall we meet beyond the river, where the surges cease to roll," Lambert moved to the front to ask if anyone wanted to offer a prayer, which was met with more tears and snuffles. Eventually the small group stood to join hands, in unison reciting a version of The Lord's Prayer. Then they looked at each other and back at the casket and one by one gathered around it to lay their hands on its glossy finish. They were dressed in traveling clothes with black armbands. At the casket they lingered, until at last the man spoke low. "If we're going to make that train ..." The women nodded and held handkerchiefs to their faces. "I know, I know," said a young woman. "It's just that —"

"We'll come back through and spend more time. You can put flowers on his grave." The man took the woman's arm. As the organ struck up a quiet rendition of the Doxology, Raylene's thoughts turned again to Lambert's sales tactics and how easy it must be to convince those in mourning to spend more, sometimes a lot more, for what was essentially a box that would go into the earth. He had failed in his pitch to her because a box would not have contained Thomas's spirit, only his flesh, which itself would not remain. As the little group proceeded up the aisle, Raylene dropped her gaze and noted five sets of footwear passing to her left.

There came the bustle of suitcases at the same time that Raylene examined and discarded her original decision to immediately confront Lambert about her sister in favor of secretly learning about how Conboie's undertaking conducted its business with the dead. She did not look up to watch Lambert, but could imagine him holding back a smile at his profitable day as the sad party of travelers hoisted their cases and their sorrow and took them out onto the street. Something about Lambert was not to be trusted and she resolved to discover more about his deviousness, if possible.

Slipping from her seat, Raylene followed the other solitary woman out to the street where the traveling party, forlorn and a bit bedraggled, were helping each other into one of the taxi-carriages that still ferried passengers about. The one gentleman turned toward the other solitary woman, saying, "I don't believe we know you."

The woman paused where she was. "I bring condolences

from the restaurant. We're so sorry."

The man nodded and turned toward Raylene, who had turned away. "And you, Miss?"

Raylene turned slightly to answer, "Yes." When the other woman frowned, she added, "Actually, purveyors of food provisions. With condolences." She gave a nod before turning to walk up the block. This detour took her to the opposite direction from her truck, passing the redbrick offices of the Kansas City Tribune, which without mob financing was probably doomed to failure. There was a Top Hat diner with a few patrons gazing outward through the plate glass window. She knew the shape and direction of this part of town based on familiarity from the time when she was five and Annie eight and they ran these streets like urchins, snitching tomatoes from sidewalk stands. That round of big city living had lasted less than a year.

Next, she passed a boarded-up tailor's shop. After the financial crash, people had gotten thrifty and taken to refashioning or mending their own clothing until it absolutely needed replacing. In the city, her mother Helen might have made a success of alterations work. She'd been handy with a needle, especially beadwork, but any kind of needlework suited her. Raylene's memories of her mother were few and fading but she still held to the idea of a mother as the heart of their family.

Now carrying her scarf and fan, she rounded the block once more and reached her truck. The mourning group was nowhere in sight. Behind the wheel, she formulated how she might learn more about Conboie's operations. To start with, she could watch where Conboie's outfit would bury this newly-deceased stranger. People with no local affiliation would likely end up at Union Cemetery and something told her to watch for them there. Uncle Ray would have approved observation as a means for assessing her opponent.

Murphy quit for the day at 4:00. Whereas his previous canvassing had turned up the gold earrings with the green stones — pawned by an Indian man — this time the owner of Capital Loan, Mr. Williams, had asserted that he had not seen the matching necklace or the missing pearl ring. A person could call this day a bust, but there was something to be said for making the effort, especially had it revealed one of the pieces and helped return him to Campbell's good graces. He wondered now, would it be so awful to lose his job over his inability to save Campbell from his own foibles? He could suffer losing his job for legitimate insurrection or disloyalty or dereliction of duty, but not for failing to rescue Campbell from the effects of his own transgressions. He wanted to think that should Campbell fire him his reputation would suffer a little but not so much as to ruin other job prospects. All the same, he'd rather not test that notion.

Were he someone else's son, he might find unfair the prospect of job loss through someone else's fault, but he had been weaned on the viewpoint that fairness was not a foregone trait of mathematics, physics, or human interactions. Life was not fair but it was still a person's duty to carry on. He would conduct himself like a gentleman when in polite company and get tough elsewhere as needed. Of course, toughness would not persuade Campbell of Murphy's worth, only delivering the goods would do that.

Before heading for home, he stopped at the office where a weekend staffer would register his presence on his day off, which could not do any harm. Leaving his Hudson in a no-parking zone, he strode hatless past one of the Missing Dog handbills pasted to a sandwich board set on the sidewalk. Good. The boss would eventually notice that.

Inside, he nodded through an open door at the freight scheduler who looked up from his desk. The Saturday secretary was not in sight, but Murphy checked his desk for the typed versions of two recent reports that he would review on Monday. One was there alongside another of those pink message slips — *A Miss Raylene called. She will call back.*

He automatically glanced around as if within his office space there would appear a clue as to why the little sister, as he thought of her, had phoned him again. She desired information relating to his boss and Annie, but Campbell's marriage would suffer, perhaps collapse, if any trace of that affair was to surface. He had seen Miss Little Moon enumerate to a man his various wrongs, and Campbell would not take that well from a woman. On the other hand, if she assisted him in finding the missing jewels, he might keep instead of lose his job.

He could almost feel that end advancing toward him from a distance. His work suited him, containing the chance to travel a bit, enjoy the camaraderie of other detectives, and to solve (among the simpler cases) the occasional tricky case. The pay he earned was commensurate with his experience and sufficient for the head of a household (though his own household had shrunk by half). And though others might not, he would admit to feeling pleasure at enjoying the diversity of people who traveled by rail, whether they be devious, illiterate, upper crust, or down on their luck. People fascinated him. Of course, if they broke the law or were indecent to other U.P. passengers, he was willing to give them the boot or see them arrested.

To Raylene Little Moon, he had tried to explain his reluctance at getting involved in her sleuthing efforts. Apart from that Pine Ridge incident, one could say she had not cooperated in assisting him at all, at least not regarding the jewelry mistakenly given to her sister. And once more, she had called without leaving a return number. He did not even know where she was lodged, otherwise he might approach her there to reiterate his position. No. It was as if she were a ghost leaving traceries meant to be noted but not responded to. He knew from experience that she was no ghost, and he knew in concept what she wanted. If he meant to keep his job, he simply could not, ought not, risk helping her.

Three

Union Cemetery was vast by prairie standards. In contrast, Pine Ridge graveyards were much smaller, one being an original grassland acre set aside by Agency officials and surrounded by a weathered wooden fence. Another had been established by the Catholic mission, which built an impressive school with a chapel and small graveyard for those who adopted Catholicism through choice or compulsion.

Raylene had changed from Annie's skirt and shoes back into trousers and boots, and pulled on her secondhand newsboy cap. She carried a coat for after the sun set. Having cruised the streets bordering the massive property, she chose to park and enter the cemetery from a side street, acres away from the front entrance. Carrying one of the wool blankets Ray had left her, she passed beneath October leaves shimmering in the late afternoon breeze.

Skirting the perimeter of the oldest plots, she headed for the zone in which she had found Thomas's cross, keeping watch for any freshly-dug grave without an occupant. There was freshly-turned soil near markers with Irish-looking names — Doyle, Kennedy, Fitzgerald. And one other half-dug grave in an open spot near a huge old stone monument, for a relative, perhaps, of a venerable K.C. family.

A fully open grave lay beyond Thomas's, further along the row, so Raylene crossed to a distant knoll bearing three or four trees, shook out her blanket, and pulled her coat on as if she were settling in to contemplate the final resting place of a loved one as a soft-focus mourner in the distance. The trees dropped a few whirling leaves onto her lap, which she left where they fell. The park-like place was peaceful all around, its solitude broken only by birdcall or the scamper of a squirrel overhead. The breeze whispered to her of places it had seen. What had once been undulating countryside perfect for grazing but less so for crops, was now planted with bodies whose spirits had crossed over. Though taught by nuns on the Pine Ridge to think in terms of purgatory and heaven, Raylene subscribed to her own people's belief in the spirit world beyond this life. Many of her fellow Lakota believed the same, that some spirits might inhabit stones or birds or hold special powers to harass the living, or aid them. Other spirits might mingle somewhere beyond where the sky met the land. Ray was spirit now. Thomas and Annie too, though Annie had left the old ways behind when she took to the city.

Images of a younger Thomas came to her now — the sheen of sweat on his shirtless body while he worked at the smithy's forge. Muscled arms and back, his cross-peen hammer swinging upward then down with a clang of steel on steel. He was young then, the hair on his arms singed in places, his face a mask of concentration. Sometimes she watched him from the closest corner. If he saw her, though, he waved her away with his tongs or simply a finger — *Get away from the fire.*

A movement among the graves broke Raylene's reverie. Dusk had fallen, blurring the features of a pair of male figures, one pushing and one pulling a wheeled cart. She watched as they lifted from the cart a coffin of a golden pine color. Whoever was being buried was of limited means, not the dead traveler from Conboie's parlor, whose kin had chosen a box befitting a prince.

She watched the men lower the casket on ropes then shovel rich black dirt into the hole and tamp it into a gentle mound.

One of them took up a wooden object to mark the plot, hammering it into place with the back of his spade. As dark fell across trees, grasses, stone monuments, and sodded swales, Raylene let her mind wander. She had heard the music of the sandstone canyons in her home country and listened now for any that the cemetery stones might make, but the only music was that of leaves in the trees, which seemed enough.

Having finished, the workers became solid black figures in a dark landscape before one switched on a torch. As she watched their cone of light move back toward the main entrance, something askew about the burial scene penetrated her thoughts. Why had the men worked through the supper hour and into dark?

There could be a rational reason. She could imagine a few: the deceased's body had been held too long above ground, requiring an after-hours burial to get it into the ground; the poor and indigent were buried late so as not to disturb day visitors to the property; the deceased was of a religion necessitating swift burial on the same day as death; an inspection of the K.C. morgue was due on Monday morning and authorities desired to empty their lockers beforehand; the workmen had tarried all day, leaving their responsibilities for nightfall.

Raylene sat a moment with these possibilities but not one satisfied her. With dark all around, she took the path that led past the new grave. Drawing close, she pulled out the pack of matches she carried for lighting campfires. Lighting one, she could make out crude lettering:

Erik Hanson

1878 -- 1936

stone ordered

Hanson was the name from the obituary for that service at

Conboie's where the casket was a fancy, shiny thing around which Mr. Hanson's mourners had gathered. But the casket she had watched being interred tonight was clearly made of plain old unfinished wood. If the family had paid for a fancy casket, their beloved had not been buried in one. Someone had lost money to Conboie Undertaking.

Raylene returned to the boarding house, driving across the tracks of streetcars, which were nearly done running for the night. Traffic seemed to grow more congested around nightclubs and saloons with names like Red & Dutch and The Living Room. On almost every corner downtown, nightclubs and saloons glowed with neon and bright lights, more drinking and music joints, it seemed, than she had noticed during previous visits. The city's reputation as "hot, wide and open" applied not just to its jazz scene but also to how it had remained wet during Prohibition. Also, for the illegal card games held in back rooms throughout the city. Thomas had run a card game at his saloon. As for "hot," perhaps that also applied to how many women bellied up to bars all over town to get their tonsils tickled by some booze. No different than men, women too wanted what they wanted. Raylene wanted a hot meal and to ask a favor of Mrs. Gunther.

"There's a plate for you in the oven," said Mrs. Gunther, laundry basket in hand as Raylene came through the door.

Raylene hung her jacket and hat in the front entry and set Mrs. Gunther's scarf and fan on the entry table. Carrying the garments she had "borrowed" from Annie's closet, she called to Mrs. Gunther, "I'll be down straight away."

A few minutes later, they met in the kitchen where Mrs. Gunther reached the oven first. She motioned Raylene to the table and set a plate of beef and potatoes before her. "Milk, dear?" she asked.

Raylene shook her head. "I'd have water or else coffee if you have some. Are your other boarders at home?"

"They each work two jobs, so they're mostly here to sleep. One of them is Italian, the other one is French. She talks like someone in the movies. I'll pour you some water. Coffee's on too."

Once her hands were empty, Mrs. Gunther settled herself opposite Raylene. "I'm going to be nosy now," she started. "Why did you go to a funeral for someone from California?"

Raylene thought a moment as she chewed a bite of savory pot roast. Mrs. Gunther seemed a steady sort, not one to trifle with her own house's standing, but through her position she would have seen a fair share of women making difficult decisions. Annie had only spoken well of Mrs. G. The woman had distinct opinions about the comportment of young ladies, though for some reason, she hadn't faulted Annie for saloon work. Raylene hated to disaffect a possible ally by explaining her own plans, which might seem extreme. But without doing so, she would not feel right seeking the landlady's support. She needed someone to trust, and her instinct was that Mrs. G was nothing if not trustworthy, so she said, "I went in order to watch Conboie's people."

Mrs. G straightened a little. "That's who handled Annie's burial and your father's."

"But Annie's took place before I reached town. I did not make the arrangements."

"In September you mean. Could your father have made them?"

"He was killed too soon after to have done that." There was nothing to gain by revealing that her uncle Raymond had done the killing.

Mrs. G rose to fetch the percolator she had left on the back burner. "So, why watch the undertaker's people?"

"The man who runs the parlor goes by Lambert. When I was last here, he wouldn't say where they'd buried Annie. Suggested I must ask Mr. Conboie, who was out of town at the time, if that was true. I planned to confront Lambert today, but I changed my mind." Raylene thought back to her hurried travels from the H-bar-H to see Thomas's body, carrying only a bundle of clothing and a few dollars for train fare. Then came the unexpected news about Annie having also died, and her heart fell to the ground. Had she even asked Lambert where Annie was buried or only asked who had paid the bill? Now she was not sure. All she knew at this point was that Annie had not been buried in the same cemetery as Thomas and someone else had been involved.

She considered it likely that Lambert, perhaps on Conboie's behalf, had been protecting the identity of whoever had financed Annie's burial, and Raylene, having traveled a fair distance, might not be expected to return again to ask. But here she was. Again.

"Could you go round to other cemeteries?" said Mrs. G. "I think there are only a few."

"I could, but now I have a hunch about Conboie's business, or at least about Mr. Lambert. That he sells fancy caskets to people in mourning but does not deliver the fancy goods unless they are present, watching him."

Mrs. G tipped her head to study Raylene. "Some sort of fraud? I hope you will not put yourself in danger."

"Mrs. Gunther, I want to be dealt with fairly."

After a pause, Mrs. G said, "I see your point, but women are at a disadvantage in a man's world. You know what I mean. Men can be dangerous, especially when a woman catches them out."

Raylene noticed the way Mrs. G blinked as she spoke that

last part, as if her words were informed by some experience she had not entirely forgotten. She said, "I am cautious when it is called for." She did not add how there were circumstances that called for taking risks and she would do so if needed. Instead, she said, "If Annie's room is available, I will rent it for an extra month. My business here should be done before then."

"You may lodge here as long as you need. Did you know that Annie boarded with me for nearly three years?" Mrs. G blinked hard. "I'm sorry she is gone. She was easy to like."

Raylene swallowed hard against a knot in her throat. "I am not as polished for city life. She took to it."

"Your riding trousers stand out. Most city women do not wear them." She touched a hand to her hair and Raylene did the same to her own, which she had chopped to disguise herself when tracking her Uncle Raymond.

"I mean to grow out my hair," said Raylene, "but would you trim it for me?"

Mrs. G bit her bottom lip, then smiled. "I don't even cut my own, but I could even yours a bit with my sewing scissors."

"I have in mind to apply for a job."

"A job! I had no idea. What kind of — Oh. Aren't you a rancher?"

"A ranch hand. I'd rather not say about the job just yet since they might not hire me."

Mrs. G paused as if reconsidering her willingness to assist. "Annie was no trouble. If you don't bring trouble here — you know I've got other girls to think about — you can stay and I'll do what I can to help."

As Mrs. G rose from the table, a phrase came to Raylene that sounded like something John Murphy would say. "I'll be much obliged."

On Sunday morning, Murphy felt an urge to attend Mass. Since his wife's departure, he had seldom attended services at St. Christopher's. Though he considered his faith an enduring one, he was not as moved by hymns, scriptures, and ceremony as when as a youngster he had attended with his parents. In those days, smoke from the censer dispersed a heady scent while readings in Latin resounded with heavenly significance. Though he no longer felt the same tug toward the mystical, leaning instead toward a skepticism suited to one who dealt in facts and evidence, Catholicism's rituals still soothed him.

St. Christopher's had been his parent's parish, not far from his father's office, until they moved to a house without a staircase for his mother's benefit. A half-Irish beauty in her younger years, his mother had nearly become an invalid after a bad fall. Now she seemed reticent to be seen in a wheeled chair at the market or Mass. A nurse-aide attended her weekly to assist with bathing and female particulars but in the kitchen, canes at hand, she reigned supreme.

Without the urgings of his wife, Murphy's father rarely attended church these days. That such attendance was said to be good for the soul had little effect on his inclination in the opposite direction. After a five or six-day workweek, he spent Sundays reading multiple newspapers, the Friday business edition out of St. Louis being of special import. On mild-weather Sundays, he would drive Murphy's mother to Westport's ice cream parlor, their favorite, and go inside to fetch ice cream cones. Sitting in their Plymouth with the radio on, they would work their treats down to nothing.

Murphy imagined that such a day as this one might find his parents on the road to Westport, the mild air of late October streaming in through the windows. This was the sort of day when he would take the wheel of his own automobile for a cruise along country roads. A drive was one of the few pleasures he indulged. Another was a good book, especially a crime novel or a mystery. But since returning from Rapid City injured and beholden to his boss, none such usual distractions could tame the dread growing inside him. He could not confide in one of the older U.P. detectives, both of whom had been dispatched to short-circuit the current roil of labor troubles in Denver.

He imagined that the ethereal beauty of St. Christopher's statues, murals, and stained-glass windows would soothe him after the trying week he'd had. A prayer or two in that holy place might also help since his prayers of late, if they could be called prayers rather than laments, had brought him no peace. This day he would sequester his skepticism in favor of praying for divine inspiration in his dealings with Campbell. He would ask for the patron saint's blessing upon his work that he might succeed in solving every case no matter how trivial and that Campbell would once more hold him in favor.

Dressed in pressed trousers with matching vest, he did his best with his tie and drew his suitcoat over his shoulders. A local tailor had opened the seams in the sleeves of his oldest shirts, which he kept in rotation, awaiting the day his cast would come off. Until then, half-on, half-off clothing would have to do.

At St. Christopher's, Murphy found himself early for the 10:00 a.m. service. Kneeling in a row at the back of the quiet nave, he realized with a jolt that he had not attended Mass in eight or nine months, perhaps since last Christmas. It had also been that long since he'd confessed. A long stretch without attending Mass required contrition, as did the lies he'd told in South Dakota and the fight he'd been in. Also, he'd been helping his boss negate the ill effects of an affair of some kind, which kept bringing Miss Little Moon and her sister to mind.

His right hand went automatically to his jacket pocket for those pink message slips, which were not there. He had not had the chance to ask either of the secretaries — Georgia on Friday, and Susan yesterday — what else Miss Little Moon had expressed. Had she sounded distressed or harried, serious or upbeat? Her messages had been so devoid of clues. He thought about what little he knew about her. There was the calm she exuded under pressure, and her unconventional looks and manner of dress, her feline walk and how she had wielded a knife. Were he to attend confession, he would admit that the little sister had aroused in him impure thoughts. Dark-eyed, dark-haired, mysterious, decisive, yet a woman of few words, the opposite of the woman he had married.

He felt that same quickening now at the thought of her and quashed it by looking up to catch the eye of an elderly woman clanking her cane against the pew in front of him as she chose a seat. He could smell the woman's bath powder, so like a grandmother's and rather like that of Mrs. Worthridge who had lost her Pekinese, for whom he had developed a distinct distaste. Not only did he dislike the dog, he disliked the woman too, primarily for traveling with a dog small enough and dumb enough to get itself lost, and also for — well, for no truly valid reason. He had no business disliking the dog or its owner in the first place. In good conscience, he should not. He felt this acutely as he sat in the pew beneath a ceiling decorated with heavenly clouds, angel figures, and cherubs. In this of all places, he needed to practice mercy and grace toward a stranger who had caused his employer to froth at the mouth. Then he might hope for mercy and grace from his employer. Words of contrition came to him, which he said silently. *O my God, I am heartily sorry for having offended thee.*

Afterwards, he prayed for mercy. Then he realized he

himself had not demonstrated mercy when Raylene Little Moon came to him for assistance.

Four

"I don't hire no women for that kind of work, even if they say they can deal. The players deal their own. I don't mind an Indian, I'm a wop myself. There's just not no women at the card games, unless they're serving drinks." This, from Ricco, the man who had assumed operations of the saloon her father had managed before his death, where her sister had poured drinks. She had reread her sister's journal of business and personal notes, but Annie's scrawls had often been abbreviated, so Raylene's plan was to spend some time watching booze deliveries and figuring out suppliers. If her father's twin Raymond had been telling the truth, someone among her father's suppliers had provided the deadly hooch that Annie drank, and Raylene wanted to know who.

Down the Block saloon didn't hire fancy people or serve fancy people, which made Raylene as likely a candidate as anyone for a job there. "I could clean up and stock shelves," she said. "I am stronger than I look." She preferred not having to serve customers who whined about their woes when liquored up, or tried to feel up the help.

"You do this kind of work before?"

"At the Lucky 7s up in Sioux City." A falsehood.

"Oh yeah? Why aren't you there now?"

Raylene looked away as if reluctant to admit to her behavior. "I cut someone who got too fresh." A half-truth from a different place.

Ricco's face lit up with glee. "Ha! No shittin'. You cut

someone? You?"

Raylene feigned nonchalance.

"Well, I'll be damned," said Ricco. He considered her a moment while she held his gaze. "I don't want no law coming round for you."

"I didn't kill him, and they wouldn't come all this way for me."

The manager now looked Raylene over again, her rough-but-clean ranch pants previously worn by Wilma's son, her denim jacket. She could detect his growing interest in someone who might protect the place's profits. If she had left Sioux City under suspicious circumstances, he wouldn't have to pay her much. Or perhaps he thought *he* could someday mess with her and not get cut. "Can you pour a drink?" he asked.

"Nothing fancy."

"Well." He blew out a sigh and waved a hand in the air. "Alright. I been through three in one month. The last one only lasted two days. You want the job you gotta start today. You can take Monday off 'cause we don't open on Sundays. Not enough drinkers to open for." He grinned slyly and crossed himself. Raylene glanced at the overflowing ashtrays and the paper scraps and other detritus filling up the corners. Before she could comment about Sunday drinkers feeling entitled to start fresh following absolution, Ricco continued, "Got to clean the johns too. That's what cost me my last girl."

To Raylene's mind, the saloon had gone downhill in the month since her father's death. It stunk now of stale cigarettes, cigars, and spilled beer. Thomas had demanded respect from customers regarding Annie and himself, and the two of them had kept the place clean out of respect for their customers. "What do you pay?" she asked.

"You'll get what that kinda job is worth, which isn't much.

The shift is mornings, four hours max. Take it or leave it."

"Cash, right?"

"Wouldn't do it any other way."

Raylene glanced around again. She had recently inspected the contents of Annie's valise, a receptacle for Annie's "important papers," its contents this time revealing an item of import to the Union Pacific detective. She had also read Annie's journal again. Besides its mention of a romantic connection with someone at the railroad, which might be Murphy's married boss, there were also names of delivery companies and those who frequented the saloon. She could not know how much detail her sister had left out, but if she could watch the saloon's buying and selling action, she might glean some information about which people knew what.

"Okay," she said. "I'm in."

Ricco nodded. "There's tools in the back room and some bottles of cleaning stuff. Say, what's your name?"

Raylene thought fast. "Call me Chiqui." The term was a variation of what Raul, cook for the H-bar-H, had murmured while caressing her with hands that knew when to be gentle and when to be firm. She missed those hands.

Ricco looked at her. "Cheeky? Ask me, that don't fit. But okay, if you say so."

Murphy's Sunday afternoon felt lazy. Given that he was still operating with a cast on his favored arm, he called on a neighbor's son to cut his lawn one more time. Murphy liked the physicality of pushing the mower back and forth, its blades slicing through the grass with a metallic zip, but he had found after his first try three weeks ago that trying to grip the handle with his cast arm threw his posture off just enough to put an extra zinger in his lower back. His father, of course, never mowed his own expanse of lawn, but this grass took no time at all for a grown man, and a little sweat never hurt anyone. Soon it would be time to trim the rhododendrons his wife had planted four years ago. The trimmer, he could manage.

After the mowing was accomplished and the youngster, Robbie, had polished off a glass of lemonade, Murphy demonstrated the use of an edger and the boy did that work too. Both the lawn and edging were slightly uneven in places, but Murphy, the notion of mercy still warm within him from his ruminations in church, let the imperfections slide. His own inclinations were to check and double check facts and figures and even the trim of the lawn, where swaths of it might need cutting on a different angle to catch toughened stems that persisted in sticking up. His perfectionist stripe was why he had excelled at book-keeping work for his father's firm. A certain amount of hairsplitting also applied to detective work, but another thought that had revisited him during prayers this morning was that he might very well lose his U.P. job in spite of his attention to detail and honesty and willingness to put in long hours. If Campbell fired him out of spite, there would be no higher power to appeal to, not Campbell's bosses, not St. Christopher, not God.

Murphy's code of honor would keep him from ratting to Campbell's wife about pieces of her jewelry having gone to Raylene's sister Annie. A man didn't do that to another man, even when the latter was a scoundrel, even when the truth might save a person's employment. You took your licks because hard luck came to everyone at some point. Perhaps that was what Murphy could feel coming his way — hard luck. Young Robbie, just now finished with mowing Murphy's lawn would join the world of working men eventually, and then he would learn how the working world worked. He paid the boy and sent him home with a pat on the shoulder.

Sunday being a Ruby-less day in the Murphy household,

Murphy would need to attempt preparing yet another meal without a woman's touch. He hadn't the creative skills for an appealing meal. It took all of his energy just to arrive at edible. Luckily, he knew how to cook scrambled eggs. With butter and salt and pepper, eggs would do.

After supper, with *The Case of the Velvet Claws* by Earle Stanley Gardner at hand, Murphy poured himself a short glass of Jameson's on ice and settled into his easy chair. He had finished The Maltese Falcon during his September travels. That story had been full of twists and turns, very satisfying.

The floor lamp gave off a golden glow as outside the front window, dusk fell. As he set his glass aside, Murphy's gaze caught on the ebony case holding a hand-carved pipe handed down from his great-great-grandfather, a Highland Scot who built railroads for the Queen in various colonies of the British empire. Burma, India, Australia. A man's man, strong of body, hard of head who married an Irish woman and whose children married mostly Irish. Various members of the Murphy clan reveled in the plotting and procuring and laying of steel in webs that strung countryside to towns to capitals to the monarchy. God Save the Queen.

Murphy opened the case and lifted out the ivory-tipped pipe and the small pouch of aromatic tobacco that his father had recently provided with the heirloom, one of the few family items remaining from that long-ago time. Though not himself inclined toward smoking, Murphy pictured a pipe-smoking man famous for the cunning way he solved mysteries — Sherlock Holmes. He smiled at the thought as his home telephone began to ring.

The time was easily 6:00 p.m., or a little after, and he had no expectation of receiving a call at that hour, on a Sunday no less. His first thought was that he hoped it wasn't work calling him. He'd had enough of work for the weekend, having hardly spent an hour without it on his mind. He let the ringing echo in the hallway before rising and putting his book aside. Lifting the phone on its sixth or seventh ring, he answered.

"Murphy?" came the reply. "It's Williams. I hate to bother you on a Sunday."

"I almost didn't answer, but you got me. What's up?" He half hoped there wasn't anything, though if the police had been to the freight yard and Williams, who was the weekend scheduler, was providing him notice of a theft or crime, Murphy would be glad for it. He could say he had already heard when in the morning Campbell sprang the news on him.

Williams blew out a breath. "This is awkward. There's no secretary on Sunday, you know that, and I was closing up, and the office phone rang, not even my own line, you know? But it was maybe two minutes to 6:00 and I was walking by Georgia's desk on my way out, so I answered. You never know what hair-brained thing someone's going to call about, and I thought it might be Campbell checking on whether anyone remained at quitting time. So anyway, it was for you."

"Is it that missing Pekinese case? We've posted a reward."

"Uh, no. Not that. Listen, I took the message but I swear to you I didn't write it down anywhere. I just thought I'd call and I'm telling you that I'll put it out of my mind after this. Consider me dumb about the whole thing."

"I'm not sure I follow you."

"It was a woman by the name of Raylene asking for you. She didn't give a number, so I said, 'That's all? Is there anything else?' She took so long at that point that I thought maybe she'd changed her mind or hung up. But finally, she said she wants to ask you who in town provides abortions."

The next morning, Raylene sat studying obituaries to be found in the stack of the newspapers Mrs. G was saving for their advertisements when Vivienne, one of the two other boarders, came into the green and yellow kitchen.

"*Bonjour!* You are the new girl. I am Vivienne," said the young woman, taking a seat across from Raylene.

Raylene looked up. "I am visiting Kansas City, both sides of it. Years ago, for a short time, I lived in the area called the west bottom." She slid the sugar bowl in the woman's direction.

"Are you settling here?"

"*Mais oui* — I mean, yes, if you are asking about America. I first lived in New York, the city, which in size was much like Paris, also very large and busy. But jobs grew thin so I am here now trying to go west."

"To California?"

The young woman's bright eyes lit up. "That will be for me when I have saved enough money from my jobs. I will go there and open a beauty parlor for the famous stars from the movies." Here, she touched her soft brown curls. "I am good with hair. I could do yours for you, if you like."

Raylene took a bite of toast. "When mine grows out I'll tie it back, but thank you for the offer."

"Forgive my boldness, you are an Indian, yes?"

"Yes."

Vivienne nodded. "In France we like the Indians and cowboys of America. There is a romance to them and their big country."

"Is that so?"

"Not the cowboys so much, or maybe yes. They are like no other. It is your country's far west that sticks in our minds as good. We did not have that in Europe, the towns made of wood and the vast unending country."

"And you did not have the fighting between the government and tribes." Raylene rarely debated with whites how native people had been driven off their lands and into poverty at the business-end of the cavalry's long guns.

"Well, yes there has always been fighting between countries and between the rich and the poor. Revolutions, beheadings, poverty, famine. The rich make up the government, which makes the laws. America is a dream for us. It lets people in, even if you are poor."

Vivienne's observations contained some truths, including that America did let almost everyone in, though when it came to claims made about the land and its riches, America's generosity was often to the detriment of the land's first people.

Vivienne asked, "Have you met Bianca? She is working in a dress factory on the east side. And I am working in a restaurant over here, washing dishes. Kitchen work." She leaned toward Raylene as if ready to hear what type of work she did.

Raylene glanced in the direction of Mrs. G, who was picking soup meat from Sunday's chicken carcass. The inward stream of sunlight cast an otherworldly glow around the woman, who though facing away from them grew very still, as if an antenna receiving the exchange at the table. "You seem to work a lot."

Vivienne cut her eyes toward Mrs. G's back as if in warning. "I have taken also some evening work at another place. Women's work." She reached for the jam pot.

To cover for Vivienne, Raylene offered, "My new job is at a stable where I board my horse. I'll ride him today." This last she spoke in Mrs. G's direction as she set her plate and cup in the sink. Leaning in, Raylene murmured to Mrs. G, "May I have a word with you?"

"Of course," came the reply.

Raylene tipped her head to suggest they move to the hallway. Once there, she said. "The Union Pacific man might come looking for me here." John Murphy was a bit of a contradiction. A conservative dresser, he wore a wedding band but drove a splashy car like a bachelor might. His behavior in South Dakota had suggested a repressed longing to cut loose. Contradiction or not, she needed him to offer his help.

Mrs. G wiped her hands on her apron. "That detective who came after Annie's death? Why would he?"

"I have not told him, but if he puts his mind to it, he will recall this house as a place he might look for me."

"I will send him away. I didn't like him poking around that first time."

"The truth is he can help me regarding my sister."

Mrs. G stood silent a moment. "I won't have him search my house again without my supervision, but do you want me to tell him anything?"

Raylene leaned closer to whisper information for Mrs. G's ears only. Mrs. G gave her a curious look. "Are you sure that's safe?"

"Tonight, yes. Perhaps not a different night."

At Brugmann's stable, Raylene parked her truck to one side and got out to admire Heinz working with a horse in a nearby paddock. He tossed her a nod as he turned a circle with a roan gelding at the end of a lunge line. After a few minutes, he worked the horse to a stop and moved calmly toward it until he had it steady beside him. He ran the leather lines across its withers and neck as he spoke low. Much about Heinz's demeanor was like her uncle's. Raymond had been expert at handling horses. "Shaping the horse" he had called it. He and Thomas had taught her to ride when she was little. She had trained Kota herself, shaping him into a cow horse that suited the ranch work she preferred — cattle, horses, open grasslands, the high-country plains with skies a wide, honest blue, taller than the world.

She had changed into her leather riding pants and ranch hat with the wide brim. Kota was due for exercise and she was overdue for the feel of his brawny form beneath her, his walking gait, his trot, his gallop. Beyond town lay undeveloped land that stretched to the horizon, some of it not yet fenced for cattle or crops. In other places, farmsteads had failed through drought and bottomed-out grain prices. That's where she would ride him, but first they would amble into town for a bit of banking business.

Heinz unclipped the gelding from the line and walked over to greet her. "Your fella, he is in fine shape. His time on pasture will not do any harm."

"I'll take him out today. I recall passing a bank downtown." Heinz scratched under his hat band. "*Ja.* You will find hitching posts nearby."

Raylene motioned toward the stable. "May I?"

Heinz pointed with one gloved hand. "He's on the right, your tack also."

Before long, Raylene had inspected Kota and checked his hooves. After saddling him, she walked him out to intercept Heinz near the gelding's paddock. "Will you call a farrier to trim Kota soon?" she asked. "I can leave money for the service."

Heinz waved a hand. "You can settle later since I have your collateral." At this he grinned.

Raylene nodded her thanks and turned Kota toward the dirt lane leading out to the road. Soon they were trotting toward town and Kansas State Bank.

After opening an account with the bank and requesting a portion of her funds be forwarded from the Bank of South Dakota, Raylene rode Kota back through town and out the northwest side. Shadows from clouds now dappled the roadway and ditch banks. When they reached open land, she judged that Kota was ready for a hard run and they were off, flying across sun-glazed, caramel-colored fields blotched with shade, bits of grass and clods of dirt flying up behind them. As she leaned low over the saddle horn, Kota's mane whipped her face. Her hat flew back on its string and her hair winged out and the air tasted ripe of fall's decay, grasses dwindling toward sleep, prairie flowers gone to seed, critters burrowing furiously in preparation for the snows of winter, coming, coming, but not yet here.

Joyriding for nothing but the pleasure of doing so was almost as satisfying as sending the loop of a lariat singing outward to snag a calf or steer, or Kota anchoring his thousand pounds in place as she wrestled a steer to the ground for branding. Early fall meant driving market cattle for days across grass and brush to reach the sales pens in Farmington, or moving others to winter pastures where they would dine on hay as needed. Fall was the snap of a campfire and the clank of tin plates, coffee steaming over hot coals, cattle dogs circling the herd until it quieted under a blanket of stars. Those nights on the prairie were when she felt closest to Grandmother Earth and the spirits of people who had always lived by the seasons.

The countryside offered flights of corn doves on the move, and higher up, bands of geese splitting the sky, and pronghorn and mule deer in shifting colors among the grassy hills. In the city, she missed these things, though the crickets in Mrs. G's side yard provided a symphony like that of home.

Kota's pent-up energy burned away and Raylene eased herself upright. At a gentle canter they arrived at a narrow stream where Raylene dismounted so Kota could wade for a drink. To the north sat a farmhouse miniaturized by distance, and to the south, a string of shining metal beads moved. A train speeding west.

A train on the move brought to mind the kinfolk passing through who had left their loved one behind to be buried by Conboie's crew. They would never know that their chosen coffin had been switched and the extra profit pocketed, probably by Lambert himself. She could not personally feature the need for a fancy box going into the ground. Better a wool blanket or a wrapper of painted paper, materials that would disintegrate as a body did. Even a cheap pine box was more respectful of the earth.

Now, though, it wasn't a question of what sort of box would suit a wormy embrace, but that such a switch was dishonorable whether designed for strangers or friends. There was only honor in deceiving enemies and that could not have been the case with Mr. Hanson. He was surely not known to Conboie or Lambert, else Lambert would have acted the friend with the man's kinfolk. Also, the burial crew had worked without the jittery laughter of nervousness, had not glanced furtively around or posted a sentry, which meant that the pine box burial had been just another job to them. Ordinary. To Raylene this suggested they were old hands at working a coffin-switching racket when no observers would be present. Added to Lambert's previous evasions regarding Annie's burial, her regard for him shrank to nothing.

Raylene shook her head. The most honest work she knew was ranch work, and she would be glad to return to it when her business in the city was done. Kota had wandered a bit downstream where a slash of green grass beckoned. She pulled a waxed paper packet from her pocket. Two slices of Mrs. G's bread, buttered and sprinkled with sugar. She went to stand by Kota as she ate. After returning him to Heinz's stable, she would peruse a pawn shop or two for items that would come in handy later today.

That evening, Murphy approached Union Cemetery's main entrance. From somewhere among the trees, an owl gave a long hoot, then another, as fallen leaves crunched underfoot. Dusk provided just enough light to see without his torch, so he followed the path leading inward. He didn't know exactly where to look, so he took the first path he came to, walking this way and that until arriving at the eastern acreage where he made out a shadowy figure sitting beneath a tree. He advanced to stand before the figure and willed himself to calm. The alarm he had felt at the little sister's last phone message had turned to barely-controlled outrage that nearly spilled over when Campbell gave him another inconsequential assignment. He had almost quit the U.P. on the spot.

"Good evening," came a quiet greeting.

He left off rancorous thoughts about being assigned to find a missing negligee left in a ladies' lavatory on last night's inbound from Denver and took a deep breath. Raylene Little Moon sat upon a blanket spread upon the grass. He said, "I would like to know what you mean by leaving me that kind of message."

"Will you sit?"

"I don't think so. I just want an answer."

"Since I haven't caught you at your office, I expressed what I need to know. I want answers too."

In her lap Raylene held a pair of binoculars. Murphy glanced left and right. "Were you watching me?"

"I'm watching that empty grave."

The lenses of his eyeglasses glinted in the rising moonlight. "The grave over there? For what reason?"

"My own reason."

Murphy's anger steamed beneath the surface of his professional calm. "I have no information to provide about ... what you asked for." He couldn't bring himself to speak the word. In the gathering darkness he could make out that she wasn't looking at him but into the distance.

She said, "I wish you would sit and quiet your voice."

"I am angry."

When she glanced up at him there were catch lights in her eyes. "I am not responsible for you turning me away from your door. You could have agreed to help me then."

"I cannot invite you to question Mr. Campbell about your sister. I am close to losing my job, which still might come to pass should word get out that a woman called to ask me about ... Well, you understand why."

"If your married boss was involved with my sister, he has little room to paint others wrong."

"Having little room might not alter the end result."

"My sister might have been pregnant. You wrote that there might be details yet to find, perhaps in the police report."

"I said *possibly* more."

"I can quote your letter."

"That's not necessary."

"If you did not want me to think that there is more to know, and that you were available to help, why did you write to me?"

Murphy could recall verbatim his letter to the woman before him, Annie Moon's sister. Perhaps he had written in consolation, perhaps out of gratitude for her assistance in extricating him from his troubles among her people. Perhaps he had written her because he ... because she ... He felt his anger deflate. He had known Raylene was smart and tough and might interpret his words the way she had. He was sorry she had lost her sister and that his job had not been to address that loss but to assist in a cover-up for Campbell's misdeeds. Such was not his to regret, but he did regret Annie Moon's involvement with his foul-mouthed boss. What could she have been to Campbell? What could he have meant to her?

He relented and took a seat upon the farthest edge of Raylene's blanket. She was facing outward so he did the same. Without moving a muscle, he found all his senses reaching toward her. He'd had a few words with her last month in the undertaker's parlor, then a glimpse through broken eyeglasses up in South Dakota, and again for a short exchange at his own front door. Now, in the gloaming, she was a non-descript shadow in a boxy jacket and baggy trousers that looked like men's work pants. He tried to register the fragrance of her, but all he detected was sun-warmed grass stirred by an evening breeze.

She said, "If Annie had been pregnant, she might have tried for an abortion."

She used that troubled "A" word so matter-of-factly. He asked, "She has passed away, so why does that matter now?"

"I imagine such a procedure comes with a dear price tag, more than she could afford. Someone else, likely her lover, would have provided some of the money. If so, the same person might have paid for her burial, and I want to know who and where." Raylene wanted to know who had held and perhaps returned Annie's affection. Her Annie, who had drawn heart shapes in her journal without attaching a name. She wanted someone to have cared for a woman who was not yet thirty who kept notes about her shoes needing new heels and which movies she had seen. She wanted someone besides herself and Thomas and Raymond to have loved Annie, whom she knew had always hungered for acceptance and love.

"Have you asked the sexton where her grave is?"

"This one is good for little except to say she is not here."

Which made no sense, given that Annie was an Indian. Murphy knew that Conboie Undertaking had handled Annie's burial in late September, and he had witnessed Raylene asking Mr. Lambert for information, to no avail. He could understand her need for the details. So much of life was lost or gained through knowing.

In the pause that followed, a bird called from somewhere nearby. Otherwise, the night was tranquil. "You are asking about something that's illegal," said Murphy.

"This is Kansas City, the crossroads of illegal activities." She paused. "I did not imagine a detective would shy from a difficult subject."

Murphy heard the challenge in her words. "I have sources inside the city police, but they might not have current names or locations. And there's the Kansas side. Your sister could have crossed the river."

"As you know, Annie boarded on that side. I'll check it."

Pulsing inside of Murphy was a desire that Raylene's request constitute the total of what she expected of him because he had come to understand that physical proximity to her threatened his composure, and experience had taught him that lack of composure could lead to mistakes in judgement. Per his tendency to construct mental balance sheets, he created one now. On the credit side was the truth that as a detective, he had some access to what local police knew; theirs was a mutual arrangement. Also, he was inclined to deliver that which the little sister's heart desired, and thereby grow closer to her.

On the debit side, his access to police reports was dependent on the detective sergeant's mood on any given day. Should Raylene Little Moon's direct talk ever reach Campbell, disaster would surely result. His assistance to her now might encourage her to overstep the barrier he had tried to erect against that very action. And of course, there was the matter of his composure.

Overlaid upon all this was his wish to protect his job, though he wasn't sure why that mattered any longer. He said, "If I secure this information, will it square us?"

"I did not make the arrangements, so Annie, as far as I'm concerned, is still missing."

"This discrepancy cannot be your fault. You were elsewhere."

"I need to locate Annie's grave. I can ask at the public cemeteries if you would take others such as Catholic. I know some Catholic ways but I am not quite one of them. You have an Irish name and you seem Catholic."

"I seem Catholic?"

"Concerned about appearances and rules."

Murphy wasn't sure how to take that. He broke rules all the time, he just didn't confess them. Switching tack, he asked, "Was Annie Catholic? They don't bury just anyone."

"We were schooled by nuns who controlled everything. They baptized us."

Murphy fell silent to digest this new information just as Raylene said, "What if in helping me you found the jewelry?"

"You told me you had no knowledge!"

"Time has delivered me some thoughts about it."

Murphy waited for more, but she sat silent. He asked, "How much do you know?"

"I know almost nothing, but I have suspicions." At this she lifted the binoculars and swept them back and forth in the direction of an empty grave in the distance.

Murphy considered the possibility that the little sister was trying to tempt him into helping her without intending to keep her end of the bargain, a classic "bait and switch," though based on what little he knew about her, he doubted it. He was tempted to think she might point him to the missing jewels. If so, he would accomplish the near-impossible by returning them to Campbell, thereby resuscitating his career. Though unsung for his heroics, his worth would be validated. He said, "I must insist that you not leave that sort of message again. I have a reputation as a man of good character."

"I recall that your good character includes following a woman, a stranger to you, across three states in order to retrieve gifts that should never have been given."

"I was doing my job."

"And now, I am doing mine."

Raylene stood, so Murphy did the same. She slung the strap of her binoculars over her shoulder and smiling to herself, folded the blanket and took up her torch. "If you decide to help, you know where to find me." Without waiting for an answer, she switched on her torch and followed its beam across the grass to the path which took her the opposite direction from which Murphy had arrived.

Murphy watched Raylene's light grow smaller until it disappeared altogether. He had not quite reconciled himself to assisting her, but he knew that he would do what was right. It so happened that what was right would also provide him more opportunities to linger in proximity to her. The very idea ran heat through him. Walking back to the cemetery entrance, he paid no notice to the evening chill.

Five

Tuesday came and Murphy wondered how he would get any U.P. work done. Yesterday had been bad enough before the dramatic message from the little sister. He had not exaggerated about how such a message could get him fired if Williams mentioned it to any of the big mouths in the office. Under certain circumstances, any of them might have a big mouth, and a few would be the type to whisper in Campbell's ear.

In spite of Campbell's flaws as a husband, about which Murphy might have sole knowledge, Campbell was a dyed-in-the-wool conservative family man, unlikely to ponder divorce, which would certainly cause his children distress, not least of which would be potential damage to the family's status in the community. This was not Murphy's problem, and yet it was. It was too late for him to refuse Campbell's jewelry assignment. Had he early on chosen differently, he might not now be in almost as deep as Campbell.

Last night he had slept sporadically, his dreams playing off his current assignment about the lost negligee by conjuring what sort of nightie the little sister might wear. His wife had worn white on their honeymoon and pink thereafter. Deciding now that Raylene would not touch a frothy, fluffy thing, his waking thought was to imagine other potential nightwear for her. But he was a gentleman, damn it. He didn't belong thinking about what Miss Little Moon did or did not wear to bed or he would be due for the confessional, for real.

When he left off thoughts about filmy garments, he replayed the rest of his exchange with the little sister. He couldn't decide if she'd outwitted him and if so, should he be her adversary instead of aiding her efforts? In the wee hours, he had decided that it was only right for her to seek her sister's Kansas City grave, and even, perhaps, to plan a confrontation with her sister's lover, though he was going to do his damnedest to keep the latter from happening. Or if a confrontation were to happen, it would not take place on U.P. property.

Before Campbell arrived in the office, Murphy handed off the lost negligee case to his junior colleague. He was about to take a walk to clear his head when a call came in that a dead dog of some floppy breed had been found in a building at the far end of the freight yard. He could picture Campbell's rage over the widow's pet being found dead after so much effort had been expended to find it alive. *Dear Jesus,* he thought, *Please don't let it be the one.*

Grabbing his jacket and hat, he called to Georgia and whoever could hear him that he'd be back. As he strode in the margin along the tracks, he could think only of Mrs. Worthridge and her imperious mien. Pacing around her hotel suite, she had bemoaned the state of a world in which her darling BooBoo could be lost. Her BooBoo, who wouldn't hurt a flea. Her BooBoo who was the most loyal companion a widowed woman could hope for. Her litany had continued long after the point had been made, enough so that it nearly rendered Murphy comatose.

Though the day had a touch of cool to the air, he could feel his dress shirt dampen from the exertion of hurrying the length of multiple football fields. Before entering the outbuilding in question, he removed his fedora and wiped his forehead with a kerchief. With his hat gripped in the hand of his cast arm, he stepped through the big open swinging doors to an interior smelling of all things railroad — sweaty men, items made of steel, solvents, grease. Two men in coveralls moved toward him from the far end.

"You here about the dog?"

"I'm John Murphy from over at operations. How are you fellas?"

"Ah, we're okay. Glad the hot weather is letting up a little. S'pose you're here for —"

"That's right."

The taller man led Murphy toward the far corner of the huge space.

"How'd you know to call?" asked Murphy.

"Seen those handbills on the way to work. It's over there." He pointed at a mound of matted hair atop a barrel full of oily rags.

Murphy looked around and chose a pitchfork with which to lift the object that had clearly been a hairy thing of just a few pounds, now shrunken in death. The mound exhibited short protrusions that were likely its legs, and a flat-looking face. It was the missing dog, alright, the correct size and colors but for the dust and grime accumulated around the rail yards, and some dried blood that suggested it had been bitten. The heat of the building hadn't helped any; he could make out the rotting smell of it. "Where'd you find it?" he asked.

"On the other side of the tracks. We were moving some old solvent needs dumping. There's a reward for finding it, yeah?"

Murphy let the mound of hair down slowly and turned toward the men. "For the right dog, alive. But that's not the one. I'm glad you called, though. It was worth a look."

"Aw, you sure? We thought we had beer money."

"Sorry, but it's not. What do you do with something like this?"

"Out along the fence line, we'd just leave it. Some critter'd come along and clean it up. But if it's found in close, maybe along the passenger tracks, we've got to dispose of it. You'd be surprised the animals we find smashed up. They get through a fence or come down the tracks from a ways away."

"How about you fellas burn it with those rags," said Murphy. "You'll be burning them."

"Guess we could." The first man looked at the other one, who shrugged. "Yeah, I guess."

"It was probably some local's pet," said Murphy. "Kind of makes for a suitable send off."

The men nodded.

"Maybe today," added Murphy, "to keep the place tidy." He put his hat back on and made to leave. "Thanks, fellas. Oh, listen, for noticing the reward poster, and keeping this place tidy—beer money." He pulled out the wallet he'd purchased after that incident in South Dakota and extracted three dollars, enough for a few rounds. "You find another one, call us, will you? We're hopeful."

The men accepted the cash and watched until Murphy had almost reached the door before they turned back to their work. Murphy stepped out into the bright light of morning and checked his watch. 8:00 a.m. Campbell would be in by now. Walking back, he began formulating his verbal report.

The boss man, Ricco, was unlocking the saloon door when that same morning Raylene arrived.

"You came back," he said.

"One day's pay won't cover my rent. I need to earn more."

Ricco laughed as if she had said something funny. "You might do alright after all." He led the way into the boxy room. "Stick around till noon, I'll win two bits. Work all week, I win a buck."

Raylene recognized what he meant, saying, "I guess half of that would be mine." She held Ricco's gaze.

He broke into laughter again. "You got some guts, but it's my bet, my money. You'll have to settle for a beer, maybe." He pointed to the kegs behind the bar. "That one with the black and white label's pretty good."

Raylene went through to the back room where a back door led to an alley. One corner held a desk and a worn oak chair, and another corner held the cleaning gear she'd put neatly away on Saturday. Along the wall were stacked cases of bottles and a large upright freezer. Her fingers itched to inspect bottles for the names of their makers, but she decided to let some time pass first.

Ricco passed by her and unbolted it. "Got deliveries today," he said. "When the ice guy comes you could hold the freezer door. I got him coming twice a week cause the freezer ain't working too good."

Raylene nodded and carried the bucket, liquid soap, and brushes to the bar's sink. Behind the bar, she had to step over a dark stain on the wooden floor that she had tried unsuccessfully to scrub away on her first day of work. The stain would live on, a reminder of the vagaries of life and the repercussions of the choices people made.

Pausing before it now, she pictured Thomas, whom she'd known as Father, prone on the beat-up floor, his life draining out of him. His astonishment followed by recognition, then acceptance of Raymond's wrath. She could conjure Raymond too, both uncle and father, bound by her rope and unaware of his own fate. Or had he seen the future? She had expected her cunning, honed through games of skill against Oglala boys, would prove sufficient against Ray. Her knowledge of herbs and poisons too. But his words had made her question those thoughts and wonder if he had actually awaited her arrival, contriving to employ her as participant and witness to his fiery plan. She would never know.

A voice inside her said *Go back where you belong and leave city things to city people.* Go for peace and sun and the sweat of a hard day's work and after work, a game of cards for nickels or matchsticks, the men's low talk and the comparing of tall tales. The swapping of duties that had been assigned. Give her rivers and the land's distant undulations as landmarks. Give her the ebb and flow of cattle on the hoof and ranch dogs racing ahead. The chill night air beyond a stall layered with sweet hay, Raul's body pressed hard against hers, and the smell of peppermint on his breath. All reasons she seldom sought out a city, including this one, but also reasons she could not go back just yet. There was no going back to those satisfactions without finishing here what she had started.

At the far end of the main room, she propped open the doors to the gentlemen's and ladies' lavatories. Because women had taken to drinking in public as easily as breathing, most public saloons offered restrooms for women, in this case a small room with one stall and a sink and mirror. This room showed scant use since she'd cleaned on Sunday, but any use at all was odd if on Sunday the place wasn't open to the public.

She had seen through Ricco's claim about being closed on Sundays as cover for what he was likely offering — illegal card games for men. Not that local officials would take much mind. They hadn't ever raided Thomas's game. But had a player gotten overheated and killed someone, they would have shut his operation down for a week or two to show they meant business. Soon enough, everything would be back to normal.

Ricco would have been foolish to forsake the gamblers itching for a card game. Money changed hands, everybody drank, they were ready-made customers. Ricco hadn't needed to hide that from her, but he couldn't know what she knew about the saloon, and she meant to keep it that way. After wiping down the lavatory sink, she glanced into the metal waste can. It held a cigarette stub with lipstick on it, and a sanitary napkin with no sign of blood. Perhaps women were allowed in on Sunday nights. Certain women.

There came a noise from the direction of the rear door so Raylene carried her bucket to the sink behind the bar in order to eavesdrop. She set the water running to get it hot and moved to peer into the back room. Ricco was at the door, greeting a man in denim work clothes. Raylene called out, "Is it the ice? I'll help." She turned off the water and crossed to stand next to Ricco, who shot her an amused look.

When the workman caught sight of her, he said, "That little thing? You gotta be kiddin'."

"Hey, help is help," said Ricco, his smile now larger.

The ice man scowled at Raylene. "Stay outta the way."

At that, Raylene stepped past both men, reaching the back of the open cargo truck first to grab one end of a bulging burlap sack which she pulled toward her. "Look out," said the ice man as Raylene hoisted the sack onto her shoulder, pivoting to take its weight across her back. The sack weighed forty or fifty pounds, about as much as a young steer. She found her balance and crossed to the back door then through it, with Ricco hurrying to open the freezer. She swung her full sack into place and turned to go back for another.

"I got it, I got it," snarled the ice man, fast on her heels. "Ain't having no girl carry more'n me. Go do something else."

Raylene looked at Ricco. Still grinning, he nodded. Back at the sink, she filled her bucket and headed for the gentlemen's lavatory as the men's voices receded behind her. Sink basins first, then toilets, then floors.

Soon after moving into one of the two toilet stalls, she

heard a voice behind her. "So, *this* is your job." The ice man in the stall's open doorway glanced at the soapy brush in her hand. "Fitting."

Raylene locked eyes with him as Ray's voice came to her — *See your opponent clearly and never underestimate.* She said, "The other stall is available."

The man grinned. "I might want this one."

"Take the other."

"No, I'm thinking this one and you can stay right there."

Raylene moved a half-step back while pretending to drop her brush. Reaching toward the floor, she ran her hand up to grasp her boot knife as Ricco's voice sounded from just outside the lavatory doorway.

"Hey Cheeky, come on out here."

Unarmed, Raylene straightened and locked gazes again with the ice man. His grin had grown wide. "Another time," he said low.

"You had better hope not," she replied as he made way to let her pass.

Murphy stood before his boss's desk as Campbell growled, "You what?"

"I went down to Freight 9 — they're the ones who called in — and had a look at the dead dog body that was there."

"And what? Jesus, tell me it wasn't that damned Peekaboo dog."

"Pekinese."

"Oh."

"By the name of BooBoo."

"Stupidest name I ever heard. Whatever happened to real dog names like Buck or Rowdy?"

"That wasn't it."

"The dead one?"

"It looked like a coyote pup."

"There are coyotes in Maintenance?"

"Injured, maybe dragged itself in." "Do you want to pay off Mrs. Worthridge so she can continue her travels?"

"Could her damn dog still show up?"

"I doubt it. Someone's got a new pet. And she will want you to pay her hotel bill for waiting around." Murphy's fervent hope was that Campbell would not soon encounter the Freight 9 workers and ask them questions about the size and color of the dog carcass. Soon this day would blend into the others, *Move along folks, nothing to see here.*

"Ah, Jesus." Campbell's face had grown red. He drummed his fingers on his desk. "Listen, here's what. Get a purchase order from Georgia and contact the widow. Get the damn hotel paid and the cost of a replacement dog and get that woman on her way. I don't want to hear anything else about dead dogs or hotels or *anything else.* Jesus. Don't bring me any more problems. I don't want problems, I want answers."

Murphy stood rooted in place, debating whether to say what he ought to.

"What?" shouted Campbell. "Don't just stand there!"
"I've had a lead, or a suggestion of a lead, about the jewelry." Campbell's face registered surprise and he planted both hands on the leading edge of his desk. "You shitting me?"

"No."

"A serious lead? What is it?"

"I'm reluctant to divulge details before something pans out to prove their worth."

"It's not a good lead then. It's lousy."

"It's probably as good as any we've had."

"But there's a catch, else you would spit it out."

"The catch is ... it requires me to help the person who says they have information."

Campbell whacked an open hand on his desk. "That's bullshit. What's 'help the person' mean. I'm the one who needs help. I need that damn jewelry."

The office had grown warm. Murphy thought how he should have closed Campbell's office door before now, but word would get around anyway. "I'll work on the situation," he said, "but I'll need time away from the office to do it." There, he'd said it.

Campbell looked ready to explode again, but then his expression softened as he bit his lower lip. "You asking for a leave of absence?"

"Paid leave."

Campbell seemed to be considering the idea, so Murphy continued. "You know I would look for runaway dogs and missing lingerie every day of every year if that's my job. I still have a wife to support." Catherine's condition was not ordinarily a bargaining chip, but Murphy wanted it clear that he wouldn't clean up Campbell's problems for free.

At last Campbell spoke. "How much time?"

"A week." He figured he could find out what the little sister wanted in two days, maybe three, if he had to verify information. A week ought to be twice what he needed.

"Five business days, that's it." The look on Campbell's face suggested he might think this a chance to be rid of a detective who now displeased him. "You find those pieces in a shop, come to me for the money to buy them. I'm not giving you cash up front this time."

Murphy nodded. "I spent Saturday checking pawn shops. The pieces aren't there. They're somewhere else."

"I sure hope your hunch pays off."

"Not a hunch, a lead."

"A *suggestion* of a lead."

"Right."

"Alright, you're on leave as of tomorrow. Today you're going to take a check to Mrs. Worthridge and explain how we have done our duty and will not finance her accommodations any longer. Wish her a smooth trip west. Pack her bags if you have to. Get that woman out of my city."

Murphy had done it. He could arrange Mrs. Worthridge's retreat, but the clock was now ticking on his finding the objects that had eluded him for the last month and his job now hinged even more than before on the little sister's word. With a jolt, he wondered if negotiating with Campbell had been madness. When he exited Campbell's office, two of the freight inspectors snapped their attention back to their work. Another one watched him all the way back to his office.

Raylene arrived just as dusk fell across Union Cemetery. She navigated through tree shadows by memory, along the paths and between old monuments and weather-scarred markers. Should she encounter an empty grave, she would note its location for inspecting another night. As she walked, she digested the textures and details around her.

At last, she reached the zone in which the recent dead were buried unless they hailed from a family with a reserved plot. As she traversed the acreage currently full of marked graves, she listened, not only for the natural sounds of night, but for the *chunk* of spade into earth. It would not do to give her presence away by walking up on a grave-digging party.

When no empty graves revealed themselves, she crossed to the area where the previous night, a grave had sat empty. Now that void now was filled with mounded dirt, empty no longer. After sitting awhile in the lee of a large oak and detecting no activity nearby, Raylene crossed the grass, acorns underfoot like small stones. At the newly tamped mound, she leaned in to light it with her torch before ambling back toward the entrance, keeping watch not to encounter the sexton. The moon was in a waning phase, headed toward blankness, which would give her extra concealment but also conceal others more effectively.

When voices reached her from somewhere to her left, she diverted in a westerly direction, proceeding slowly from one patch of darker shadow to the next until from a distance she could make out two people reclined on a blanket, their cigarettes like red eyes in the dark. Away from city traffic, their voices carried to her, one in a female register, the other, male. Lovers, then, or else companions who preferred to speak their thoughts into the dark, which negated the need to hold one another's gazes or read expressions. Night was a great equalizer.

Retreating toward the older section, Raylene plotted a course for the sexton's cottage. While inside the cottage that one time, she had identified a small kitchenette off the main room and two closed doors, one she supposed led to a room for bathing and toileting, the other to a bedroom.

A person such as the sexton might lead a quiet life after hours, or maybe not. Perhaps since a street car ran within a block of the cemetery entrance, he took himself of an evening to one or more of the city's jazz joints and drinking parlors.

On her route to the cottage, she caught sight of a form bent over a granite grave marker so she paused in place, close enough to make out the outline of a woman's hat and coat. The figure seemed to be placing flowers. It stood still for a minute, maybe two, during which time Raylene thought she heard the murmuring of prayers. From her childhood came a memorization exercise required by nuns. *Eternal rest grant unto them...*

When the figure moved away, Raylene advanced to the walkway that ran alongside the sexton's cottage, ready to turn away should its front door open. A glow of interior lights lit the cottage's windows, but otherwise the place sat quiet. Raylene moved close enough to walk the perimeter of the cottage's narrow gardens, not quite trespassing since all the cemetery's land was public. The backfire of an auto on the closest street reached her and then came a sound reverberating through a window at the rear, the presumed bedroom. A rhythmic sound, dull from outside, but likely sharp on the inside: metal striking wood. She stopped in her tracks to listen. Four whacks then a pause then four whacks. This went on for half a minute, maybe longer, much too long for hanging a picture or repairing the hinge of a cupboard. Someone inside was building something.

The whacking stopped, so Raylene pivoted and made her way back to the street.

That evening, as Murphy waved goodbye to the taxi cab carrying Mrs. Worthridge to the U.P. passenger depot, he felt a great fatigue descend upon him. He was used to dealing with people who had been robbed or injured or who refused to speak up for fear of implicating themselves in a crime they knew something about. Rarely did he encounter people, either victim or perpetrator, who couldn't turn off the faucet of their words. His telephone call to Mrs. Worthridge at the Crown Hotel had lasted nearly twenty minutes during which time he had managed two or three sentences of explanation and an offer of remuneration. The rest of the time he had listened to her hysteria at the news that her BooBoo had not been located.

In his estimation, the woman's theatrics had been just that — performance, surely tinged with honest grief, but performance nonetheless. Such was probably how she operated when seeking accommodation from those outside her orbit. And perhaps within. Well, he had accommodated her hysteria and the need for payment of her hotel account. Management had sent a maid to assist with packing the lady's delicates and wardrobe, then a taxi had been called. In the lobby, Murphy produced a ticket for train passage westward, and loaded the BooBoo-less woman into the taxi that now, finally, was turning a corner to disappear from sight. He sighed deeply and made a mental note to call the office about dispatching someone to seek out and remove the reward handbills. That would be the end of that.

His preparations and encounter with Mrs. Worthridge had eaten up much of the afternoon and now he faced the choice of heading home to see what sort of soup his housekeeper Ruby had left for him to warm on the stove, or, and this sounded infinitely more appealing, he could head uptown to what was left of the dining district after the big crash. Many establishments had not reopened. He paused a moment to consider his choices. Any Missouri restaurant worth its salt offered beef, the sort of fare he'd been raised on. But tonight, he needed a change, a meal to start him back on a winning track. Something exotic. Italian noodles, maybe, dressed with red sauce or meatballs. For that he would head to Johnny's Taste of Italy.

Six

The next morning, Murphy's alarm clock nearly made his head implode. What on earth had he drunk last night? More accurately, how much had he drunk of Johnny's house wine, though Johnny's wasn't where he had spent the whole evening. A block and a half up from the restaurant there sat a joint that let local jazz musicians jam on weeknights. For whatever reason, Murphy had felt like he needed to live it up a little before taking on the little sister's goal of locating a practitioner of illegal medical procedures. He had walked up to Red's for a nightcap accompanied by hot horns and piano licks. Had he really sent drinks to the women at one of the front tables who seemed to be with the piano player? Drinks for the piano player too, but it was the women who had caught his eye, dressed in ways that accentuated all the right curves. One had gotten up and sung a song Murphy recognized.

Next thing he knew, the bartender was plying him with coffee and he had wobbled his way back to his coupe. Somehow, he had made it home. Driving home, his thoughts had pivoted back to the word for that medical procedure, *that word*, as he now thought of it, but having never discussed the subject out loud, he needed to work up to speaking about it to his contacts at police headquarters. They would, Dear God, think he was asking for himself. Instead of facing that task first, he decided to telephone cemeteries associated with the Catholic diocese. Once he located Annie Moon's grave, he would take on the stickier mission.

He would typically shave and dress before thinking about breakfast, but he needed coffee or sugar or something. Wearing his robe, he went to the kitchen to start some coffee perking and rummaged about for the makings of toast. Disjointed as his thoughts were, he recalled the little sister's previous advice about water so he poured himself a full glass and drank it down. Cream for coffee. Bread. Was there any of that peach jam left? Catholic cemeteries. Probably three or four. His city directory might not call them out as such. Or maybe it would. Just then the telephone rang.

Murphy half-stumbled into the hallway and picked up the handset. "Hello?" he said.

"Son!"

Murphy winced at his father's voluminous cheer. "Ah, good morning, Father."

"Are you alright?"

Murphy couldn't tell. From the inside, he sounded like he felt. Blurry. "I'm grand," he lied. "How are you? How's Mam?"

"We're grand. Listen, I wanted to catch you before you left for work. Your mother requests your company at Sunday supper. You declined last month and then you broke your arm on that trip north, so it's two months and your mother's been counting. She's about to call you herself. And then ... you know."

Murphy knew what "You know" meant — tears plus admonitions about what a mother's heart needed. Perhaps a bit of begging. The begging would do him in. He was their only child and it was true that he had accepted fewer invitations to his parents' home after Catherine took ill. When she had been unable to leave the house, he had at first made excuses for them both and stayed home to assuage the fear that seemed to grow within her like a cancer. But over time, his staying or going had not seemed to change Catherine's outlook, and he had joined the occasional family meal so that parents and aunts would not feel entirely abandoned.

Eventually, he tired of fielding questions from his elders about the state of Catherine's care and her mental capacity and his own intentions regarding her. On one occasion roughly three years back, he had carried dishes into his parents' kitchen and found his mother weeping over a sink full of suds. "Am I not to have grandchildren?" she had asked, tears wetting her cheeks, and he had felt her sorrow deeply.

"Right," said Murphy now. "I do know, and, well ..."

"Do come. For your mother."

What could he say to that which had always been implied but was now made specific — that in keeping his distance he was breaking his mother's heart. "I have a new assignment that might require I work the weekend." Following silence on the other end, Murphy continued, "Perhaps I can stop by, not for supper, but afterwards for a visit."

His father, a man of few words, sighed. "She'll take what she can get. You know she'll cook enough in case you come for supper."

"Likely enough to feed all the poor in Dublin. Tell her I'll stop in *afterwards*, okay Da?"

"Alright."

When they signed off, Murphy moved back to the kitchen where he slumped into a chair mulling over the sorrow of mothers but pleased that his father had not detected his hangover. At least he hoped so. At last, he roused to fetch a mug from a cupboard and moved to the coffee pot steaming on the stove. As he was pouring himself some and fantasizing how cream and sugar might cure a headache, there came the sound of a key in the back door. With his thoughts still on parents and children, he had the odd sensation of being his younger self arriving home on his bicycle after school; he had always entered through the kitchen door after setting his bike against the back porch railing.

In the midst of his flashback, he started at the sight of Ruby, his part-time housekeeper, arriving with hands full of a coat and purse and a shopping bag with basics purchased from his household cash. Her bag would contain cornflakes, a loaf of bread, and a pound of butter. Perhaps the fixings for soup. *Ruby? — What day was this?* — Dear God, he was in his robe when he should be dressed.

Murphy's face went hot, but rather than flee so that Ruby would be greeted with a view of the back of his uncombed head and his plaid robe in retreat, he pushed his eyeglasses up and waited until she registered the sight of him.

He marshalled a friendly but contrite look. "Good morning. My sincerest apologies. I got distracted and am running late. I'll get ready for the day and leave you to start in the kitchen."

The young woman had frozen just inside the kitchen door, her eyes shifting from Murphy to the stove's clock to the mug of coffee on the counter. She always let herself in after he left for work, but here he was, standing before her in a state of disrepair. He said, "I'll be working away from the office today. That's thrown off my timing." Hoping for a graceful exit, he turned away.

"Mr. Murphy — your coffee?" said Ruby to his back.

He answered as he walked away. "A change of plans — I'll go out to breakfast this morning."

Headed to her afternoon stop, Raylene thought back over her morning. She had met Ricco at the saloon and cleaned for two hours. At one point, a delivery of beer had arrived, three kegs from Dooney Bros. Brewery, a name she recognized from Annie's journal. When the opportunity arose, she had remarked to Ricco that the saloon seemed to go through plenty of beer. "Probably hard stuff, too," she added, keeping her tone casual.

"Pretty steady," said Ricco. "Some customers have come here for years. They like the labels they're used to."

"Anything sell best?"

"Everything sells." He had gone back to counting cash from the prior evening, but she pushed the subject further.

She said, "I suppose you get a couple of deliveries each week."

"I place orders when I need 'em."

"With the big distributors?"

Now he looked at her funny. "You worked a saloon before, you know how it works."

She shrugged. "Not in this city. I am curious where your hard stuff comes from."

"I didn't hire you to be curious."

Raylene raised her open hands. "Curiosity is natural."

"Well, nosy people get themselves hurt. Sometimes."

Raylene shook her head as if to suggest she wasn't going to push him and went back to sweeping. She did not need him pitching her out of the place. Not that knowing exactly who brought deliveries and what they contained would bring Annie back — it wouldn't — nor would she singlehandedly shut down a bootlegging operation if she thought it was the one supplying bad booze. In their day, Federal agents had not always succeeded at that. Still, a hole would remain in her understanding of Annie's passing without some knowledge to fill it, and that might require she fabricate an opportunity to spy on the saloon when it opened for the lunch trade.

Now, though, she was headed for another public cemetery to try to find Annie. Elmwood was in the northeast of the city on Fifteenth Street. Kansas City was organized with avenues running north and south and streets running east and west, none of which mattered when she was a child on foot or using the streetcars while visiting, but now that she was driving about the city, she was developing an orientation to that layout. She also had a map.

Before long, she parked on the street near Elmwood's entrance and walked in under foliage of yellow and gold. Leaves swirled in the breeze and patterned the grassy lawns. Park-like acres rolled away to the distance.

She followed a lettered sign pointing the way to the sexton's cottage, which was slightly larger than the one at Union Cemetery. Outside the cottage she found an older man trimming a rose bush, one of many hugging the cottage. She stood to one side quietly until the man looked up from his work.

"Can I help you?" he asked.

"I am hoping to locate a recent burial."

"You found the right person." He waved a hand at the pile of thorny debris lying near his feet. "Fall clean-up."

"The hips make good tea."

"Well, my wife, God bless her, would've said the same. She was good for all that stuff. This here's her favorite — yellow rose of Texas." He removed his gloves. "Help yourself if you want, but watch for thorns."

"If you would look up a record ..."

"Yes, of course. I forget myself when talking about roses." He motioned toward the cottage. "Follow me. My better half had the best hand for setting down last name, first name, and dates, but she'd admit I'm not half-bad at it myself."

He led the way into the parlor of the cottage where curtains had been drawn back from the windows. Raylene stopped just inside the doorway as the sexton stepped to a large desk on which stacks of leather-bound ledgers rested. "It's all by year, of course, month and date. Got all the records going back to the 1870s." At this he beamed a little like a proud papa. "Course not all the way back to the beginning of settlers in these parts. We're not *that* old, but still we've got a couple thousand."

One of the ledgers lay open on the desk near an ink stand and fountain pen. The sexton ran a hand gently across the open page. "Tell me what name and roughly when we would have completed the burial."

"I'm looking for Annie Moon. She died the week of September 19th and would have been buried before the 26th. That's what I was told. If not Moon then Yellow Moon."

"Moon. That's unusual, shouldn't be too hard to find. Her body was sent here from elsewhere, or was she from nearby?"

"She was here."

"There's just shy of two pages with all the records from early September," he said, flipping pages. "I'll check back to the first. Won't take any time at all but you can have a seat while I look." He gestured toward a nearby wooden bench.

"Standing suits me."

"As you like. Let me see ..." He first turned back a page, then leaning closer, ran a finger slowly down the right-hand page, murmuring "Moon, Moon," until he reached the bottom. He turned to the next page and proceeded in the same manner.

Raylene found her heart was beating hard and willed it to calm. Her sister would be buried here or else at one of the other cemeteries, a fact over which she had no control.

At last, the sexton looked up. "I'll check once more," he said, "but there's only these pages. My writing's not the finest — all that digging, you know — but I take care with the records since my wife ..." His shrug ended the sentence.

Raylene waited until he repeated his previous procedure. She found herself following his finger's motion with her eyes.

When the man uttered not one word of discovery, no *urp* of pleasure at having found a clue, no stutter of breath at a treasure revealed, she knew that Elmwood provided another impasse.

The sexton straightened and shook his head. "No such record for a Moon, sorry to say. That name would stand out. Did someone tell you she was here?"

"No. I am checking all the cemeteries."

"Ah. There's some bunch to check. A big one east of the city limits, for instance. And there's some connected to the Catholics and two or three on the Kansas side — we all belong to a trade group of sorts — I don't suppose you'd want the Huron Cemetery, unless that's your people."

When Raylene shook her head, he added, "If you called, you might get through unless they're like me, digging and pruning and all."

This begged another question from Raylene. "Does Conboie's crew do actual burying here?"

"I handle everything, except it takes extra hands to lower a casket. So, if it's their customer and I haven't got enough help, I might press them into service."

"But they wouldn't work on their own here."

The sexton puffed up a little. "It's my job to complete any burials. There's none without me."

"I thank you for your time," said Raylene. She was wearing her saloon-cleaning clothes and the old barn coat given her by Billy Horse.

"Want some of those rose hips?" asked the sexton, a catch in his voice causing Raylene to pause as she made to leave. "I'll pull them for you if you'll have some."

She looked back at him. His eyes were soft and he looked a little hopeful. "I suppose," she said. "If you have the time." He had been pleasant with her, which made it easier to linger a few more minutes.

The man's smile grew wide. "Got my gloves right here. Snippers would work too. I'll strip a bunch. You from around here?" He continued his patter as he led the way, Raylene nodding now and then or providing the briefest of answers. Before long, she had a pocket full of the dried hip berries. After they exchanged goodbyes, Raylene returned to her truck and took out the penciled list of cemeteries she had made the previous night. She was just getting started.

Murphy took his breakfast at a diner not far from Union Station, but knew better than to breach the office for the use of a telephone while he was on leave. When paying his meal tab, he procured a handful of nickels in change. He could use the public telephone at the corner of 25th and Holmes near the Louis George library branch. When done with his calls, there would be time to drop in at the L. George, where he might borrow "The Postman Always Rings Twice" or an issue of Startling Detective Adventures magazine, which in a recent issue had told the story of a "Karpis-Barker" gang moll married to a Prohibition-era runner of whiskey from New Orleans to K.C. Even if somewhat exaggerated, that story had to have been based in truth, since he knew the named culprit had in real life been caught and sent to the slammer.

The pay telephone booth was littered with cigarette butts, which Murphy kicked into its corner before pulling out the pocket notebook on which he had listed cemeteries and their phone numbers. Those under Catholic administration included Mount Saint Mary's and one further north called Resurrection. To show his good intentions, he would include Mount Calvary, which lay west of the river. He had identified a Jewish cemetery, but figured he could skip that one. Were he a betting man, he'd put money on one of the others.

The day was nice, so he left the phone booth door open as he pulled nickels from his pocket and set to work calling. Before long, he knew what he had suspected — that no one with the name Moon had been buried with Kansas City, Missouri's Catholics. Though he rang more than once, the phone at Mount Calvary on the Kansas side was not answered.

October 28, 1936

Dear Catherine,

I know a week has not quite passed, but it will by the time you have received this, and I thought I would write before work overtakes my schedule. This time there will be no travel, no mistakes to be made on an Indian reservation, but as much or more than before at stake with Campbell.

Do you remember that your parents were displeased that you married an accountant who became a detective. They would rather an accountant for a son-in-law. I thought that you objected, too, but I was so sure of my career change that you agreed. You just wanted a peaceful home, am I right? What woman would not? I have only the one marital experience (with you), but I suspect most women say very little and hope everything works out for the best.

Because you will not pin me with your clear blue eyes, I will mention that my work week has taken a dark turn. I have been phoning today in search of a burial record (with no success thus far) and next will come a pursuit that I will not describe other than to mention that overheated discussion we had one time. Just that one, as I recall. Do you remember what you said and what I said? Of course you might not. I hope you do not. I would like to forget it myself.

The Colorado Rockies, if I have it right, are plowing headlong toward winter's cold days and nights, but here in K.C. our days are pleasantly cool after another brutal summer. What a difference it makes to be at not much higher than sea level. Leaves on trees here are just now turning fall colors. Winter, of course, sneaks up across the plains.

That is all my poor right hand can take. The doctor will set my left arm free tomorrow — hoorah, and I will visit my parents this Sunday evening. I know they keep you in their prayers, as do I.

Yours truly,
John

Later that afternoon, Raylene parked her truck on 30th Street in the old part of town, which was home to her father's Salem Avenue saloon. The saloon was now Ricco's to manage, but its history as Thomas's endured within her. Walking a counterclockwise circuit, she perused the businesses fronting Salem and around to Derby Avenue, some of which had closed in the last few years.

On her stroll, she passed a laundry, a second-hand store, and a building marked YMCA that looked operational. Almost in line with the alley that ran behind the saloon sat a business making sacks used for hauling grain. Morton Grain Sacks. A person inside the workshop's doorway, or standing on the curb in front of it, would have a reasonable view across 30th to deliveries in the alley behind Ricco's saloon. Also, those selling grain sacks might have customers such as breweries or distilleries. This was a place to know better. She went inside.

A dozen machines with women sitting at them were clattering away as lengths of sack cloth were fed between presser feet and toothed guides that dragged the material under powerful needles looped with heavy thread. The sewing women flashed looks at Raylene, but every one of them held her place. Their glances drew the attention of the only man in the large room. Hands on his hips, he stood watching the workers before sauntering over to stand within shouting distance of Raylene. He looked her up and down before speaking loudly. "If you're looking for work, I got no room for you."

Women of various shades of skin color worked in a smog of cotton dust suspended in the air, which told Raylene that her heritage wasn't a problem. A place like this would prefer workers who harbored few expectations of decent treatment or pay. She said, "I thought you might need someone to stack and count your goods for delivery."

"I've got a nephew who does that."

"You might need extra hands. I'm looking to work afternoons."

The man pulled himself up to his full height and stuck his thumbs in his waistband. "I know you speak English because we've been speaking English. But you're not getting my meaning."

Raylene feigned a look of innocent neediness. "I have a truck I could use for making deliveries."

"You? Have a truck?"

She nodded.

"You have a truck that runs."

"Reliably."

"Well, I'll be." He glanced around as if she might have brought it inside with her. "Where's it at?"

She motioned to the doorway and led him out to the sidewalk, where she pointed at her truck, close enough to hit with a rock.

"The green one?" said the boss man.

"Yes."

Out in the light, she could see that he had a fine layer of cotton dust in his hair and along his shoulders. Before the day was out, he would shed powder like a dog does water. He gave her a look that said he didn't believe her. "Let me see you start it up."

She pulled the key on its short leather thong from her pocket and walked over to the truck. Climbing in, she fired it up. Through the windshield she watched him shake his head as if at a sleight-of-hand trick. She shut down the truck and went back to where he stood silently working his mouth. "You load here in front, is that right?" she asked.

He nodded.

"If you don't want me counting or bundling your sacks, I

could wait at the curb until you have a delivery to go to a customer."

While waiting for his answer, she glanced down the alley she'd been scouting. Near each back door was a trash barrel or two pushed close to the brick buildings; also, the odd pedestrian cutting through from 29th to 30th.

At last, the workshop boss spoke. "No, I stand by what I said."

Raylene shrugged. She had had another thought but didn't want to give up this possible contact. "I might come around someday to ask again."

"You can ask, but don't expect anything."

She nodded.

The man looked at her as if waiting for her to move first, but she stood her ground and waited until he turned back toward his workshop and disappeared through its door. When he was gone, she went back to her truck and moved it one space closer to the workshop's entrance, which offered the best line of sight to the alley. Then she settled back in her seat and watched from her open window for signs of alley activity.

Murphy arrived at Union Cemetery as dusk was falling. He did not know where he might find the little sister, but he had called the boarding house and had not found her there. For some reason, she had spent recent evenings in this cemetery, so he watched for her as he strolled within its cocoon of peace. When he spotted her, he drew close to her sitting place and stopped.

"Hello again," said Raylene. "Join me if you'd like."

Murphy took a seat on Raylene's blanket. "I telephoned Catholic cemeteries today."

"Did you have luck?"

"None. There's Mount Calvary on the Kansas side. When I

got no answer, I drove over. I found the sexton, whom I will say was reluctant to leave off what he was doing, but he did cooperate, and he checked the records and Annie was not there. He had buried no Moon in September."

Raylene fingered the rose hips in her coat pocket. "There was no Moon at Elmwood either."

"I believe you told me that your father is buried here at Union."

"I have seen his grave."

"Could your sister have instead been buried in Kansas? There's a Mt. Hope, that's an old one, and a Memorial Park. And a Maple Hill. My research says Maple Hill is more recent."

Raylene shook her head. "I wondered about that, but I cannot imagine a reason."

"She boarded over there, yes? So perhaps she had other dealings there and ..."

"But she worked on this side, my father's business was here." She paused. "Also, who would have arranged it? Your boss, perhaps."

"Well, I —" Murphy had pondered what exactly Campbell had been to Annie and what had attracted her to him. The one photograph he had seen of Annie showed her as nice-looking. Campbell, rough as he often was, might have been a tender paramour. But would he have arranged Annie's burial? Perhaps, if she were precious enough to him for the gift of all that jewelry. He could have paid for a nice casket and a quiet, shady place, but most likely within the city where he resided and they both worked. Or ... had Campbell paid to have her buried elsewhere in order to distance himself from her death?

He was not about to ask these questions of his boss. Reasoning that Raylene would have thought this all through as well, Murphy did not speak his thoughts aloud. He would call the Kansas cemeteries and find Annie's resting place. Somehow it had become important that he be the one to tell Raylene that he'd found her sister.

Raylene said, "I could not get information from Conboie & Son. Mr. Lambert was smooth in his avoidance and I have since begun to wonder whether Conboie runs the place. Mr. Lambert seems to have oversight." She looked at Murphy. "Would he give you the information?"

The problem was, should Murphy question either Conboie or Lambert, either one might easily alert Campbell that Murphy was snooping around about his private matters. He knew how that would end. He said, "I doubt it. If he would not tell you, he was probably sworn to secrecy or paid to keep quiet."

"This city runs on secrets."

Didn't they *all* have secrets, thought Murphy. The little sister too. A person could simply not know everything about someone else. It just wasn't possible, not even between married people. Not even between siblings. He spent his days trying to locate objects secreted from the railroad or damaged by those who meant to remain unidentified. Those items, however, were not bodies.

He said, "Could Mrs. Gunther shed light on Annie's private life? Who she knew, or miscellaneous details she has not confided to you? Or perhaps there's something you have heard that you don't realize is important." Murphy mentally kicked himself. Though insignificant details could lead to revelations, he did not mean to treat the little sister like the subject of one of his U.P. cases. She had her own concerns while he had his, though he was finding it easier to see her quest as the more important. She had lost much. Would he go to similar lengths regarding his mother, for instance? Or his father? Very likely so.

Raylene said, "Mrs. Gunther is a watchful sort but she does not know my sister's whereabouts." After a moment she added, "I am ready for the identities of abortion providers."

Murphy swallowed hard. "I have been thinking about how to request them."

"If it is awkward — and I sense it is awkward for you — you could say it is on behalf of a case you are working. Would that be implausible?"

"One problem is that the railroad has no interest in such subjects, so why would *I* as a Union Pacific detective be asking?"

"You could be asking for your boss."

"Surely not!"

"Then for a private case you've taken on."

Stunned, Murphy reached around in his thoughts to detect whether they had been breached by the woman sitting three feet from him. Police work and private investigators were glorified in the stories and magazines he often read. They were smart. They were dogged. A part of him wondered how he would acquit himself as a P.I. After Campbell fired him, which seemed almost inevitable, would he return to his father's accountancy, seek a spot on the police force, or hang out his own shingle? He could not see himself behind a desk all day, not again. Police work was attractive, but the force itself was probably too corrupt for his taste, so a P.I. shingle might be his best option. An optimist at heart, he felt up to the challenge but at the same time somewhat unprepared. It helped that he did not have a wife at home to disabuse him of the notion.

Raylene sat cross-legged. Once more she wondered why he found abortion so unspeakable. As with naming body parts or diseases or wounds or the dead, everything had its proper name. She said, "You will have to use *that word*."

Murphy kept his voice steady. "Of course."

"You will have to ask for abortionists, plural."

"I agree."

She sensed an unnatural stillness attached to John Murphy whenever he was near. His was the manner of creatures seeking signs of danger in their immediate surroundings. Of course, she might prove a danger to him, but she would rather assist him if he would continue helping her. She said, "This seems extra hard for you."

"I will manage to get the list you need. But there's no guarantee Kansas City even has any."

"Wherever there are men living alongside women, there will be pregnancies that are wrong for the women. This is true everywhere, thus legitimate abortionists and also profiteers." She wondered to herself how often women would be found living without men in their homes, men in their beds. In Catholic convents, of course, which had produced the nuns who reigned over the Pine Ridge Indian School students. Now that she thought of it, perhaps some nuns were unduly harsh to due to their chaste lives. She said, "When you identify the local abortionists, I will take my questions to them."

Not a task for me, thought Murphy. He had investigated deaths on the rail system but for some reason this seemed worse. He rose to his feet and bid Raylene good night.

When he had gone, Raylene sat in the falling dark. She had binoculars and a torch with her and was at ease on her own. Stunt-diving bats had appeared above the trees. She closed her eyes and slowed her breath and let her mind drift this way and that across the city, north to the banks of the muddy Missouri and west to the Kansas River and back. Though Raylene's grandmother had sometimes said that spirits have many threads that tie them to the living, Raylene could not perceive the spirits of those lying underground in this place who did not belong to her. Thomas's spirit was that of a warrior gone to the sky. Raymond, Thomas's identical brother, had surely gone there too. But the spirits of others buried here were likely nearby, keeping watch over bodies communing now with tree roots and worms. Annie's spirit too was waiting release. *Patience, sister,* she thought. *I will find you.*

Seven

Outside K.C. Police Headquarters on Locust Street, Murphy paused to pull a kerchief and wipe his brow. The day was cooler, a portent of bigger changes coming, but beneath his suit jacket the underarms of his shirt were damp. His back too. What an ordeal he had just been through.

His day had started with his phone call to the beat sergeant for the city's downtown sector. The sarge invited him in, so Murphy slid a fresh notebook into his pocket and drove to the station. There he greeted the desk sergeant and others as he was waved through to offices in the rear. From the time he had left his house, all the way through the station and especially while making small talk then getting down to the subject at hand, he could feel the engine of his discomfort chugging along, turning a furrow inside him.

"You want what?" said the street crimes detective Murphy had been referred to.

"You heard me."

"I heard, but why are you asking?"

Murphy employed the ruse Raylene had suggested.

"You're moonlighting?" responded the detective.

"After a fashion."

"You are or you're not." The detective shook his head. "Can't believe the U.P. likes its detectives working side jobs. Thought they keep their people pretty close."

Murphy feigned nonchalance and lapsed into a type of detective-speak he sometimes used with the dicks at police headquarters. "A guy's gotta do what he's gotta do. Don't broadcast it, alright?"

"Ah, don't get hot, I'm no rat." The crimes man grinned as if he'd discovered information that might come in handy sometime. "Sure you don't need it for yourself, or your ... whoever?"

Murphy narrowed his eyes and flashed the gold band on his finger. "Last I knew, I'm still married."

"Sure you are. Same for me. But that's nothing. Lots of guys are married."

Murphy felt his ire rising. His marriage and his thoughts about his marriage were nobody's business but his own. He said, "Keep it to yourself, why don't you. You got those contacts or do I have to go knocking on doors all over town?"

"Alright, alright. I got them in a file. Good thing the sarge likes you."

Murphy knew the sarge liked a bottle of Jameson at Christmas, Murphy's favorite too. That was how much he liked Murphy. A brand-new bottle's worth. The police detective continued, "Ain't made a bust since the last complaint against one of them. Usually, it's someone ends up in the hospital, or dead. Otherwise, the chief says don't roust 'cause you never know who's behind them."

"Behind them?"

The crimes man lowered his voice. "Who's behind the operation. If they've got a sponsor." When Murphy gave him a quizzical look, he added. "Are you dense? The mob's got all kinds of operations." He tapped his pen on the folder he was now holding. "The one on the west side might be close to Gargotta's gang. You know, he almost went away."

"You're kidding me, right? What do they care about ... you know."

"Who's gonna ask them? Not me. They got interests all

over, not just booze and girls, and I can tell you from experience they don't take kindly to interference when nobody's been hurt. Fair warning."

"I hear you." Murphy nearly snatched the folder from the detective. He pulled out his notepad to copy down the names and addresses. There were three. "That's it?" he asked.

"Ain't it enough?"

"Well, yeah. It's more than I started with."

Murphy handed back the folder and shook the man's hand. As he made for the door, the detective called after him, a grin in his voice. "Hey now, good luck with that ... private case you got going."

Murphy noticed the winks and grins from others at nearby desks and ignored them. Sometimes silence was better than a retort that could be twisted into fodder for gossip. He retraced his steps down the hall, waved a hand at the beat sergeant behind his desk and nodded to the front desk sergeant as he went out the front.

Now he was on the street, his half-on coat gathering fresh air to cool him. There was no telling how valuable the contacts he'd gotten would be to the little sister. The most recent date on the crimes contact list was from January, three quarters of a year ago, which meant that if he accepted Raylene's assessment and the crimes man's description, no K.C. abortion practitioner needed to fear the law. Fear or no fear, he had kept his part of the bargain with Raylene.

After Raylene finished her morning's work at the saloon, she drove to Browne Grocery, a longtime K.C. business serving all comers. Spending a little time and effort on a drive across town to purchase deli meats would not, in her estimation, undermine her surveillance efforts. For the rest of the afternoon, she would position herself at the foot of the alleyway across 30th where with some sliced meats and a thermos she had borrowed from Mrs. G, she could last for hours.

This morning, she had found what seemed a clue to the influx of booze into her father's saloon. While wiping bottles behind the bar, she spied a slender stack of cut paper squares tucked behind stacks of spare glassware. When she was certain Ricco was engaged elsewhere, she sneaked a peek at what turned out to be tan-colored labels printed with a solid yellow circle and black lettering reading Fine K.C. Bourbon. She slipped a label into her pants pocket before Ricco strode into the room.

"Cheeky. Whatcha doing?" he asked.

"Wiping bottles. I can do up those glasses too." She pointed at a handful of dirty glasses in the steel sink.

Ricco studied her a moment. "Nah, I'm pouring tonight, so I'll get 'em."

Raylene paused to rinse out her rag before emerging from behind the bar. Studiously ignoring Ricco's gaze, she crossed to the closest table for patrons and began to scrub at its pitted surface. Eventually, Ricco returned to the back room and Raylene finished wiping the rest of the tables and cleaned the floor.

Later, she was in line to order at Browne's with that booze label in hand. Turning to the person behind her, she proffered the label and asked, "Excuse me. Have you seen this bourbon around town?"

The shopper behind Raylene was a woman of roughly forty-five holding a shopping basket in one hand and a purse in the other. She looked from the label to Raylene. "I don't drink."

"Thank you anyway." Raylene turned back to the counter,

where she placed her order. As she was paying, she held the label out and asked the clerk at the register, "Do you know if there's a company called K.C. Bourbon?"

"Can't say I've heard of it," came the answer.

Raylene nodded her thanks, paid up, and went out with her package. She had not seen such a label in her father's saloon, but if K.C. Burbon was a product name, why wasn't the distiller's name also on the label?

Back on 30th, Raylene's preferred parking spot was taken, so she claimed the spot to the west of it and resigned herself to a less than perfect angle of view. When thirty minutes had passed, she caught movement on the sidewalk and slid her gaze that way. It was the Morgan Grain Sacks boss walking with someone toward a Ford sedan parked just ahead of her. She went back to watching the alley while the parting conversation on the sidewalk drifted to her in snippets. Something amicable about schedules and whether the size of the order could be met. Before long, the Ford started up and drove away, leaving street dust and exhaust in its wake. Suddenly, the Morgan boss man was at her truck window. She drew her arm inside.

"Aren't you the one who came looking for a job yesterday?" he asked.

"I am."

"And didn't I tell you I don't have a spot for you?"

"You said that."

"Well, what are you doing here now? I told you I don't have nothing for you. If you're going to stake out my business or bother my workers, I'm not having it."

"On your advice, I abandoned the thought of working for you."

"What are you doing here outside my business?"

Raylene waved a hand toward the buildings. "To be

accurate, I'm outside the lamp store."

"Don't act smart with me. You've got no business here. Move along."

She gave him a benign look. "This is a public street."

The man began to fume, but Raylene had her own reason for watching the alley and she meant to do so for as long as possible. She had gotten a look at the cartons of bottles stacked in Ricco's back room. There were a few bottles of tonic, vodka, and a whole bunch of colas; other soft drink bottles were empty. Ricco was due for a supply of hard liquors and she wanted to see who delivered it.

The boss man huffed off to his workshop and Raylene turned her attention again to the alley. There — in the minute or two she had been otherwise engaged — a small delivery vehicle had pulled in at roughly the right spot for accessing the back of the saloon.

The front of the vehicle in the alley was nondescript, giving nothing away, the back half of it was in shadow. She exited her truck and crossed 30th for a better look up the alley, which had a slant of sun along one side, but not enough to illuminate any name on the truck. She was deciding whether to stroll in that direction when there came the sound of a car pulling up behind her.

"Hey there — you!" came a male voice.

She turned to find a squad car parked at the curb, its engine running. An officer thrust a finger in her direction before stepping out, leaving his driver's door open.

"What's your business here?" he asked.

The question struck Raylene as odd. She was standing on a sidewalk in the old part of town. Was that a crime? "I am looking into that alley," she said.

"For what purpose?"

"Do I need a purpose?"

"Is that your truck over there?" The officer motioned across 30th where Raylene's truck sat.

Clearly, the Morton's man had called the police. "That's mine."

"Maybe you need to get in it and drive it away. You're not to be bothering people around here."

Raylene spread her hands. "I have business to take care of, but alley signage prohibits my parking in the alley."

"What kind of business would you have in this alley?"

Now she'd done it. In this city, a policeman could be in cahoots with bootleggers, with burglars, with almost anyone. She didn't mean for him to know what she was after. "I ... am watching to see if my ... husband comes out of the saloon with a girlfriend."

"Is that the husband who didn't put a ring on your finger?"

Of course. Raylene's only ring was the one she had taken from Thomas's lifeless body, which she now wore on a leather string around her neck. "He pawned it," she said of her imaginary husband.

"Uh huh." The officer slipped his nightstick from his belt and waved it now for emphasis. "Here's what I have to say to that. Husband or no husband, ring or no ring, we've got regulations against loitering, so you need to cross back over and climb into your truck, or whoever's truck that is, and be on your way."

Raylene glanced up the alley. She could make out male figures, one being Ricco's shape, carrying crates across the short span from vehicle to building. "I'd like to finish what I came for."

The policeman slapped his palm with the nightstick. "Your business might be legitimate or not, but you're going to take it elsewhere, or I'll be obliged to take you and your business downtown and you can sit while contemplating the error of your ways."

Raylene sighed. Regular life in a city like this was enough to impede the pursuit of truth. "Officer," she said, "I accept your invitation to move along." She threw a glance at the vehicle in the alley, but if her instincts were correct, it wouldn't be there for long and she would miss her chance to note the markings on it. If it even had markings.

She went back to her truck. Since the officer was watching, she drove a half-dozen blocks before turning north and circling back to the top of the alleyway. From 29th Street, she could see that the vehicle that had been near the saloon was now gone. She would have to wait for her next saloon shift to discover what had been delivered.

When the telephone rang in the boarding house hallway, Mrs. Gunther got up from the kitchen table and answered it. "Well," she said after a moment, "we have just sat down to an early supper but I can certainly ask her to call you." After another moment she said, "Alright, hold on."

Back in the kitchen, she told Raylene, "It's your railroad detective."

"He's not mine," said Raylene.

"You know what I mean. I told him we were eating supper, but he insisted."

"I apologize for the interruption."

"For a few minutes, this was the first time in days that you've been able to eat my cooking while it's hot."

"I know." Raylene rose and went to speak into the telephone.

"I'll bring you those contacts you wanted," said Murphy.

"Right now?"

"How about after you've eaten."

Of course, she wanted the contacts Murphy had procured,

but as evening fell, other subjects of interest arose. Her previous evenings in Union Cemetery had only served to whet her appetite for observing the after-dark workers. She felt certain that something would materialize from all that furtiveness. "I will be going out after supper."

"On the town?" asked Murphy?

The less Mrs. G knew, the better. Raylene said, "To my usual."

"Then I can find you there."

"Casual clothing, okay? We should look ordinary."

He described what he wore when mowing the lawn. She agreed to his wardrobe suggestion and they signed off.

Fall was doing its trick of slicing daylight by a few minutes per day, reducing the useful hours for watching others at dusk, but Raylene was glad to have spent time tonight at Mrs. G's table. In conversation, she had learned a bit more about Annie's time at the boarding house.

At twilight, she made her way around the cemetery's outer acreage and eventually to a freshly-dug grave left standing empty. Given the six-pointed stars on some of the nearest grave markers, she felt she walked among the Jewish dead. That star symbol was the extent of her knowledge about Jews. Also, that Jesus was a Jew betrayed by Jews, unless she had that wrong. Many of the teachings and lessons required by the nuns for reservation students to memorize made little sense to her. That there existed a great spirit overseeing the workings of earth and sky paralleled her people's creation stories about Grandmother Earth and spirit beings. But to her mind, people could be wise without the talent for multiplying fish.

As usual she chose a spot in the deep shadows beneath trees and spread her blanket upon a cushion of fallen leaves.

She was just settling in when Murphy came along, raising his left hand a little. His cast was clearly gone. "Let's not speak names," she said as he joined her on the blanket, "in case anyone overhears."

He said, "I think it's time you explained what you are watching for in a dark cemetery."

"Did you bring those contacts?"

"Yes. But now I've decided that if you want me to hand them over, you must tell me why you are watching that empty grave. That's got to be what you are doing because you did that before."

"Move over here, will you?"

Murphy's pulse leapt as he paused to ponder the meaning of her request.

"If we are spotted," she said, "we should look like people who know each other well enough to sit in the dark talking." Raylene patted the spot right next to her. "I have seen others doing the same."

Murphy took a breath and resettled himself inches from her left hip. To calm his thoughts, he replayed his trials at police headquarters and how the list of contacts burned hot in his pocket. He did think about sin sometimes, but ferrying these particular contacts to another person who would use them for good did not seem a sin. More like a transaction, as in business. He said, "Okay. Tell me what you're doing."

She did not figure Murphy for trouble in the matter, so Raylene, speaking low, described having observed a short service in Conboie's salon for a gentleman traveler and how later, when out of curiosity about Mr. Lambert's disposition to subversive tactics, she watched as a pine box went into the grave marked for that same traveler. "The casket I observed during the service was fancy, with brass fittings. Top notch. Very different than the pine box they later put into the grave labeled for that same man."

When Murphy had digested her words he said, "Do you know —" just as Raylene touched his arm and motioned with one finger toward a pair of workers, one leading a large-wheeled cart, the other walking behind. The pair stopped at the empty grave and proceeded to lower a rectangular pine box into the ground.

When the workers began shoveling dirt atop the box, Raylene spoke just above a murmur. "Then another night there was a fresh grave with a marker, but no obituary that I could find. Something strange is going on."

"A person could be buried without an obituary."

"It appears they can also be buried without the casket used in a service and presumably paid for at Conboie's parlor. Both of those things are happening."

After the workers tamped the dirt into place and added a wooden marker, Raylene lifted her binoculars and detected that one of them was a black-skinned man. He wore no straw hat now, but she thought he might be the one she had seen arrive with a shovel that day she had visited the cemetery's ornery sexton. Later she would examine this new marker.

But instead of heading back along the path they had used to reach the gravesite, the two workers rolled their cart toward Raylene and Murphy, whose proximity to an exit now seemed obvious. "Lean toward me as if whispering a secret," said Raylene. "Obscure your face."

As the workers' voices grew louder. Raylene lifted a hand to Murphy's shoulder and pulled him toward her, angling her face beneath the brim of his fedora. The advancing men were speaking about someone referred to as "Lamb" or "Lam." Turned away from the speakers, Raylene only made out "getting caught" and something about "dough."

Then Murphy's hands were pulling her into an embrace,

his cheek against her ear. He murmured, "You smell good."

She shushed him.

He was thinking *warm cotton* but it was probably her bath soap. He had finally decided what made her look different from when he'd met her in September — her hair was shorter, cut just below her ears, with bangs now. She looked almost oriental.

Raylene felt the heat of Murphy against her as the voices of the workers retreated up the path. He was nothing like Raul, who had followed ranch work all over the west, landing at the H-bar-H, the massive operation she had exited in pursuit of Raymond. There was something to be said for leaving someone behind — sometimes you hungered for them more than when they were beside you. John Murphy was right here, warm and close, smelling of spicy aftershave. He was a man whose arms felt nice around her, but he was also a man who wore a wedding ring.

She pulled away from his embrace and lifted his ring hand before releasing it gently. He sucked in a breath, perhaps in reaction to his arm being a bit weak. She said, "We had better check the marker on that grave, and you owe me those names."

As Murphy disengaged from thoughts of Raylene's lips on his, he heard a tinge of regret in her voice. Or, perhaps that too was his imagination.

Eight

At the start of her saloon shift, Raylene noted two new crates of booze atop the dwindling older supply, but Ricco's presence kept her from examining any of the bottles. He seemed agitated while counting the previous night's cash receipts, so when she was done putting her cleaning supplies away, she asked, "Are you okay?"

"Why?"

She shrugged. "You seem out of sorts."

"Got people breathin' down my neck is all." When he noticed she hadn't moved, he asked, "What?"

The time had arrived for her to come out with it. "What is K.C. Bourbon?"

He frowned. "What's it sound like? It's booze."

"Is it made by someone local?"

Now he scowled. "Across the river, but it's K.C. over there too. You wanna complain about my choice of booze?"

"I have personal reasons for asking."

"Oh, yeah? I got personal reasons for ordering what my customers will drink, but you tell me yours."

Late at night while lying in Annie's room, in the same bed where Annie had slept, Raylene had given this plenty of thought. If there was a legitimate distillery with that K.C. name, Ricco wouldn't have its labels lying around. The distiller would themselves label their product. "I don't think there is a distillery anywhere nearby for that label. Nothing legal, anyway, so I figure someone's cooking it."

Ricco stood from his desk. "You know what? You need to stick to your own business. You got no idea what it takes to be in this business in this city. Whatever you think about it, you're wrong."

Raylene stood taller. "Then I'll ask this. Do you have a sister?" When Ricco narrowed his eyes as if deciding whether to answer, she pressed him. "Do you?"

Finally, he said, "It's none of yours, but I got two."

"If one of them dies from drinking bad booze, you might want to know where she got it and who cooked it." She grabbed her coat from a nearby chair and said as she exited, "Or perhaps you are the type who does not care."

"This is it," said Murphy an hour later to Raylene. She had greeted him as if nothing had passed between them the previous evening, but he felt sheepish anyway and tried to corral his thudding heart. Now they both studied the three-story apartment building that had seen better days. He thought maybe she was wearing different trousers than the worn ones he had seen her in before. Even so, in the pale light of a fall afternoon she looked like someone exotic from a mystery novel. He said, "I wish you would let me accompany you."

She smiled at his chivalry, or else naiveté. "A man would not be welcome in the conversation, and you are only here now because you insisted."

"You didn't say I couldn't do my own investigating." His presence was a reversal from his intentions of the previous evening. Then, he had planned to completely avoid this portion of Raylene's search. But during the night he had dreamt about Raylene leaving one of these providers only to encounter one of the mob's goons on her way out. Some big lug of a guy who didn't like that she wasn't white. Murphy's dream-self had watched the drama play out from somewhere above and beyond, as if he held a movie camera in his hand and had no way to intervene. As the goon marched Raylene away, he himself had jolted awake, his bedclothes tangled as if from a struggle. Also, there had been their embrace in the cemetery, which while not a sweethearts' embrace had somehow altered his perspective about her potentially dangerous pursuits. He said, "I want you safe so you can provide me that clue to the jewelry. There might be danger in questioning the type of people who ... do this type of thing."

"I will only be asking if my sister sought their services."

"But they're not doctors, they're opportunists. Criminals."

"How do you know they're not doctors?"

Murphy opened his mouth to reply but instead snapped it shut.

Raylene said, "Years ago, this was an ordinary thing for women to seek from other women until medical men — because doctors were almost always men — decided that no others should earn fees from such procedures. Then Christians declared it a sin, so now there are those who are willing to help women or else profit from them on the sly. I would rather seek a medicine woman for the care of women's bodies. Their spirits too." After a moment, she added, "Are you well? The day is cool but you are sweating."

"It's nothing."

Raylene nodded and started for the building's front door, then stopped and returned to Murphy who had watched her walk away. From her coat pocket she handed Murphy the bourbon label from Ricco's saloon. "Can you investigate who makes this bourbon? If it is actually bourbon and not tinted wood alcohol."

Murphy studied the label a moment. "It's a moon, right?"

Raylene paused. She had wondered if anyone besides her

would think that. The yellow circle did not have the blotches of the moon's so-called face, but she herself had made that leap. She said, "It might be."

"Your father was Yellow Moon. Did he cook jake?"

"I cannot feature him having the time."

"Then maybe labeling his own?" Murphy mentally reviewed what he knew from the police report. "Your sister died of so-called natural causes. Are you thinking it was booze?"

"Bad booze has killed many people." She paused to wave a hand toward the apartment building. "Or Annie's death could have been from another cause of little concern to authorities regarding an Indian girl."

Murphy had no reply because ... well, because the woman standing before him knew how things worked in the big city around them. For the last time, Raylene turned toward the building and Murphy watched her go. Inside apartment #5, there would be talk about that which he had only a rudimentary perspective. Still, he couldn't help but imagine some sort of danger lurking there because people who engaged in surreptitious activities did not like being questioned about their actions. And you never knew who might turn violent.

As he drove away, Murphy conjured the women in his orbit: his mother, three aunts, the secretaries at U.P., including Georgia of the glorious gams, and could imagine none of them finding their way to apartment #5. He wondered about Ruby, who at twenty was old enough to be married and young enough to join the current trend of women taking lovers before marriage, which incited another thought: Women, women, everywhere, and not a one for him. Except Catherine, of course. Poor Catherine, who would dress only for the sanitarium but never again for a night of dinner and music, and never again for her marriage bed. *Poor Catherine,* but not only Catherine. Also, *Poor Murphy.*

The building's small lobby held a hallway leading to ground-floor apartments at the back. Three rows of mail boxes lined one wall while a staircase commanded the other. The odor of frying onions hung in the stairwell as Raylene made her way upstairs to #5. Pausing there, she thought about her sister in their earlier years, carefree and always making plans to leave Oglala. Always looking forward, counting the days until exams were over, until the break at summertime, until school was out for good. Annie hadn't at that point gone places, but she intended to go places, she had made that clear.

Had Annie landed here on #5's doorstep, anxious of heart and hopeful that help could be found within? And had she found help or harm? Raylene took a breath then rapped firmly on the door.

Later that afternoon, as prearranged with Mrs. G, Raylene answered the ring of the bell when Murphy arrived. At the doorway, he said, "Are you sure this is alright with your landlady? My impression is she doesn't much care to let gentlemen in. Or maybe it's just me."

"She runs a proper house for women, so she is cautious about admitting men. I see you dressed the way I suggested. You might be glad for it."

Murphy put a hand to where his tie was missing before leaning in conspiratorially. "How did your visits go?"

"I completed two, but we'll save that for later."

"I have news for you."

Raylene brought a finger to her lips and motioned him in.

Murphy said, "Why am I coming in? Oh my! Something smells terrific."

Raylene motioned him forward. "Let's say hello." She led him back to the cheerful kitchen.

Mrs. Gunther turned from the pan of biscuits she was sliding into the oven. "Hello again, Mr. Murphy."

Murphy, hat in hand, gave a cordial nod. "Hello, Mrs. Gunther, and please call me John. I've got to say, your house smells like heaven."

Mrs. G's smile telegraphed her susceptibility to compliments.

Footsteps sounded on the wooden hallway stairs and a moment later, the boarder named Vivienne came into the kitchen, dressed in a slinky black number that hugged her lithe figure. Her hair was done in curls. "*Bonsoir!*" she said "Good evening!"

Raylene introduced Murphy. Vivienne held out a hand for him to shake, then paused to study him once his hand was in hers. "Mister Murphy, we have met!" When he blinked at her, she released his hand and said, "In one of the clubs downtown, just this week. Thank you again for the drinks."

Murphy's eyes grew wide. That would have been the night after Campbell granted him leave to find the jewelry, which, Dear God, was only good through the coming Monday. He recollected only snippets from his night out of food and much drink, but quite a bit about the next day's hangover. Now he wondered if he had made a fool of himself.

Vivienne continued, "You were a *bon vivant.* Very drunk, and very generous. The music was good, *non*?"

Raylene and Mrs. G both turned to study Murphy, who nodded. A faint memory came to him of a nearly empty wallet after buying drinks for good-looking women and the musicians they seemed to be with. He said, "I hope I did not overstep."

"Not at all!" said Vivienne. "A woman likes a gentleman to

find her attractive. Sometimes a little overstepping is in order." She gave him a wide smile and motioned with the coat she had over her arm as she addressed the group. "I am off. They are letting me hostess tonight. I'm sure I will be ... under the glass."

"Scrutinized," said Mrs. G.

"That's me," said Vivienne. She leaned toward Raylene and said, "I trust you two will supervise the inspection."

"We will be quick about it," answered Raylene. Vivienne nodded, waved to all, and went to catch the taxi that had been summoned.

"No use getting her good shoes soiled," said Mrs. G, "especially if she is being assessed tonight for a better position."

"Under the glass," said Raylene.

Mrs. G said, "Supper will be ready soon."

Raylene thanked her. To Murphy she said, "I have something to show you upstairs."

"You do?" Thoughts whirled round in Murphy's head, not all of them pure. Of course this was not an assignation, so whatever was upstairs must relate to the little sister's quest. Dutifully, he followed her up the staircase. She was wearing the same pants he had seen on her at the cemetery and again he thought how more women were wearing pants as if doing so gave them special powers.

Raylene stopped in the doorway to a second-floor room at the front of the house. "This is it," she said, stepping through, "Vivienne's room."

Murphy stopped where he was. "Miss Little Moon, I — I'm not ..."

"We agreed you would call me Raylene." She looked around as if to guide Murphy's gaze. "Mrs. Gunther told me that you had examined Annie's room."

"Well, yes, but it's at the back of the house."

"You checked those places a person might hide valuables."

"It was unoccupied, so my search was brief. Also, unproductive." Still in the doorway, he locked eyes with Raylene. "Has Vivienne something to do with the jewelry?" His thoughts took off: Could Vivienne have been an accomplice, hiding valuables on Annie's behalf or had she purchased them from Annie? Her demeanor of a few minutes ago, though, suggested complete nonchalance, so he discarded the notion that Vivienne might have stolen them from Annie.

"Vivienne did not know my sister. She arrived just after Annie's body was found. But this was Annie's room until the week before her death."

The information hit Murphy like a brick. "*This* was Annie's room? For how long?"

"Roughly two years, almost three. This *boudoir* — Vivienne's word — is where Annie lodged until moving to the larger one you examined."

In spite of his experience at presenting a neutral expression during interviews and investigations, an astonished Murphy stared into Vivienne's room. He had not thought to ask about Annie having resided in a different room. From the police he'd received Annie's purse to give to Raylene, and had been assured that Mrs. Gunther had examined and packed Annie's modest wardrobe. When his search had yielded no jewelry, he had checked pawn shops before following Raylene's trail toward her home country. *This* was a room he had not examined.

Now he took in the details: though the room's furnishings were sturdy and plain, there were feminine touches all around that made it look elegant. An embroidered dresser scarf atop which sat various jars and bottles. A floral scarf draped over the off-white shade of a floor lamp. The bed was made up with a white chenille bedspread and pink pillow slips. Chagrined, he asked, "Is Vivienne allowing me to search?"

"If Mrs. Gunther supervises."

"This is what you meant about helping me find the jewelry?"

"My sister loved hiding things when we were young — she tucked notes in my schoolbooks, sometimes inside my shoes. If she found something worthwhile, an intact pencil or a length of fishing line, or some other small item, she hid it until she was ready to use it or trade it. This room would have been the perfect place, because no one would have interfered."

Murphy studied the space for a moment. He would have to roll back the rug and —

"Supper's on!" came the call from downstairs. "Come while it's hot."

"That's for us," said Raylene.

"Me too?"

"My lack of being here most evenings does not play to Mrs. Gunther's strengths."

"Does she know about your outings to the cemetery?"

"She knows nothing about them and I intend to keep it that way. This evening you can help me make up for the suppers I have missed."

Murphy rubbed his hands together. Their search could wait if home cooking was at hand.

"Another portion for you, Mr. Murphy?" asked Mrs. G a half-hour later. The three were sitting at the kitchen table where, except on holidays, boarders were served.

Raylene watched in amusement as Murphy patted his stomach. "I'd better stop at two. Mrs. Gunther, your cooking is as good as — maybe better than — my own mother's."

"It's nice to do a version with beer. Another biscuit?"

"No, but they are the best around. Were I to board with you, I'd weigh twenty pounds more." Over supper he had described his arrangement with Ruby and the soups she left for him to reheat later. Now he cleared his throat. "Ah, Mrs. Gunther. Raylene tells me that you have the final word about whether I may look for the missing jewelry in what used to be Annie's room, now Vivienne's."

"The items you came for last month," said Mrs. G, "when you looked behind drawers and under the bed."

"People hide things under loose floorboards," mused Murphy aloud.

"Absolutely not!"

Murphy's heart jumped. "I beg your pardon?"

"You will find no loose floorboards whatsoever."

"I only mean that people hide valuables, sometimes quite well."

Here, Mrs. G looked at Raylene and back to Murphy. "Raylene told me that you are helping her find Annie's resting place."

Murphy felt it necessary to bolster his position. "My assignment was Catholic cemeteries and a couple of other miscellaneous details. I even visited the one Catholic cemetery on this side of the river. Annie is not buried there."

The landlady's face softened. She shook her head and looked off into space. "A mystery, indeed." Then she looked pointedly at Murphy. "You must keep after it until you find her. Teamwork is sure to win out."

The concept of "team" had not entered Murphy's original calculations. He had developed an appreciation for the little sister's intuition, her curiosity, and her gumption, but it probably did not help that being near her made his blood run hot. And by God, he wanted that jewelry. He nodded at Mrs.

G and looked at Raylene. "We've been a bit like a team."

Raylene said, "You have been a help and I thank you for that." She had been pleasantly surprised at how useful Murphy had made himself so far, but she needed more, perhaps somewhat illegal help from him.

Mrs. G said to Murphy. "If you're in this together you might as well have a look."

Murphy was ready. This could be his big break.

Mrs. G led them up the stairs to Vivienne's room, where Murphy got down on the floor to check under the bed before sweeping his arm all the way to his shoulder between the mattresses. Raylene and Mrs. G emptied the closet, laying Vivienne's garments gently atop her bedspread, the final item being a royal blue dress. Murphy paused at the sight of it. He remembered that dress from his night on the town, how it had shone sensuously in the lamplight of the night club where he now half-recalled a light-haired woman wearing it as she smoked languorously. "Go ahead," said Mrs. G as he reeled his thoughts back to the room.

The closet was lit with a bare bulb in a fixture overhead. Murphy scanned its walls and floor and though he could see it clearly, ran his hands along the closet's inner doorframe. The shelf above held only a shoebox with the label from a downtown store. He handed it to Raylene who opened it to extract a pair of practical black shoes. Shaking them, she shook her head at Murphy.

Next came checking under the rug followed by a search behind the one framed print on the wall, and the desk, which held only writing paper.

Standing before the dresser, Raylene looked at Mrs. G. "How shall we do these drawers?"

"We can't very well take everything out. Too intrusive," said Mrs. G. "You and I can feel around between items." She turned to Murphy. "We can pull them out so you can check beneath and behind."

Murphy agreed and the three set about doing that. The dresser was an olden sort made of multi-colored woods finished with a clear gloss. Its drawers held locks requiring a skeleton key that Mrs. G explained had decades previously been misplaced.

The top two small drawers held sundry items such as shoe laces, trinkets, and a passport. The next drawer down was larger and held lingerie items and sleepwear. Murphy looked at the floor until the drawer's exterior was presented to him.

The bottom-most drawer held folded pants and cotton socks, and a winter set of flannels. Once again, there was no jewelry. After Raylene slid the last drawer home, she motioned to Murphy to take one end of the dresser. Together, they lifted it away from the wall and Murphy examined the back of it, getting down on the floor to run his hands under its scrolled skirt.

"Damn it!" he said, standing. Then, "Sorry. Forgive me."

Mrs. Gunther narrowed her eyes momentarily, then gave him a wry look. "Apology accepted."

"The nightstand," said Raylene, as they set the dresser back into place.

Murphy nodded and checked beneath its top and the shelf below. He got down on the floor and ran his hand up under it. "Nothing," he said, standing and brushing at his pants.

The three looked at each other, then around the room. There were no other frames on the wall, no other closet or furniture. A robe hung from a hook on the back of the door, but Murphy was not about to check pockets in Vivienne's garments. If Vivienne had found any jewelry, Mrs. G would surely have heard about it, and he believed the landlady would share that knowledge, if only to assist Raylene.

"There's nothing else," said Mrs. G.

Raylene pointed at the table lamp, which resembled a vase converted with fittings.

"The shade is intact," said Murphy. "I checked."

The threesome stood in silence before Raylene stepped closer and switched the lamp off. Lights from the hallway and closet cast a pale glow into the room from two sides as she unplugged it. Cradling its hollow ceramic body, she turned the lamp's bottom up. "There's a hole with cotton in it," she said to the room.

Murphy stepped forward. Sure enough, white wadding showed in the channel where the power cord ran up through a wide hole in the base.

"What use would cotton be?" said Mrs. Gunther, leaning in to look.

Adding his hands to steady the lamp's base, Murphy extracted the wadding, which seemed to have a solid center.

Raylene set the lamp back in place as Mrs. G watched Murphy open the wadding to reveal pearl earrings with clips of gold.

"My word!" cried Mrs. G.

Murphy held the earrings out for Raylene to see. Even in pale light, the pearls gleamed as if lit from within. He had given Catherine a string of pearls as a wedding gift. She had worn them almost every day, and also as the orderlies escorted her to the sanitarium's transport vehicle. "Do you think your sister hid these?" he asked Raylene.

"I couldn't say. She favored turquoise."

Mrs. G simply shook her head.

"They're not shown in that photo I had of her," said Murphy.

"The one you lost," said Raylene. "But are they on your list?"

"No."

"If your boss doesn't claim them, they would rightly belong to this household, and that means Mrs. Gunther."

Mrs. G put a hand to her throat as Murphy nodded. He tucked the cocooned earrings into his pants pocket. His money was on Campbell and his wife.

When Vivienne's room had been restored, the three trooped back downstairs to the front hallway. "I think we'll take a walk around the block," said Raylene, pausing by the coat rack to hand Murphy's coat to him and take her own. She gave Murphy a pointed look.

You'd better take an umbrella from those by the front door," said Mrs. G.

"Mrs. Gunther, I can't thank you enough," said Murphy, taking his coat and reaching for his fedora. "It's been a pleasure and ... eye-opening."

Mrs. G said to Raylene, "I think this neighborhood is safe enough, if wet at this point. Still, I'm glad that Mr. Murphy — John — is with you." She waved them off as she headed for the kitchen.

Murphy's evening had been a roller coaster. First, immense pleasure at being in the company of Raylene during a delicious meal cooked by someone who knew her way around a kitchen, followed by finding jewelry that was a disappointment for not being on his list. All things considered, he was still on the hook for the missing rose-gold ring and emerald necklace, and he had no clue where to find them.

Nine

Standing outside the boarding house, umbrella in hand, Raylene said to Murphy, "I would like to compare progress from earlier today."

Murphy, wearing his fedora, reached to open her umbrella and hand it back.

Raylene led the way from the front stoop to the sidewalk. "Did you have any luck with that label?"

Murphy frowned into the gathering darkness. "Yes and no. I managed to ask two of the senior street crimes officers down at headquarters. I got mostly shrugs and blank looks until one of the others by the name of Rossi spoke up. He says he's seen K.C. Bourbon with other designs on the label. One had a tree in front of a river. Another one had a burlesque dancer. He figures it's just a label that's being printed for hooch being brought in, or made locally."

Raylene had wondered as much. "Did he suggest who is supplying it?"

"He seemed disinterested in who. From what I gather, unless there's a big dust-up, or a bystander of the upstanding-citizen persuasion who gets hospitalized from drinking it, they're not going to worry about a little booze."

"Upstanding citizen," said Raylene.

"No offense to your sister. From what I saw of the police record, they didn't suspect her death as involving foul play. Sometimes people think that drinkers deserve what they get. So, if it was booze, well, nobody made her drink it." He could feel himself being more loquacious than normal. Was he trying to impress her? Again, he offered, "No offense."

"If the police don't care, they won't be of any help."

"Someone in the booze racket knows someone high enough up to keep it from being a problem. A commissioner, maybe, or Chief." He could have added, but didn't, that drinkers just want drinks, they don't care so much who's making the stuff. The ones who want girls, they don't think is there something I ought to know about her, they just want a girl. Same with gambling — *Show me to the tables.*

The sporadic rain was pattering on the umbrella Raylene carried and on Murphy's hat and coat. He said, "How did your ... um ... conversations go?"

"The first one was no help, a retired doctor so ancient I wondered if he could see the photograph I showed him."

Murphy perked up. "Would that be the photo I lost?"

"I rescued it from being lost, so now it is mine."

"But it shows the jewelry, at least the necklace."

"And it shows my sister. Not your sister or your boss's sister. A sister takes the top spot. Plus, I still have another visit to make and I need to show her likeness. I cannot know what name she might have used."

They came to the misty glow thrown by a streetlight on the corner. Murphy stopped and looked under the umbrella's leading edge to catch Raylene's eye. Their bubble in the mist felt secluded. He felt his body reaching toward her but restrained himself. "The earrings are a find," he said, "and I am glad for them, but that photo shows the missing necklace."

She locked eyes with him. "If your boss's wife wore that necklace on special occasions, there might be a photo of *her* wearing it."

"I don't believe I'll ask about a photo of the wife."

Raylene shrugged and turned the corner, proceeding

clockwise from Mrs. G's. "Would you like to hear about my second attempt today?"

Murphy reined in his irritation at knowing the little sister had the photo he needed for his search. He couldn't exactly wrestle her to the wet sidewalk to see if she had it on her. He would need to convince her to lend it to him. During investigations, he was adept at evincing answers, even from those who initially resisted, but he had to admit that any attempt to extract the photo of Annie from Raylene was likely to fail. He said, "Okay, tell me about your second visit."

"The second location was also an apartment in a duplex, this time with a woman performing the duties. She said business is steady but cannot recall my sister coming to her."

"How about the third address?"

"I didn't pursue it because I learned that the practitioner had been prosecuted last year and left town afterwards."

"So, that's the end of that."

Raylene paused on the sidewalk. She knew what he wanted, which was for her to be done with that line of inquiry. "It's not the end. I was given the address for a woman on this side of the West Bottom who practices oriental medicine. I'll ask her."

As Raylene moved forward again, Murphy mulled over the idea of someone practicing Chinese medicine in K.C. For a time after Catherine's departure, he had used a Chinese laundry downtown. He had figured the owners to be descendants of those who laid track for the railroad lines. In the K.C. area alone, there were tracks for the Chicago, Milwaukee and St. Paul; the Atchison, Topeka and Santa Fe; those for the lines of Missouri, Alton, St. Louis, Rhode Island, Southern, and San Francisco railroads; and of course, the U.P. lines. He hadn't used that laundry since Ruby began working for him, but even if legislation still prohibited Orientals from owning property, they could probably lease or rent a laundry business.

The two walked in companionable silence, in and out of the glow cast by streetlights and front porches. Occasionally a vehicle rolled by. A light rain still pattered upon them, not steady, but enough to wet the sidewalk. Murphy's coat glistened with it.

At last Raylene spoke again. "I know your job is on your mind, but I have a task that I could use some help with. At Union Cemetery."

"A task?"

"Tomorrow evening, at dark."

Murphy held up a hand. "That's Halloween night, and this rain is supposed to keep up."

"A little rain won't stop people from a jaunt to a cemetery on Halloween, but the good news is that shady burial crews won't want to work with a bunch of potential witnesses wandering around."

Murphy could not see her face beneath the umbrella's brim. "You don't want to be caught out, but you're asking me to join in? Are we talking about something illegal or only dangerous?"

"We should dress for the weather and I will bring a spade for each of us."

"Are you serious?"

"Now might be the time to change your mind about us being a team."

"I didn't say that."

"Sturdy boots would be in order. A hat, perhaps a slicker."

Murphy said, "You have already suggested that you observed fraud at Union Cemetery. Now you propose to do something illegal there." He didn't know whether to be mortified or thrilled at the notion of a woman who would take such risks. He opted for thrilled.

Her voice came soft but clear. "Everyone should go to jail at least once."

Murphy nearly choked. "Wha — What?"

"I quote my Uncle Raymond. He did not want our people to be afraid of standing against those who would cheat our family or allies or friends. He was righteous about doing only right unless someone had clearly done him wrong."

"He must have been tough, but I have to wonder if Lambert's crew is cheating you, your family, or an ally."

"Raymond *was* tough. My father too. Now I meet them both in my dreams."

So, thought Murphy, she had lost an uncle in addition to her father and sister, while he had lost almost no one but Catherine. Though still alive she was lost to him, and he still had both parents and four aunties, two of them back east, and a smattering of cousins in various cities. When it came to family, he was relatively rich. He felt presumptuous to ask this of her, but they were cocooned within the mist and the dark all around. The night felt private, with no one else strolling beneath streetlights. He asked, "Do you have other family?"

A moment of silence ensued during which Murphy thought Raylene might not answer. Then came, "I have many who are like family to me, my *thióspaye*. I also have a whole nation. It has been reduced, but it survives."

Murphy wondered what exactly kept him from turning Raylene down flat. For some reason, he wanted to see what she planned to do after dark, with spades. On the one hand, she wasn't simply a woman asking for help. She was compelling and sure of herself. (*Dear God*, he longed to feel her in his arms.) Detection by authorities would be next to nil, and ... he had always prided himself on trying to do the right thing.

On the other hand, he couldn't be sure that her idea of the right thing aligned with his. If they were caught, word would get around and at the very least he would lose his job. If they were arrested, he might no longer seem employable.

There was no use arguing with himself. He could not possess knowledge about a wrong and do absolutely nothing to right it. They were rounding the corner on the homestretch to the boarding house when he said, "Please tell me that something about this task of yours will address a wrong against your sister or your family."

"I cannot say for sure, but I think so. Indirectly."

Murphy sighed. He said, "I'll wear boots and the jacket I keep for fishing."

Raylene smiled to herself. To Murphy she said, "Tomorrow then. Under the trees where we last met."

Where I tried to hold you, thought Murphy. *Where you made me want you more.*

Rain fell steadily overnight. In the morning, after scrubbing the saloon while keeping out of Ricco's way, Raylene drove to Swope Library, the one closest to the Negro high school. There she would not look out of place as she scanned local newspapers and a year's worth of local magazines for articles about local mobsters and their crimes going back to fall of 1935. She was looking for arrests, convictions, acquittals. She found a few, some of which read like personality profiles containing appreciation for those who took risks or made a lot of money breaking laws. She understood. People who had lost a lot and scrambled for what they had could look at a conniver and see a prince.

The next morning, Murphy dressed carefully and gathered his raincoat and hat, but before driving to the office, he called first to see if anyone expected Campbell. It was Saturday, but you never knew.

Having been told that Campbell was not in the office, Murphy called Campbell's house. Ordinarily, he would only call with late-breaking news on a case that required authorization of extraordinary funds or instantaneous travel, but this seemed important enough.

Recognizing the voice that answered, he said, "Good morning, Mrs. Campbell. I hope it's not too early to call. This is John Murphy. Is your husband in?"

"Work, again?" came the reply. "There's already been a call this morning. He hardly takes a day off but Sundays." She did not sound miffed, more like someone reciting the words expected of a spouse.

"Sorry, yes. That's the railroad, always wanting more. I hope you are well."

"Quite well, thank you, but Pherson was about to take the dogs around the block. They enjoy getting wet while he does not. Can I tell him what it's about?"

Murphy thought fast. "Ah, no ma'am, I'm on a confidential case, but he might tell you, if it's allowed."

Mrs. Campbell sighed. "Alright. Hold on while I catch him before he gets out the door."

There came the sound of ladylike heels on a hard floor as Murphy pictured the house's rather grand front entry where a telephone sat on a table atop black and white tiles. He'd been just two or three times beyond the big entry doors to catch a glimpse of a banister leading to the upstairs and tall windows casting patterned light all around. There had been money on the missus's side, thus the jewelry.

After a minute, he caught the solid thumping of footsteps growing closer, then Campbell's growl coming down the line.

"That you Murphy?"

"Yes, sir."

"I thought you were hot on the trail of what I asked for."

"I have been, and I did find something. I'm not one hundred percent sure, though, because it's not what you identified as missing." He had the cotton-wrapped earrings in his pocket.

There was a pause. "Spill."

"It's not the necklace or the rose-gold ring. It's earrings."

"The hell you say. Where'd they come from?"

Murphy could picture Campbell's florid face growing redder. He said, "They were well hidden in a different room that Annie had previously occupied in her boarding house. I found them last night."

"You told me you had checked that place. Now you're saying you didn't?"

"It turns out she had switched bedrooms before her death. So, I checked one, but not the one I didn't know about."

"I thought I was paying you to find out everything. So, these are not like what you found before."

"Those others matched the necklace. These are large pearls set in gold. The clasps have the shape of a leaf where they grab the earlobe." Murphy could feel himself holding his breath. If these jewels belonged to Mrs. Campbell, he might expect a reprieve from his boss, or at least an extension of time to find the other items.

"Hang on a minute."

Murphy waited, listening to the sound of his boss's shoes on the hard floor. Then dead air followed by muffled sounds in the background, a bit of what sounded like dogs whining. Then the sound of heavy footfall again, and Campbell was back.

"You're sure about where you found them?"

"Yes, but no one reports seeing Annie wear them."

"That son-of-a-bitch!"

"Mr. Campbell. Isn't your wife nearby?"

"What? Oh. You got those items?"

"Right here."

"Give me half an hour to walk the damn dogs in the damn rain. I'll come out when you ring."

Murphy blew out a breath. What could he do but agree?

Leaving the library, Raylene returned to Down the Block and stepped in, dripping water from her coat and hat. Inside, she found a bartender on duty that she hadn't met before. A tall, beefy man with sallow skin. When she stated her intent to speak with Ricco, he asked, "Who's asking?"

"Tell him Cheeky. I work here mornings."

"Oh, you're the one. You lasted pretty good so far."

Raylene nodded. "Before you signal him, I'd like to ask what you know about the stack of K.C. Bourbon labels tucked behind the bar glasses." She motioned to the far end of the bar.

"Those? They're for a special recipe. They run short of help, we put the labels on."

"Have you had other labels with other names?"

"Same name, but it'll have a different picture, like a train or a —"

"Shut up," said Ricco from the doorway to the back room. "That's none of yours to talk about." There was no telling how long he'd been standing there.

"But she works here," said the bartender as two regulars came in and took seats at the bar.

"Shut up and serve your customers," said Ricco. To Raylene, he said, "What do you want?"

"It's payday."

"I was surprised you kept working after insulting me like you did."

"I am often accused of stating the truth."

"Well, I'm not like what you said. About sisters. So don't go spreadin' it around."

Raylene motioned with a sweep of hands that took in the saloon, the bartender, and the two drinkers. "Do you want to talk out here?"

Ricco rolled his eyes and frowned. "Come into the office, I'll get your pay."

She followed him into the storage-office room and waited by a stack of soda crates while he unlocked a desk drawer and drew out a cash box. "I have more questions," she said.

"I'm getting' tired of telling you — Just work, don't ask. You don't shut up, I'll have to can you." He held out three dollars to her. "That's for five days. You haven't worked tomorrow yet."

Raylene nodded but did not take the money. "If you answer my questions, you may keep the money."

Ricco frowned. "You runnin' a scheme?"

"I have a few names and I have you figured as someone who has connections. Am I right?" Subtle flattery, not enough for him to see through, but enough to inflate his sense of self.

He shrugged, but offered no denial. A good sign.

She continued. "I am learning about some of the men running certain networks, taking advantage of local businesses not willing to complain about the nature of what is above board and what is not. Do I read this right?"

"Maybe."

"What interests me is —"

Ricco broke in. "I think I got you figured out. When I first got here, I asked around and the guy who used to run this joint was some Indian who got himself killed after hours. Once I got to asking, I heard stories. Some other Indian speared him." He studied Raylene for a moment. "I peg you as related somehow.

Daughter maybe, though there was a daughter died here too. That the sister you meant?"

The way he spoke about Thomas and Annie both dying in this place relit the coals of sorrow banked inside Raylene. Raymond was gone, too, of course, but somehow his death had come to seem inevitable. She just could not accept that Thomas had known he was selling tainted goods. Off label, perhaps, but not tainted. He was too honorable to cheat the customers who provided his livelihood. And he would not have let Annie drink something that he knew could kill her. Ray blamed Thomas, but he must not have known how this city worked behind the scenes. Now that she knew better how things worked, she could not walk away without learning more details.

Ricco was watching the doorway that led to the front, but Raylene could tell he was listening for her reply. She kept her voice low so it would not project to the drinkers or barman. "I mean to find who cooked the poison that my sister drank while working in this bar. Before you came."

"Is that what killed her?"

"It also blinded someone else I know. Not ordinary booze. Something worse."

Ricco rolled his eyes. "How do you know she got it here? And even if she did, and I'm not sayin' she did, what do you think you can do with the kinda people that cook that stuff? You're a skinny little nothin'. I'm the one that saved you from the ice man."

Raylene studied him. He was angry, no doubt, at being bullied by the types who insisted he buy their booze at a cost that he might resent. He might be a person to deflect his own lack of power by making someone else feel low. She said, "You saved *him* is what happened."

He laughed loudly. "That's rich. How d'ya figure?"

With a motion smooth as ice, Raylene slid her boot knife from its hiding place and held it up so it gleamed in the light.

Ricco's mouth fell open before he said, "Jesus Christ, is that legit? You carry that?"

"I do."

"Well, damn. I never figured you for being that tough."

Raylene put her knife away without explaining that not all weapons were for offense. Silence fell between them before she said, "Will you tell me if you're buying bootleg booze from the same source as the previous manager? I need a word with whoever that is."

"A word, huh? You're askin' for trouble and I don't want it comin' back on me."

His reply was meant as a warning, and Raylene had heard many warnings in her lifetime. She said, "You will not know if you are serving bad booze until something goes wrong. If it kills one of your regulars, who do you think the police will come for? Not the ones who cook it. They'll come for you."

Ricco rubbed his chin stubble with his free hand. In the other he still held the cash. Then something inside him deflated and he looked away as he spoke. "There was a guy doing delivery for a big outfit. He's got a box truck. But soon as I opened the place after the Indian died, he started right in trying to deliver twice the amount I'd ordered, and I said no and we had what you call a *falling out*. I still gotta buy it but someone else delivers now."

Raylene stood silent for a beat to let Ricco realize that the sky had not collapsed following his disclosure. Then she asked, "Who was that first delivery man?"

"Went by Duke."

"Was it his truck he was using, could you tell?"

"That guy was no slouch at liftin' crates, but now this one by the name of Lam calls, which I figure for some kinda nickname. The one making deliveries is a Negro."

Raylene knew who Lam had to be. "Anything else?"

"The Lam guy says, 'Seems like it's time for you to order a case or two.' That's how it works. You don't say when you need more. He tells you, then he shakes you down for the cost plus his cut."

I bet he does, thought Raylene. *I bet he thinks he's golden.* "Lam would have a boss," she said. "Just nod when I name the right one."

Ricco made a face. "Don't bother. Used to be Pusateris's racket, but he built a legit nightclub just outside the city. Now it's Gargotta's. His ring does booze and girls."

"I read a newspaper story about a raid where they picked up some of Gargotta's girls." This brought to mind Vivienne and her hostess work. Girls rarely got a pass. She told Ricco, "You can keep your money."

He looked at the bills and shoved them into his pocket. "Don't forget I told you not to do this. If they kill you, don't come cryin' to me. I'll just say I told you so." He looked pleased with his joke.

Raylene squared her coat and made to leave.

"Hey," said Ricco. "You comin' to work tomorrow or not?"

Raylene held his gaze. "If I come back, I want honest pay for the work you don't want to do."

"Oh, *now* you're by the rules. You probably want what the Feds say. Two bits an hour.

Raylene nodded.

"That's a buck a day."

"Good math."

"Don't get smart. I'll think about it. But at least, if you're not dead, come back and tell me what happened."

"You will know what happened by whether Lam ever calls you again."

"What if he does call?"

"Then you will know that I have failed."

Raylene turned and went out through the bar, which now had four drinkers at the brass rail and the same bartender yukking it up with them. She crossed the floorboards that were dark with the blood that had soaked in to become a part of them and felt a dip of sorrow. She did not yet have the physical evidence to make her case to Charles Gargotta, but she knew where she might procure some evidence after dark.

Ten

Raylene left Ricco's saloon (she had to begin thinking of it as *his* now) and drove through a light rain to the West Bottom, which belonged to Kansas though it sat east of the Kansas River and west of the Missouri state line. Kansas City occupied both sides of that river, with people and goods flowing freely both directions.

She was certain she recalled West Bottom streets from years past, but driving around now, she found otherwise, cataloguing mostly industrial buildings — wholesale liquors, metal manufacturing, furniture makers, wool and tallow, harvesting machines, and more. Train rails crisscrossed this portion of land. Smoke from industrial stacks and laboring engines hung in the air. The rumble of passing trains provided a rolling refrain.

All around was the wet green smell of the rivers, but nearest the Kansas River lay stockyards, and across that river a processing plant, so that westerly winds moved the odors of cattle and manure and the tang of blood all day long. This brought to mind the cattle drive Raylene would have missed after leaving the ranch. By now, her fellow cowhands would have driven the yearlings to Rapid City for loading onto rail cars headed east.

Instead, her goal now was a single-story building with spaces for let at the approximate address she'd been given the previous day "between Forester and the viaduct." Her street map had been of limited help and now the slashing rain and window wipers flipping back and forth largely obscured the numbers on most buildings. Due to this section of land flaring south and east, West Bottom streets sometimes branched at angles, perhaps as they had arisen in the days of wagons and mule teams.

After narrowing her search to two square blocks, Raylene parked and pulled on her western hat and went into a wholesale drugs business, skirting men in business suits moving about inside. At the reception desk she was directed another half-block east to an elevated train bridge. Parking closer to that location, she eventually found the building with a painted advertisement for milled flour on the side of it and peeling paint on the front door. Asking inside, she was sent around back to what resembled an alley where she found a door with a small glass window painted over with characters formed of red slash marks.

As when she had visited the other abortion providers, she thought now about Wilma Manheart and the daughter she had birthed who would never grow to feed herself or dress herself. A child with bright dark eyes but no language. Lizzy Manheart might live to be fifteen or twenty but would never attend school or kiss a boy or bear children of her own. Still, her mother was as fiercely attentive to her as she was to her son, who could do all of those things, only in his own muddled way. If she'd anticipated the effort required to tend such a child, would Wilma have ended her pregnancy? No one could have predicted the challenges ahead when Lizzy entered this world. No babe could know, no child could look ahead, no parent had the vision to look into the future and see whether their own children would be better off or worse off than themselves. There was only hope for the future, and sometimes hope was sustenance.

The door gave a jingle as she opened it and another as it

closed behind her. She stomped her wet boots on the rug just inside and slapped the mist from her hat. When her eyes adjusted to the low light, she absorbed the narrow view to a counter behind which sat rows of apothecary jars labeled in more of those foreign characters shaped similarly to a few she had seen on gravestones in a back section of Union Cemetery.

All around was the fragrance of herbal smoke, unlike the prairie sage with which she was familiar, but pleasant indeed. A petite, Oriental woman of indeterminate age came through a split curtain behind the counter and motioned Raylene forward.

When Raylene emerged from the herbs shop thirty minutes later, the sun had come out and a strange warm breeze like the last breath of summer danced around her. Inside the shop, she had used pantomime and shown the photograph of Annie. The herbalist spoke limited English, but Raylene had learned that Annie had indeed visited to ask about ending a pregnancy, offering to pay with the fancy necklace in the photo. The proprietor, Ling Sue, had declined the necklace as something that might arouse the suspicions of buyers or authorities when later sold.

On the pavement outside, Raylene stood a moment, stunned at the thought that her sister might have stood on this very spot while contemplating her predicament, only to leave empty-handed but for a stick of penny incense the lady had sold her. Raylene now held such a stick as a symbol of her sister's last weeks.

In the emerging warmth, puddles on the streets began to steam as did the saturated ground. All around, steam rose to drift in thin sheets. Raylene returned to her truck and drove to the Jackson County Court House where she might obtain some details about death records. After that she drove through the misty streets to a farm supply store, followed by a Five-and-Dime and lastly, a round of inquiries at the photography studios listed in Mrs. G's city directory, two of them near downtown.

Back at the boarding house, Raylene called Murphy to ask him to bring a tool she had not been able to secure. "If you have one," she said. "Also, an extra torch. I think the fog will give us a little cover."

"I have a hand drill I can bring, but I've got to say that your plan is sounding stranger and riskier by the day."

Raylene chose her words carefully to present a challenge few men — and she hoped Murphy was in that category — would be hard pressed to resist. "Then do not come. I can do this myself."

Murphy, in stocking feet in the hallway of his home, hesitated. The little sister was all in. She would move ahead with help or without. He asked himself again, did he want to be in this with her? It was one thing to help her locate Annie's grave, which itself was no crime, and another to commit an actual crime. Then again, what if it was not a crime to unearth a fraud in the manner she seemed to be proposing? He could only hope she had her observations and facts straight.

"Good night," said Raylene down the phone line.

"Wait," said Murphy. If Raylene was indeed correct and some sort of fraud was being perpetrated on innocent purchasers of undertaking services, that fraud surely involved cheating a variety of Kansas City residents out of hard-earned money. Helping to shine a light on such cheats might improve his own reputation with U.P. and around town. She had also suggested a tenuous connection between fraud at Union Cemetery and Annie's death, though he wasn't certain how she would reconcile that. But he himself had already reaped a slight benefit from helping her thus far — those pearl earrings.

After that pause for thought, he said, "I'll come."

Raylene let out the breath she had been holding. It seemed that Murphy was made of similar stuff to that of her father and uncle, Yellow Moon men. She said, "Let's meet outside the east border, which is Locust Street. I'll wait for you at 9:00."

"Alright, I'll meet you there," said Murphy, trepidation surging through him. What was he getting himself into?

By the time Murphy was driving to his rendezvous with Raylene, the ground fog had grown thick as soup, eddying around his vehicle as he steered it along the shrouded streets. He had left a bowl of gum packets and wrapped candies on his front porch for trick-or-treaters who ventured out on a night like this, the sort of night which could befuddle a person in their own neighborhood.

He located Raylene's truck parked halfway between two streetlamps, each like yellowed alien orbs floating above the sidewalk. As he pulled in and exited his coupe, Raylene climbed out of her truck wearing a dark poncho cut from oilcloth. He made out black stripes painted on her face. "What's that get-up you're wearing?

From the back of her truck, she lifted a second poncho and held it out to him. "My objective is for us to look like pranksters. If we are noticed by others out on this night, they will think we are in costume."

"Looks like a costume."

"The color will blend with the fog and protect our clothing."

She did not say *Protect us from a decaying body*, but Murphy understood the implication. He marveled at her willingness to view a stranger's corpse. He knew of no other woman who would.

When he had donned the poncho and returned his hat to his head, she showed him a small jar and said, "You get face paint too."

He held up a hand. "Not for me."

"It will be better if we go unrecognized. Casual observers will see stripes and not the details of our faces."

"Is there another option?"

"You could try blackface."

"I guess I'll take stripes."

Raylene dipped her finger in the black paint and swiped it across Murphy's cheeks. He held very still, as if his skin registered fire, not paint. "There," she said. "Ready for the eve of *Dia de los Muertos.*"

"What's that, code for digging up graves?"

"That is the Mexican celebration called Day of the Dead. A friend of mine describes feasts and parades."

"Catholics have All Souls Day and All Saints Day, without feasts or parades." Raylene seemed to inhabit a world so different from his, yet that was part of her allure. He adjusted his poncho. "Are we ready?"

"This spade is for you."

Murphy took up his torch and the tool he'd brought, and with a spade tucked beneath on arm, followed Raylene, who carried a spade and a duffle bag. Inside the cemetery they found a path and followed it in the direction he associated with where he had almost kissed her under the trees.

After fifteen or so minutes of advancing slowly, Raylene stopped. "I think it is that fresh mound just ahead."

Jesus, thought Murphy. *She really is ... we really are ... going to do this.* He rifled his memory for a mystery novel or true crime story that involved digging up a grave, but he couldn't recall any. Almost all those stories involved graft, or murder, or escaped prisoners, or armed robberies. Not graves. No one dug up bodies, the way doctors reportedly once did when studying human anatomy. What would a dead body offer by way of clues to assist Raylene? Perhaps clues to the mystery surrounding a death, but also decaying flesh and stinking juices. In his work for the railroad, he had yet to observe a decomposing body up close. When there was a death, lawmen were called to the scene. He supposed there was a first time for everything.

The fog had grown even thicker so that it parted and swirled around them like spirits rising from their sleep. Raylene looked left and right as if she might make out approaching figures, then shone her torch on the grave's wooden marker. Bending close, she read out the name on it: Ourbon Kansa. This was the grave she'd previously contemplated.

There were numerous reasons this marker was false. For one, Kansa was the name of a native tribe from the area, not a surname for ordinary people. Also, among other symbols, plenty of nearby grave markers displayed the many-sided Jewish star. To Raylene's mind, Ourbon Kansa sounded very un-Jewish.

Murphy asked, "Was this one not in the obituaries?"

"Not there and not in courthouse records. There is no death record."

"Maybe they're making up names for unidentified people."

"Even if the coroner had held the body while notifying relatives or some such, there would be a death certificate in the name to be used for burial. Officials could use John Doe or Jane Doe but there is no recent deceased by those names."

Murphy knew that if one of his parents or aunts died elsewhere and was buried with a phony name, he would be mighty unhappy. Perhaps these were people whom no one was looking for. The little sister could be wrong, she had to be wrong sometimes. When the dark form that was Raylene moved to the head of the black dirt mound, she pulled from her duffle bag a tarpaulin and a small hand saw.

She said, "From what I recall of this area, water in the soil should drain toward the foot of this grave. We would do well to remove the dirt from this end." She loosened the wooden marker at the head and spread out the tarp and set to work with her spade at the head of the black mound.

Murphy set to work adjacent. The soaked dirt was heavy and before long he could feel the pull on his lungs. He thought he could hear her breathing hard too, muffled by the mist. They worked in silence for a while, their spades *shlushing* into the wet earth. *Shlush*, lift, turn, and slide the shining soil onto the tarp-held mound, which grew larger by the minute.

The fog imparted an otherworldly quality to their labors. The longer they worked, the more Murphy realized that his previously broken arm was sorely in need of rehabilitation. Laboring like this might do it good. He also thought they might get away with Raylene's plan. Clearly, she wanted a look inside the pine box without unearthing the whole thing, and they were making progress in a cocoon of heavy, wet air that seemed to embrace them. Distant sounds arrived as if from an even greater distance. Murphy stood his spade upright a moment to rub his left forearm and ask, "Any progress in your other search?"

Raylene added another hump of mud to the growing mound. "I found the herbalist in an obscure place. She uses special herbs to induce a spontaneous abortion. Annie had gotten a lift there and offered payment using jewels —"

"The jewels I'm looking for? Did the herbalist still have them?"

"The necklace was too fancy for payment and Annie did not return on another day." Here, she looked off into the thick air as if looking for Annie in the distance. "You know what that means."

"That the necklace is somewhere and maybe we can find it."

"It means Annie was pregnant, perhaps not too far along, but she did not end it with an abortion, at least not in Kansas City."

"The woman saw jewels?"

"A necklace with green stones."

Murphy's pulse shot up. Could the herbalist have been lying about not accepting the necklace in payment, or had Annie disposed of it elsewhere?

"There will be no pressuring the herbalist," said Raylene, returning to her spade work.

"But you have her address."

"Her livelihood is tenuous at best. I will not help you attempt to secure from her something she does not have."

"She might have told you a falsehood."

"She told all without any pressure. Had she something to hide, she would not have divulged what she did. Drop that thinking, will you? I am trying to say that my sister was likely pregnant when she died. When she died, her pregnancy died with her."

For the moment, Murphy abandoned thoughts of the jewels to recall his wife, whom he had assumed to want all the usual things that went with marriage and home, but who it turned out actually feared having a child. She had told him she would not, could not bring an infant into the world. About that one subject, she had been quite forceful, whereas his own expectations had been for children. Since her departure, he had looked back on his dismissal of her fears and recognized his inability to apprehend her fragile state of mind. When his thoughts turned dark, he imagined that their opposing positions had driven her further toward an untenable existence, which meant that he had had a hand in her breakdown. To change the subject, he said, "Would your father have asked for an autopsy?"

"Perhaps, because he did not suspect tainted booze, but his death came too soon."

"So that's that, then." They had removed the mounded-up portion of the mud. Now came work below ground level.

Raylene understood that Murphy might think *That was that*, but she knew a thing or two about her sister that others did not. Somewhere there existed a lover who was father to Annie's unborn child. Though she knew her sister was capable of ending an unwanted pregnancy, she thought Annie unlikely to take a lover casually. Money was important, of course. A person had to live, and recent years had been rougher than most, but Annie would not have accepted money in exchange for sexual favors. The cash Annie had left behind might have been saved during frugal living, but a portion of it could as easily have come from a lover who intended it for purchasing an abortion, or for setting up a household.

While she worked, Raylene pictured the boys that Annie had favored on the reservation. The majority had been handsome with well-sculpted bodies from farmwork or heavy labor. Not for her a pimply sort who slurred drunken words of lust or love. Fastidiousness earned high marks, a bath before courting, hair combed and relatively clean for school or community gatherings. One Pine Ridge boy who attracted Annie's attention was Two Toms, who had met with a machinery accident and been taken to the Rapid City hospital. He returned with cologne purchased in that city and was never without a dab of it until the bottle finally ran dry. As was the case with young people, Annie's tastes developed over time, so a sweet-smelling city-slicker seemed entirely possible, perhaps someone more polished than not. Over a spade full of mud, Raylene said, "Describe your boss to me."

Oh dear, here it comes, thought Murphy. "Well, he's older than I am, maybe forty-plus. His people are Irish with some Scottish thrown in. Hard-headed, always certain he's right. Pretty fair with assignments, except for lately. Oh. I took those pearl earrings to him today. He seemed astonished, but glad to have them. Those may have earned me an extra day or two on leave, plus my suggestion about finding more pieces soon."

"I would like to know what he looks like, and if he bathes."

If he bathes? "Um, he smells like a man, I guess. He's kind of fair-skinned with thinning hair on top. Turns red when he's aggravated. He's not fashionable, if that's what you're thinking. Given to cigars, but sometimes just chews them." Murphy worked his spade as he thought a moment. "I don't know what Annie saw in him, but then I'm not sure what women see in men generally. How they choose a man, or settle for a man."

It always comes down to attraction, thought Raylene. She herself found little appeal in the looks of men resembling her father. Fathers, plural, both Thomas and Raymond. Or the classmates she grew up around, swaggering, angry kids who endured, as they must, the indignities perpetrated by whites running Indian schools. Angry boys who looked like they could be her brothers held no appeal for her. Just once she had fallen for an older, half-blood boy who had kicked and cursed school officials who tried to cut off his braids. Rather than submit, the boy had run away. For a whole year, Raylene nurtured a flame for him, always wondering whether he had found a place where he could be himself.

Her tastes ran to slightly older types grown beyond their randy, brainless years. She measured them by their ability to control their appetites. Raul, back at the H-bar-H remained rangy and strong, even without the hard riding that cattle work required. He had adjusted after his roping accident without more than some occasional grumbling and a round of hard drinking. He then mastered new skills in order to work and live the way he wanted among the ranch hands. She found his character as attractive as his hungry body.

Now she thought about Murphy, who cut a fine figure in a suit but also wore the impromptu poncho well. To his credit, he was taking this risk alongside her. She asked, "Does your wife know that you will shovel mud in exchange for help with a case?"

Murphy straightened and stood stiffly upright. "Why do you mention my wife?"

"She probably sees you neat and pressed on most days. This is surely a different side of your work."

Murphy thought back to what the little sister could not know about Catherine and him. Once again, he balked at explaining Catherine's plight, this time because it might suggest a husband opening the door for a different woman to step through, which was in opposition to his vows. Instead of saying, *Something makes me want to do this for you, do this with you,* he cleared his throat. "This is not quite like my U.P. work. I thought you might be taking on too much for one person, so I'm helping."

After a pause, Raylene said, "I think my uncle found that necklace in Annie's things before anyone else began looking." Or was Uncle Raymond actually her father and Annie's? He was a father to them because he helped raise them, and she was learning to accept that she might never know whether he was more than an uncle.

"A different uncle or the one you referred to as deceased?"

"The one who rides with my father in my dreams."

Discouraged, Murphy lifted his spade vertically and slammed it downward. The sound it made hitting something solid registered just as competing voices and warbling laughter reached them through the fog. Murphy and Raylene both looked at Murphy's spade, then at each other. He lifted his spade from the mud and she brought hers to her side and stood silent. They were two gray figures in swirling mist.

Raylene cocked her head then pointed northward. Murphy nodded. The two of them stood watching as dark shapes took on human forms, advancing in their direction along the paved walkway. There came an exclamation. "Hey, look. People!" Raylene and Murphy had been noticed.

Two couples approached, females in costumes trimmed in feathers and men in what looked like top hats. One of the men said, "Fancy finding you here."

At this, the others chuckled and a nasally female voice said, "Hey, Vinnie, pass me that flask."

"Looks like you're digging. What for?" asked the second man.

Raylene spoke up. "We are playing a joke on my ... brother."

"What's the joke?" asked the first man.

"A pretend-grave. I will climb in and be covered up to my neck. A different friend will lead him through here on the way to their party."

"Oh, *ick*," said the other woman. "What a mess."

Chiming in, Murphy said, "I'll turn the garden hose on her later." With his free hand, he pantomimed spraying water around.

This got the revelers chuckling again. "Oh, now I gotta pee," said the second woman. The two women linked arms and set off south down the path. After a moment, the two men followed them.

Raylene and Murphy watched as the murky figures dissolved into the gloom. When the group did not reappear, the two went back to the head of the grave and recommenced removing the last few inches of mud from atop the head of the pine box.

When the mud was reduced to a smeared film of black with wood showing through, Raylene said, "It's pine, as I thought." She put down her spade and wiped her gloved hands on the front of her poncho. Letting herself down into the hole, she reached up for the tools Murphy handed her.

He said, "Maybe we need to think this through. You don't know what you might hit with that drill. Could be someone's face." Not only that, even if she could identify a corpse buried in the wrong coffin, it seemed unlikely that local law enforcement would put much energy into apprehending and prosecuting fraudulent undertakers who were also longtime local business people. They might instead want a cut of the surplus profits that Conboie's flunkies were pocketing. Worse yet, upon reviewing Raylene's allegations, they might prosecute her for digging up the evidence. He knew that authorities didn't take kindly to her type.

She said, "The center is best for a pilot hole. Then I can enlarge it."

"You don't know how tall the corpse is, or how wide. What if you damage it?"

Raylene thought a moment. "I don't think I will, but all of this was so I could gather evidence and I plan to do just that. Will you listen for anyone coming?"

Murphy took a breath and let it out. There were people out and about all over town. More were bound to show up in this place of the dead. Not to honor those in repose, but to shiver with glee on a spectral night in a cemetery. He felt certain that someone else would come along and the ruse about their prank would not hold up with an open burial box beneath Raylene's feet.

Raylene had placed the drill point and begun turning the

handle clockwise. The sound of her work was slight and wouldn't carry far. The handsaw would be another matter. There would be no mistaking the sound of its metal teeth being drawn through wood, even muddy wood. But he wasn't about to quit this place and leave her on her own. "Do you want me to do that?" he asked. In for a dime, in for a dollar.

"If we are caught, it will be better if you haven't handled the actual break-in." She stood a moment to address him. "By the way, I have left most of my cash where Mrs. G can find it. For bail money."

She was right about the former, of course. A surge of relief pulsed through Murphy, followed by a burp of guilt about the latter. He swept his gaze around as if standing guard.

After twenty minutes or so of drilling and sawing, Raylene straightened to stretch. "In spite of the chill, this is hot work."

"I can take a turn," he said. They'd been incredibly lucky not to be apprehended thus far, but time was ticking away.

"I almost have it."

Murphy checked his watch. 11:30. He said, "Almost the witching hour," which after he'd spoken, sounded like nonsense from some dime novel. They had enough worries without adding superstition, which was Catherine's type of fantastical thinking. Back then.

He marveled again about sneaking around in a cemetery with a woman he had fantasized about, imagining her as intense and dangerous with a certain animal appeal. He had witnessed the first two and felt the third as a hunger in his loins. "Raylene," he said. That name still felt new and slightly forbidden in his mouth. "Do you ever think about me? When I'm not working with you?" He felt his face go hot in the cool mist.

She looked up from sawing and considered him, muddy gloves, smeared black lines on his face where he had scratched an itch. Though his question had been earnest, he was taking this risk with her, which meant he was made of tougher stuff than his business-suited detective work might suggest.

From somewhere in the mist came the screams of cats fighting. Fastening her gaze on his, she thought through her answer. "When you are being more a help than a hindrance, I think about your assistance. Also, how your wife is ... somewhere you have not explained. And how some parents would condemn their son's desire for a Lakota woman, even if she finds him ... Well, I will say yes, I think about you." She smiled to herself and turned back to her work.

He stood there, working her words over in his mind, trying to decipher them as either a barrier between them, or an opportunity, no matter how small.

When she'd pushed and pulled her saw two more times, the rough-cut shape fell into the pine box. She lifted it out and stood looking down.

"What do you see?" he asked as he imagined a decaying corpse with slashes where her saw had cut through a neck.

"Looks like straw."

"What?"

"The casket is packed with straw."

Murphy stepped closer to the edge and peered down. "They don't pack bodies that way."

"Straw is perfect for other things. And that explains why this coffin is not buried deeper."

There really wasn't room for both of them to stand below, so Murphy watched from above as she stuck her gloved hand into the opening and moved it around before withdrawing a dark-colored bottle with a screw cap. She looked up at him, smiling widely. "This is what that strange nonsense name on the marker meant."

"Ourbon? Oh. Bourbon? I thought this dig was about

casket fraud. Fancy ones being swapped."

"After that first casket scam, I kept watching and detected this enterprise, which I think is also a scam. Pull Mrs. G's Brownie from my bag and take photos, will you? It's loaded with film and there are two extra bulbs. The bottle and the hole are important."

Murphy did as she asked, saying, "Photos might be turned against you by the cops."

Raylene waited while the flash lit up the mist around her. "I know to use caution with the police, but if the photos turn out, they will help my cause." She worked the bottle back down into the packing.

"Your plan might backfire." Of course, he did not know her exact plan because she kept so much to herself. Not secrets exactly, but almost.

She said, "I will take the rap. Let's fill this hole and get out of this place."

"Wait," said Murphy. "If photos will help you, wouldn't one of those bottles be of use?"

Raylene reached back into the box and brought the same bottle out, which she slid under her poncho and into her coat pocket.

As Murphy returned the camera to the carry bag, voices signaled the arrival of more figures from the fog. "Hey!" came a male voice with a twang that suggested southern roots. Murphy straightened quickly.

Onto the grass, three figures advanced, becoming less ghostly and more solid. "No way," said another male. A third voice joined in. "That's crazy."

As the figures moved closer, Raylene reached for the handle of the spade she'd been using and slid the tool toward her.

"Hey, fellas," said Murphy. "What a night, huh?"

The bareheaded three looked like teenagers, their hair and coats glistening with moisture. One turned to the others and said, "Looks like we caught us some grave robbers."

"Just a prank on a friend," said Murphy, taking a cue from Raylene's earlier lie. "A pretend grave. We're wrapping up."

The stranger who seemed to be the leader turned to his buddies. "Seems like the po-lice would want to know about this sort of thing. Might be glad to catch burglars in the cemetery. Stealing bodies or whatever."

"Yeah," said another. "Bodies or worse."

The first, one, advancing closer, looked down at Raylene, whose gaze flitted from him to the other two, gauging what they might opt for in terms of trouble — three against two. The first one rearranged his shoulders as if to fill out his coat more. "I'm thinking," he said to Murphy, "that if you got any pocket money on you, now's the time to share it. Then we'd be too busy to care what the hell you're doing."

Murmurs of agreement came from the other two. The squeakiest one declared, "That's right. We could use us some more liquor."

Murphy took a step sideways drawing the strangers closer so that the straggler was standing on the excavation tarp. He held his hands up. "I don't think you want to do that. Get the cops after you."

The first one grew bolder. "They'll never find us in this fog. Gimme your wallet."

Murphy dropped his hands in slow motion and slid his left hand under his poncho as Raylene whipped the bourbon bottle from her coat pocket and pitched it at the leader, calling, "Look out!" The teen half-turned to catch the flying bottle as Murphy swept his spade up off the ground to glance off the other's head, sending him backwards with a shout into the thug behind him. Raylene swung the flat of her own spade against the back of the closest teen's knees. As that one folded with a cry of pain, she dropped her spade in the hole and scrambled up.

The second of the three was uninjured. "Oh fuck, you killed him," he moaned as he rolled out from under the leader, whose head oozed blood.

Raylene leaned to take the pulse of the injured one. It felt steady. He seemed to be coming around. As she made to stand, she caught movement from her right and pulled her boot knife free as the second teen lunged for her. Instinctively, she stepped toward him and brought her blade up through the front of his coat, slicing it open and ending with the blade tip poised just beneath his chin. He had reached for her shoulders but with a yelp, flung his hands wide and stepped back. "Jesus Christ," he cried, picking at his split coat.

She pointed her knife at him. "You and your friend with the bad knees, get this stupid friend of yours up off the ground and walk him out of here. Take him for stitches, and while you are at the hospital, ask for some brains." When he stood gaping at her, she growled, "Get going!"

The other two helped the leader up. He was moaning now, a good sign. As the three limped away, the leader braced between the others, Raylene put her knife away and looked at Murphy. They stood blinking at each other for a moment. Then she said, "I guess we had better get this hole filled. Are you okay?"

He nodded, stunned by the enormity of what had just transpired. He could have killed that kid with his shovel and Raylene could have sliced the other one.

"Your intuition was good," said Raylene, breaking into his thoughts. "The edge can kill but a glancing blow stuns. He will have a headache, worse than a hangover, but enough to make him think twice next time. That's one *coup*."

Murphy tried to slow his pounding heart. "One what?"

"Bragging rights for touching the enemy but leaving him alive. Killing isn't the only way to win." She had picked up her shovel and moved to the mound of mud. "Let's finish here in case they do send the cops."

"They're headed for the hospital. We might have an hour."

"Hospitals have telephones and we don't know who their fathers are." She moved the muddy bottle to her canvas bag then lifted her shovel to the mound on the tarp. *Shlush*, lift, step closer to slide the ooze down into the hole.

Murphy moved to the opposite side and did the same. Before long the hole was filled and mounded once more. They removed their ponchos and rolled them into the filthy tarpaulin. Raylene had brought cold cream and clean rags. They cleaned up a bit before heading east through the mist. By the time they reached their vehicles, Murphy's equilibrium had returned. The whole night had been dreamlike. The fog, the digging, the costumed revelers, and the dopes who tried to rob them.

At the rear of Raylene's truck, he handed over the rolled tarp, saying, "If your plan is to take that bottle and the photos to the police, maybe I can help."

She wiped her hands on her poncho then laid one on Murphy's damp sleeve. "We made a good team tonight, and I thank you."

His heart warmed to her words, but once again he felt helpless to make a move toward her. They were both wet and muddy and the police could be on their way to arrest them. Instead, he helped her neaten the gear in her truck bed and close it up. She had the camera bag with her when she cranked the engine to life. Within a block of rumbling away, her truck disappeared into the mist.

Eleven

Before his marriage, Murphy had attended Catholic Masses with his bride-to-be, who was relatively new to Kansas City. Her religious upbringing had been Protestant and sporadic, but she had pledged to raise their children in the Catholic Church. He was certain now that she had given her word without knowing what troubled thoughts and behaviors would later plague her.

Now, as 8:00 a.m. Mass began in St. Christopher Parish, he sat in the back-most pew, his mind drifting beyond the familiar elements of worship and the colored light shining down through the windows above the transepts, beyond the glow of polished wood rails and pews and the hushed quiet of the faithful, all the way back to his narrow view that young women who attracted his attention would naturally possess a perspective about work and home life similar to his own.

Those notions had undoubtedly taken root in him through proximity to his parents and their traditional marriage and home life, which resembled so many others he had observed in his youth. His friends' activities had mirrored his own, including their adolescent-fueled fantasies about sex with unidentified females they found in random girly magazines passed about by upperclassmen. If they imagined the future at all, they imagined their future wives as ladylike, reading Ladies' Home Journal to polish their feminine arts.

He had been suckled on tenets of sin and guilt, and came to know well the inside of the confessional for misbehavior such as studying those girly magazines and talking Lucy Bales into letting him kiss her while feeling the bra-armor beneath her sweater. He had used milk money to purchase comic books when his allowance was gone. There was his lie about his old Schwinn C being stolen from outside the Star Movie House when in fact he had traded it to the teenager in the ticket booth for three months' worth of free admissions. He had satisfied himself in bed late at night, and in the shower. Most of those behaviors, impulsive or planned, delinquent or otherwise, had been duly confessed, earning heaps of Hail Marys for penance. Throughout childhood, he had attended confession regularly, but in later years attended only when convenient. He thought he felt himself growing wiser into adulthood.

But perhaps he had not. For instance, he had let Catherine believe that his career as an accountant was solid when in fact, even at that point he resented his father's expectations for him within the accountancy and knew that his scoliosis would not withstand eight hours in a chair every day for thirty years. Not even *almost* eight hours and *almost* thirty years. When he switched to his U.P. position, he sensed Catherine's un-expressed disappointment that he was willing to spend his days around greasy railyards and throngs of the general populace. Now that Campbell was likely to fire him, he felt a slight relief that she was not here to witness his downfall from the work he had begun to master. This was followed by a surge of guilt over his relief. There seemed to be no hiding from guilt, ever circular and sure to dog a person's coattails.

Murphy did not hold Catherine's psychological frailty against her, she was simply who she was, but he had oversold himself and also married outside his faith against his parents' wishes. And they had been proven right, not because of Catherine's inadequate religious upbringing but because his match with her had not resulted in grandchildren before faltering. Even worse, he now wished for a reprieve from his marriage to a wife who would never return to his home, his bed, even to his city. Still, he wouldn't carry these thoughts to confession.

Just last night he had gloried in three whole hours with Raylene in the cocoon of cemetery fog while they broke the law — Thank God, not for a dead body. He had even injured someone's son. Like a human automaton, he had lifted the spade and swung it at that kid's head. With that act, something had broken open inside him. Driving home last night he had felt it, a current like a cold, deep river pushing against an impasse inside of him. He had lain most of the night feeling his heart beat in his chest and neck until eventually he had slept like the dead of Union Cemetery. This morning, he felt like a freer version of himself, but he didn't know if that was a good thing or not.

All through Mass he sat in a swirl of his own thoughts while the familiar Latin flowed around him. Now he realized that Father Flannagan was signaling the altar boys to bring the wine and water as worshippers rearranged themselves and set aside their Missals and hymnals. The organist started up again as people at the front stood to move toward the communion rail.

There were only two others sitting in his row, now rising to their feet, but he couldn't make himself join them. He could not accept the sacrament when he knew that he had not and would not confess the decisions and thoughts now troubling him, especially those regarding his immutable, everlasting marital vows.

Late afternoon. The fog of the previous night had continued through morning, but now the temperature had dropped a bit and a light mist hovered at street level. By nightfall, the dew would settle on lawns and bushes, fence poles and roofs.

As Murphy guided his coupe past his house to turn into his driveway, Raylene caught his glance toward her truck at the curb and then at her perch on the top step leading to his porch. From a distance, he looked somber.

She waited for the sound of his vehicle idling and the garage door going up. When it closed with a thud, she knew that soon his front door would open. It did.

Murphy came out onto the porch and she looked up. He studied her a moment then said, "Is everything okay? I wasn't expecting you."

"I'm fine, just wasting time until you returned." She lifted a magazine from beside her.

When he saw it was Ladies' Home Journal, he flinched. "You read that?"

"I borrowed it from Mrs. G in case your neighbors sent the police. They would think me harmless."

"Had I known you were coming by, I would not have lingered elsewhere. Will you come in off the porch?"

Raylene glanced around. They did not seem to be drawing attention. "I once entered a woman's house without her knowledge, but I won't again."

Murphy asked, "What happened?" He watched with interest as Raylene slipped her left arm from her coat and rolled up her shirt sleeve.

When she held out her forearm, he could see it was dotted with many small scars as if a dozen small comets had struck her. "Buckshot?" he asked.

She nodded as she ran her right hand along the markings. "A few are still in there. I was lucky she was a poor aim, or perhaps she only meant to wound me when she came home to find me with her husband." She rolled her sleeve down again and slipped out of her coat, folding it upon her lap. "He had convinced me that he was unmarried and I believed him. Or, I wanted to believe him. I think she shot him too, later, when her aim improved."

Murphy shook his head. He was learning that Raylene would share only small bits of her past and pressing her might compel her to quit a conversation. He said, "If you'll wait a minute, I'll be right back." He entered his house, letting the screen door bang gently behind him. He was gone two or three minutes then returned with two tall glasses of soda pop. He handed her one and sat down beside her on the leading edge of the porch. "I could use something stronger," he said, "but it's a little early."

"Rough day?" She took a sip from her glass. Root beer.

Murphy took a generous swallow. "I need to see my parents tonight. Once a month they host our extended family for supper and I haven't gone but twice this year, so I owe them." When Raylene sat quiet, he went on. "I'm an only child, so there are certain expectations ..." He shrugged. "You don't have brothers, am I right?"

"You are right."

"Did your father ever tell you he was proud of you?"

Raylene watched the mist hanging low to the street. Eventually, she said, "Neither my father or uncle would have used those words. As a child I heard some praise, but eventually they expected I had learned sufficient lessons about taking actions to be proud of. They both taught me that women could be warriors." She had spent long hours riding and roping and mastering games of speed and agility in order to compete with the boys who always expected to win. Such pursuits were not for Annie, who would watch from the sidelines cheering, sometimes for Raylene and sometimes for a boy she fancied. She and Annie had never squabbled over hair ribbons, dolls, or dresses. Those were luxuries and it was a luxury to argue when survival of the family and community meant total cooperation. She said, "Does your father place a weight on you?"

Murphy gave a small snort. "It's mostly unspoken, but I feel it. I expect to be fired from my job any day now and I should warn him. Both of them."

"At supper."

"Afterwards."

"And you would rather not."

Murphy nodded. He had nearly finished his soda but Raylene was only a third into hers. He could feel the slow loosening of his thoughts and the partition he had constructed around his feelings for the woman sitting next to him.

She said, "Tomorrow I will take the film from last night to be developed."

"That's good, I guess." He half wanted the photos not to turn out so that she would still have multiple goals to achieve in his city, but to wish that was unfair when in fact he could not help but root for her success. He changed the subject. "I think you wore those pants when I first saw you."

She brushed a hand along one leather-clad leg. "They're nearly indestructible. My own design. My muddy clothes are being washed."

"I vaguely remember your horse."

"Kota." Her steadfast companion. She had trained him herself using all the skills that Ray and Thomas had taught her. None of that "breaking" a horse bullshit, just firm but fair shaping of his willingness to work under her command.

"You don't see those spotted ones often."

Her thoughts about Murphy softened further at his recollection of her cow pony, the friend whose loyalty she treasured most. A horse, though loyal to its person, was a herd animal. Its community came first, whereas people often chose personal profit over the common good. She glanced at Murphy, who was staring into his empty glass. He was dressed for something official, church maybe, but there were bits of grass stuck to his dress shoes. She could sense the churning inside him and his effort to control it. She said, "I detect that you ventured from the sidewalk."

He looked down at his trousers and shoes. "After lunch I went to a spot I like. A giant statue on a hill above the city. From the top you can see for miles. It was hazy today but I could make out the Kansas River moving. I like to think about where it goes, and the Missouri too, how far they roll and what they encounter on the way. Boats, bridges, waterfowl, deer coming down to drink. Little boys with their fishing poles."

As a girl, Raylene had fished the streams and rivers of South Dakota. Not with Annie, though. Annie cooked dinner sometimes but would never handle a live fish or slit one open to extract its entrails. "Do you fish?" she asked.

"I did regularly as a boy, but now I have to make time for it, which I haven't this year." He sounded wistful. "Rivers seem alive, don't they? Streams too, bringing rain water or meltwater that formed somewhere else and might have fallen on some other continent. All that water on the move."

His words transported Raylene to earlier times when a length of string or fishing line with a hook on the end and a squirming earthworm enabled a mere child to bring home a meal. John Murphy might not know it, but he was talking about the connectedness of the earth's water to its lands and wildlife. The great cycle of renewal. She said, "I am ready for a drink of something stronger."

Murphy perked up. "I have whiskey, also vodka left from ... well, some gathering or other. I think there's probably some plain soda for mixing."

"Whiskey neat, please."

"Will you come inside for it?"

"Not unless you tell me about your wife who doesn't live here."

Murphy gave her a startled look. "Where did you get that impression?"

"Though your address was on the letter you mailed to South Dakota I called your office to invite you both to an event for which I needed to address invitations. I was told there was no reason to include your wife's name."

"What sort of event?"

"There is no event."

"Oh." He smiled wryly while gathering up their glasses. "Now I need a drink."

In a few minutes, he came back through the screen door to join Raylene on the porch. Handing her a highball glass of golden liquid, he lifted his own. "To a satisfactory outcome with the police."

Raylene clinked her glass with Murphy's. "Thank you." She took a sip and let its heat coat her mouth before swallowing.

"Smooth all the way down," she said.

"Jameson. My father's favorite, and his father's before that. We have that in common." He looked out at the street lights coming on and the last of the mist lying heavy on the lawns. He took a big swallow of his drink then said, "Okay, here goes. Things were good for some time. I changed jobs soon after our marriage and she was agreeable to that, at least it seemed so, and we were typical newlyweds. Then a couple of years ago, almost three I guess, she had a breakdown of some kind and became fearful and started doing things like ... setting fire to my books. In the living room. Something went wrong in her mind. The doctors said that current medications are sometimes worse than the malady. There's no cure, but quiet and calm surroundings help. Now I write to her in care of a sanitarium in Colorado." He took another slug of his drink. "So, I am here and she's there, and she won't ever return. Sadly." After a moment, he said, "I would like to kiss you."

Murphy's honesty dismantled the last of the barriers Raylene had begun erecting against him during their first encounter in South Dakota. He didn't touch her now, but waited, his desire palpable, beckoning her own desire. A surefire antidote to her daily revisiting of her family's deep losses was the relinquishing of herself to that which sustained life. To small pleasures where she found them, and to life-affirming intimacy with the right person. This man, at this moment, seemed the right person. She said, "If you want, I will come in for a while."

His face registered surprise. "You mean it?"

"For an hour, give or take. You are due somewhere else this evening."

"But I could — No, you're right. An hour, then."

They both rose and he opened the screen door and held it for her and she stepped far enough in so he could close the heavy front door, casting the entryway and living room into shadow. She motioned to the front window and he crossed to close the drapes there. A window on the adjacent wall held sheers that were closed and drapes that were open, letting in a bit of ambient light from the street. Just enough.

She crossed to the sofa and setting her drink aside, pulled its pillows down onto the hooked rug. She doffed her coat and Murphy did the same. Taking a seat on the rug, she patted the spot next to her.

Murphy took a seat beside her as blood began rushing to his brain. He watched as if observing from two places at once — at a remove and also up close. His pulse pounded as she rose to her knees and reached for his left hand, turning the gold band on his third finger until it came free. She set the ring on the sofa seat, saying, "We will leave your wife out of this." Then she unbuttoned her denim shirt and pulled it free from her pants and set it aside. Beneath, she wore a plain cotton undershirt, and this she took off too.

As Murphy worked at his own buttons, he drank in the sight of her, more intoxicating than whiskey. Her smooth, tan skin, lighter below her throat and face. The indents of her ribs, and the small moons of her breasts. Her breath was coming faster and he was nearly dizzy with desire when she tapped her mouth with a forefinger and said, "You may kiss me here, but only once. I prefer my kisses in other places."

Murphy knew then that the path he was on had changed direction and he would follow it to wherever it led.

Twelve

On Monday, Murphy made it to KC police headquarters by ten. Ruby had arrived at eight to straighten his house and make soup. By then he had cleaned up any outward traces of Raylene's visit, washing and drying the highball glasses and straightening the rug and sofa. This was after an extended evening with his father, sipping Jameson while discussing the ramifications of losing his U.P. job. If or when he lost it. The whole time his mind languished back in his own living room, on the rug, with her.

Outwardly, his living room had looked unchanged in the glow of morning, but for him it now held a certain significance. It was the room where the floral rug was now special and the air around it infused with possibilities. Had anyone asked, he could not have said how everything about his life could be different, but inside, he knew it was.

Three aspirin and breakfast at the Daily Diner had helped alleviate his hangover, and three cups of coffee doctored with cream and sugar had primed him for convincing the desk sergeant of Raylene's need to speak with a detective.

Seated on a bench in the lobby, he knew it was too early to expect Raylene, but this was his last day of leave from work. At 4:30, he would meet Campbell at the office and face the firing squad, so today of all days, he must help Raylene. After breakfast, he had called Mrs. G's house and been told that Raylene had left for the morning or perhaps for the day. Mrs. G could not say where she was headed, but he knew she had probably delivered her film for processing and would return to pick up any prints at a designated hour. A rush photo job would cost extra, but he knew that the cost would not stop her. Last night he had been so taken with the nearness of her that he had not thought to ask which studio she had found to accommodate a same-day turnaround. She might be there now unless she had other business to attend to while waiting. At the station he would try to steer her to the most sympathetic of the detectives on duty.

And when she did arrive, would she look any different to him? How would she act toward him? Last night, she had said as she made ready to leave, "I have given Mrs. G something to hold for you in case tomorrow goes wrong. I am fairly certain it will lead you to the last of the jewelry. Perhaps it will save your job." If such were indeed the case, he might be redeemed in Campbell's eyes and also his own father's.

At the time he had simply stared past her words because in that moment, the missing jewelry was no match for his thoughts about the taste of her skin which exuded the taste of earth and salt and sky. And then there was the feel of himself inside of her and the heat of their bodies pressed one to the other. He had not kissed her mouth until she was dressed to leave. In the doorway, he had kissed her as a lover would, pulling her to him and detecting the perfume of whiskey on her lips and tongue, and the taste of himself in her mouth. As she descended his front steps and walked away into the night, he had stood watching. She had not looked back, but climbed into her truck and fired it up. Hearing the truck engine, he felt a stab of panic that he might not know her again the way he had known her for the past hour, seared now into his brain.

Sergeant Franklin, at the desk today, was sure to doubt her claim that booze was buried in Union Cemetery, but he himself had seen a pine box buried by a crew after dark that seemed to be the same box he had witnessed Raylene cutting through on Halloween night. The one she'd taken a bottle from. Raylene was the one suggesting a link between that booze and local bootleggers or mob bosses. A photograph might lend credence to her story, but he knew that local cops often treated local mobsters with more deference than they'd treat people passing through, which was how they'd view Raylene. Her boarding status with Mrs. G wouldn't count. Her final words came back to him. "... in case tomorrow goes wrong." He was going to do his damnedest to see nothing did go wrong.

When the traffic cleared at the front desk, the sergeant looked over at Murphy. "You gonna sit there all morning?" he asked.

"If I have to. You're sure you didn't take the statement of a Miss Little Moon?"

The sergeant flexed his face. "No Moons this morning. No full ones, no little ones, you already asked me that."

Murphy shrugged. "Then I'll keep waiting."

"Suit yourself."

Three of the four benches in the lobby were now occupied. An elderly man in rough clothes sat to Murphy's left. Murphy waited, arms crossed, trying to imagine some other place besides this one where someone besides himself would take her claims seriously. But his mind kept circling round to the previous night in his living room and what they had done to each other and with each other. When he realized he was becoming aroused, he stood and went out through the glass-fronted doors into the fresh fall air. To curb the heat inside him, he mentally replayed last night's post-dinner scene with his parents and what his father had left unspoken about his looming dismissal from U.P. Thoughts about his father cooled his blood in no time.

When he stepped back into the station lobby, Sergeant Franklin looked over from papers he was fiddling with and said, "Maybe she's not coming."

"She's coming," said Murphy. "She's got to."

Raylene started early for Saint Ives Photography studio, arriving before it was open. The proprietor, whom she'd met on her reconnaissance earlier in the week, had agreed to process her film promptly, for a fee. She told him, "We only exposed three frames." Then she left for the Brugmanns' stable. She needed to clear her thoughts about her tryst with John Murphy, who had displayed a lusty hunger for the many pleasures two bodies could produce. Her remedy for almost any mental turbulence was a good, long ride on her trusty piebald, his gentle nickering as she saddled him up, and his bottled energy ready to burst forth at her signal. She had neglected him the last few days. Two hours of riding the straw-colored Kansas grasslands would steady them both.

At the stable, she made small talk with Heinz and met his nephew, who was visiting from just outside of St. Louis. She had brought lumps of sugar for her equine friend and spent an hour currying and brushing him till his coat shone like polished stone. Though she would repeat all this work afterwards, she combed his mane and tail before saddling him and walking him out to the lane. Snakes had not yet gone to ground. They might be out on the roads or in open spaces between shrubs, sunning themselves in the waning warmth of the year, so she carried Raymond's hunting knife in the scabbard on her belt. Only a snake that struck her horse would be in danger from that knife.

In her saddlebags she had a thermos of coffee and two sandwiches provided by Mrs. G. If she chose, she could stay out most of the day and make it back to the photography studio before closing time.

The day was bright, with fluffy clouds here and there overhead. The air had the feel that came with a change of seasons — modestly warm and cooled by a breeze. She rode Kota at a walk to the outskirts of town then turned down nearly every country road they came to, crossing open land where it wasn't fenced. The land had been refreshed by the recent rains, with patches of grass still green. They came to a stream no wider than Kota was long, and she let him drink his fill. After some time, they circled back to the stream and she fed him the oats she had brought him as a treat, then he nibbled shoots at the water's edge while she ate one of her sandwiches and sipped coffee. When it was time to return to the stable, she gave Kota his head and tucked in as he powered up to a gallop, dirt flying out behind them. Together, they were the sun and earth, stirring the breeze across the grasslands. In her heart she was Kota and he was her. When he slowed, she steered him back in the direction they'd come.

Back at the Brugmann place, she picked his hooves clean and washed and brushed him until the effort registered in her arms. After he had lipped the last of the sugar cubes from her palm, she leaned in close to breathe into his nostrils. Speaking low, she told him that she was trying to resolve the dirty booze problem she was certain had killed Annie. Also, that what she planned might backfire but he was in good hands if for some reason she didn't return. She walked him out to the pasture, opened the gate, and sent him through with just his halter on.

Heinz appeared as she stood watching Kota amble across the pasture toward a dozen horses grazing contentedly on good pasture grass. She pulled a wad of cash from her pocket. "Here is payment for Kota's boarding thus far, and some extra," she told Heinz. She glanced across the pasture toward the far horizon. Only a month ago she had left her ranch job to pursue answers to her questions regarding Annie's death, but that month felt like a lifetime. She said, "Of all the horses I have ever known, he is my favorite."

Heinz, who was a reticent sort, glanced calmly at her then looked away and spoke in the direction of the pasture. "You sound like someone who might not return."

She stood silent a moment watching the horses. "I'll be back if things work out."

"Do you need help of some kind?"

"No. I just have something I must do."

"Is it about your father?"

"My sister."

He nodded and watched Kota join the other horses. "Your Kota is prize horseflesh, and I will gladly keep him in good condition so you can take him home again."

She liked the sound of that. After bidding Heinz farewell, she went to her truck and started it. When she rolled around past the barn, she slowed to glance back at the pasture. From that vantage, Kota was a dot in the distance. He looked very far away.

Murphy had waited almost two hours in the police station lobby before his revolving thoughts about the previous evening cooled sufficiently for him to apply a detective's approach to locating Raylene. In an alcove set off from the main lobby, there were public pay telephones he could use to call around to find the studio that was processing film for Raylene. If he timed it right, he could catch her there so he could offer his assistance with filing a police complaint.

After phoning two studios and finding their lines busy, he reached one other, which had no rush order for Raylene Little Moon. He tried a fourth — no cigar. Then he tried again with St. Ives, and bingo — film for Miss Little Moon was currently drying. Next, they would print any viable negatives. They had promised to have her order completed by 3:30 p.m. Relief washed over him. After signing off, he threw a wave in the direction of the sergeant's desk and headed for his coupe, passing two cops duck-walking a drunk into the building. He could be waiting for Raylene in front of the studio by 2:00, but before then he needed to make a call away from the fine-tuned hearing of the desk sergeant. From a phone booth around the corner from police headquarters he phoned Campbell at U.P.

"You're supposed to come in at 4:30," said Campbell when he finally took Murphy's call. "Or do you have news for me?"

"That's the thing," said Murphy trying to avoid a wad of gum stuck to the receiver of the phone he was using. "I have a solid lead, but I can't provide it until tomorrow." By then he would know how he and Raylene had fared in making out complaints at KCPD.

"Your leave was just to today."

"*Through* today," said Murphy. "You gave me five working days and that includes today, so I'll come in tomorrow and bring you the lead." He did not know what Raylene had meant by leaving something with Mrs. G for him, but if she meant to provide him a lead, she would keep her word.

"Alright, alright, Jesus Christ. That had better be a good damn lead," growled Campbell.

"It will be." Murphy was done worrying about his job. Now he wanted Campbell to admit that he, Murphy, had accomplished more than anyone else could have regarding the jewelry, which not being U.P. business, should not be hanging over Murphy's head.

By 2:00, Murphy had fitted his coupe into a parking slot in front of St. Ives. Foot traffic in this part of downtown was thick, with people headed for nearby businesses and The

Golden residential hotel. As was his habit on a stakeout, he imagined personal stories for each of the passersby, complete with friendships, spouses, jilted lovers, and jobs they either relished or resented. For the latter, he sometimes conjured overbearing bosses who needed help from employees to solve their personal troubles. He was beginning to think he would rather have no boss at all.

Raylene arrived in front of the photo studio at 3:15. She was not surprised to find him there. Any detective worth a paycheck could have figured out which local photo studio had agreed to process her film. When he stepped out of his auto and up onto the sidewalk, she said, "Hello again."

Now that she stood before him with windblown hair and the glow of fall around her, all of the personal things he'd contemplated saying to her flew out of his head, plus there were pedestrians passing them by and a clerk watching them through the windows of the studio. "Hello to you," was all he came up with.

Raylene led the way in, advancing promptly to the glass-top counter. "You have an order for Little Moon," she told the clerk.

"It's in the back. I'll get it. I think Mr. St. Ives said only two looked printable." He turned and went through a doorway behind the counter.

Raylene stood at the counter and Murphy gave her room by standing back. He could make out splatters of mud running up the legs of her pants. Her boots were creased with mud between heel and sole. She had likely been somewhere off the sidewalks and streets of town.

Mr. St. Ives, a mustachioed man wearing a faded brown work apron, emerged from the back carrying a white envelope. When he saw Murphy, he said, "Sir, we'll be with you in a minute."

"That's alright," said Murphy, stepping forward. "I'm with her." He liked the sound of "I'm with her." How great it would be if that were true, if he *was* with her.

Opening the envelope, the man slid out a sleeve of negatives and two black-and-white prints. "I tried an 8x10 first," he said, "but the image blew out. These 5x7s are the best we can do. I burned them a little extra and increased the contrast. They don't look like much." He held them out to Raylene.

She said, "You're right. They're blurry."

"I told you it would be the same price whether they're any good or not. I can't be responsible for whether people can take a decent picture. I'm not in charge of that, only developing whatever's there."

Raylene knew that conditions had been poor when Murphy had snapped the photos. Grousing to this man would get her nowhere fast. She glanced at the prints. "They will do."

"I'll pay the tab," said Murphy, stepping forward with his wallet.

"I paid already," said Raylene.

"Before seeing the work?" said Murphy. He looked at the proprietor.

The man shrugged. "It was a rush job."

Murphy gathered up the sleeve of negatives and the larger white envelope and handed them to Raylene, who put everything back together.

Outside, yellow and gold leaves from nearby trees skittered along the sidewalk. Murphy said, "I don't see how those photos will help your case, but I guess there's not much way to make them better. At least you have an actual bottle." A crispy leaf blew right toward him. He lifted his foot and brought his shoe down on it. "I've given some thought to the best way to approach making out a complaint with the police. Do you want to hear it?"

"Of course."

"Here's the thing. Anyone can waltz in and report something they think is lawbreaking, or make a complaint about someone who has done them wrong. Not civil stuff, although it doesn't hurt to have a police report if you're taking someone to court over their failure to pay you for contractual work, or situations like that. But criminal complaints are scrutinized before being investigated. They can't completely take the complainant's word because that person could have a vendetta against someone. A sergeant of detectives decides whether to assign a detective to look into the facts, take statements, gather evidence, that sort of thing. So, you want to put your best claim forward and tell them exact dates and locations, in this case where you witnessed the fraud about the coffin you think was switched —"

"It *was* switched."

"Okay, I believe you, but they won't unless they investigate and corroborate. Also, that complaint is separate from the matter of the grave we dug up, which wasn't a grave but a holding place for hooch, yes?" When Raylene nodded, he continued. "So, they'll need two statements from you — the name of whose coffin it was that got switched and the date of the funeral and the switch if you know them. Any pertinent details. Then there's also the matter of the coffin that you have the bottle from. Figuring how and why there's a coffin of booze in the graveyard is a separate matter, even if they're somehow related."

"It was the same crew working after dark," said Raylene.

"I believe you. Still, detectives would have to stake out the cemetery in order to apprehend the culprits. But that's *if* they want to figure out *who done it*, you know? I'm just trying to prepare you for being disappointed about how they choose to move forward or not. And you can't count on them telling you what they determine from an investigation, because you're not the party wronged by either of those incidents. In one case, some unsuspecting coffin buyers were duped, and in the other — I guess it would be the public because Union Cemetery belongs to the city. Do you follow me?"

"Yes."

"I can swear out a statement about how I helped uncover that coffin of bottles and took the photos but you shouldn't get your hopes up about how they respond. *If* they respond."

"That will not be a problem," said Raylene.

Murphy let out a breath. "Good. This is Monday, which means Detective Sergeant Dunphry is assigning detectives. I think it'll be him. The trouble is, he's not the straightest stick in the woodpile — oh, in case you don't know it, you won't want to go in armed."

"Armed?"

"I don't think they would frisk just anyone, but they might choose you. They might not find your boot knife, but up on the Pine Ridge you had a hunting knife and you wouldn't want them to accuse you of planning to threaten them." He had personally benefited from her carrying that knife, but it might not take much for police to accuse someone like her of being a danger.

She said, "They must see ranchers wearing knives."

"Especially west of the river, but all this cemetery stuff happened on this side, in the city. And, you don't look like a rancher. You look like a woman." He just wanted her on the right side of whoever they ran up against.

"I understand your point. I will not wear a knife to the police station, you have my word," she said.

"Good." He glanced up the block, past the hotel and a

famous old restaurant that opened for dinner. "I'm parked right here. Which way is your truck?"

Raylene pointed. "That way."

"Downtown on a Monday is always busy like this. If you're ready to go, I'll meet you there."

"I am ready to go." She put a hand on his sleeve and felt the warmth of him beneath her palm. His was a warmth she now knew. She knew the passion of his kiss too, which had surprised her by making her hungry for more. He was headed to the police station and she was not. She said, "I will see you."

He paused a moment to parse her words, but thoughts about whether it would be Detective Dunphry reviewing their statements had taken over his mind. He leaned in and gave Raylene a hug meant to communicate that he would help her with every fiber of his being. When he got to his coupe, he looked back, but of course she was walking away. In a minute, she was out of sight.

Late afternoon traffic was heavy, but Murphy still reached police headquarters within fifteen minutes. All nearby street spaces were taken, so he parked in a public lot and hurried back to take the front steps two at a time to the upper landing and the glass entry doors. With a look of curiosity and amusement, Sgt. Franklin glanced up while speaking with a middle-aged couple pressed against his desk.

At times Murphy found the lobby of police headquarters too library-quiet, with people speaking in hushed tones. Very occasionally an angry citizen would complain in full voice. This time, all the benches held people either huddled in twos and threes as if over coffee, or sitting stock still, hands in their laps and blank looks on their faces. Whenever anyone moved about, their shoes clacked on the marble floor.

Murphy stepped to a spot just inside the front door to wait, hands in his pockets.

After a few minutes, when the couple was sent back to sit and wait, the sergeant glanced over. "You again?" he said, a half-smile on his face.

"This time she's coming," said Murphy. "There's traffic," he added. "And parking's a mess."

"Sure," said Sgt. Franklin, beckoning to a businessman who had been waiting.

Murphy began watching the entrance, mentally replaying what he had twenty minutes ago explained to Raylene about the utmost importance of details. Dates and times, descriptions of those involved. Corroboration being important, he could attest to which evening they had spent in the foggy cemetery uncovering the hooch-filled coffin. Without spilling about the run-in with the teenagers, of course.

After a bit of waiting, Murphy checked the clock on the far wall, which now read 4:35. He felt like a watched pot with the heat beneath it ramping up. *Patience, patience.* Raylene's truck tire might have gone flat. She might have run an errand on the way. He didn't think she was the sort to get cold feet. He reminded himself that he was an old hand at making statements to police and Raylene was inclined to make decisions in her own time. He had found that out last night when she invited herself into his home and into his arms. *Patience.*

At the hour mark, it occurred to him that Raylene wasn't coming. He stewed a moment. Hadn't they agreed to meet at police headquarters to file a report? Or two reports. She had the bottle from that crazy grave robbery they'd pulled. She had photos that were foggy with not much detail, poor enough they might have been staged. And while the other incident of the coffin being switched after dark was farfetched, he believed her story whole-heartedly whether anyone else would or not. But still ...

Outside, the day was taking on that golden glow of afternoon and Murphy began to rethink his exchange with Raylene outside the photography studio. Had they agreed to meet here? He replayed joining her at the studio at 3:15 where she picked up her film and prints. On the sidewalk out front he had explained about the criminal complaint process and the vagaries of police cooperation. She had listened and chimed in and agreed not to wear a weapon. They had parted to head for their respective vehicles but — now he thought back, he realized she had not said, "I will meet you there in fifteen," or, "If you get there first, wait for me," or even, "I will see you there." What she had said was, "I will see you," which was not at all like a promise. More like a farewell.

The realization stunned him. Raylene had some other plan than meeting with police. For a panicked moment he thought she might have hightailed it back to South Dakota, but she would have hinted at that, wouldn't she? His ego wouldn't let him think she had left town on the sly, nor would his heart.

To think clearly, he needed distance from the half-dozen conversations now echoing within the lobby and the clacking of footsteps in the hallway from which a detective called citizens back to an office to give their statements. He turned for the door just as Sgt. Franklin looked up.

"Next time," said the sergeant.

It might only have been a friendly acknowledgement by a copper who had seen a lot of craziness, but Murphy ignored the comment as he pushed out to descend from the landing, his feet barely touching the steps. In a few minutes he was behind the wheel, sitting in the quiet of his coupe, thinking.

What in the world was he missing about Raylene and the police? He did not know whether her background included run-ins with police, which might give her pause about entering Kansas City's headquarters. But she seemed to be made of sterner stuff. If she meant to make out complaints to the police, she would do so. And if she wanted to spur an investigation before the culprits could move the casket of booze, she would not hesitate. Wearing his detective hat, he asked himself: Was she hesitating or had she no intention of involving the law?

Perhaps the latter.

In which case, why make a point of photographing the bootlegged bottle and coffin? It was true that police might not investigate either of her claims. Or they might take so long in considering the merits of her claims that she'd leave for home before any investigation was concluded. He had to ask — Would she even care about the finalization of an investigation regarding buried booze or fraudulent casket sales? It wasn't as if she herself had been a victim. He thought back. She had not mentioned suspecting her father's burial of being tainted; she had mentioned finding his grave but not being peeved about how or where he'd been buried. Annie's burial — that was another matter. He knew it had taken place just before Raylene had arrived to view her father's body. So, Annie's casket was not the concern. The problem was a lack of a confirmed location for Annie's grave, and rightly so.

A knock on his driver's side window startled Murphy. The one knocking was a lady with a death grip on a carved wooden cane, the sort that old timers sometimes carried.

She spoke as he rolled down his window. "Mister, you going to come out of that spot? Aren't any others closer in."

"Yes ma'am," said Murphy. As he backed out, the woman motioned to a mud-caked Ford captained by a man Murphy figured for the husband.

Out on Locust Street again, Murphy glided along with the

traffic headed south until reaching Sixteenth, where he turned right and pulled over to the curb at the next available opportunity. There, he sat with his auto idling as he tried to reconstitute his line of thinking about Annie's burial. They had not located Annie's grave, but Raylene seemed to have gone quiet on that matter, focusing instead on the bootleggers or booze runners or whoever was burying booze in phony graves.

He began sifting through his recollections of Raylene's remarks about booze. One had arisen when they stood before the apartment of the abortion provider, touching on Annie's death as being from "natural causes." Raylene had said, "Booze kills people." Could that be the sticking point? If Raylene thought that booze killed Annie, who was only twenty-eight, she would not take aim against regular booze makers and the products that people drank every day without harm. She might, though, turn against illegitimate booze makers and booze sellers. But then the logical thing would be to seek the help of police. Even for his U.P. job, he didn't singlehandedly apprehend thieves and scoundrels. He might delay someone until police arrived, but he played by the rules and operated within a detective's boundaries.

Of course, Raylene wasn't a cop or an average citizen. He had seen her stand down those ruffians in the cemetery; also, some rowdies up in South Dakota. With his broken arm and eyeglasses, he could not aid her during that incident. She succeeded by herself. That was one of the first times she had astonished him, but it hadn't been the last. Now he wondered ... could she be after hoodlums involved with hooch? *Dear God, she might.* And if so, she would find them dangerously resistant to anyone questioning their conduct or their profits. He took a breath and let it out slowly. On her own, she was probably soon to be in danger.

Raylene's wool blanket fell softly onto a golden carpet of cemetery leaves gleaming in the last rays of light slicing through trees on a nearby knoll. The blanket was one from the truck that had been Uncle Raymond's. He preferred the old wool blankets passed down from his and Thomas's parents, who had likely gotten them from their parents. She had only met those relations during childhood. Her childhood and ancestors were both long gone.

She knelt with her knees nearly touching Thomas's grave and thought again what a shame it was that Thomas and Ray had crossed over from life at such a distance from one another. Though plagued by differences in their later years, they resembled two halves of a single person, a double father for her and Annie. You had to know them well to tell them apart.

She smiled as she recalled stories about how Thomas and Raymond had fooled her mother's people in Oglala, one twin appearing at a gathering for a betrothal or for the arrival of a newborn baby, taking leave just before the other "returned" in similar clothing but with a different horse. Not for a death ceremony, which was too sacred for foolishness, but for occasions when good-natured pranks perpetrated against relatives and acquaintances were permissible.

To the cemetery she had carried some dried twigs of wild sagebrush she had collected from near the *makhósica* expressly for the purpose of saying a prayer over this grave. Not only a prayer, more a remembrance of who Thomas had been.

First, she layered the sagebrush twigs atop the grave's mound, followed by a few handfuls of golden leaves from those on the ground, enough to make a small heap. Then she stretched a little to place her mother's silver ring and turquoise ring atop the spot where she thought Thomas's heart would lie below. She knew he had carried her mother with him always, even when he left to seek work beyond the reservation. He'd left them all. And perhaps there had been no other choice. Was it a choice to stay and be unable to provide for your family? Raymond had done the same, as had so many. But each time returning, they shared the truths they had learned and all morsels of sustenance.

Raylene turned her face toward the setting sun and closed her eyes, as she had been taught, to detect that which was unseeable. Lessons from both fathers: that eyes could still see with one's thoughts unobstructed by the shapes and textures of the world. *Your seeing mind*, Raymond called it. She sat this way for a time, holding Thomas and Raymond in the dancing light behind her eyes, and in doing so understood that Raymond believed it necessary to destroy Thomas for serving hooch that could kill. That had killed. She was sure of it now. Poisoned hooch that killed Annie was real.

In the saloon there had been two warriors. Ray full of anger and vengeance and Thomas in shock at Annie's death. Before his own death Ray had followed his own teaching — *Know your opponent. Think his thoughts.* He had delivered prairie justice by sending Thomas to the spirit world.

She liked to think there were horses on the Other Side for riding and racing, hooves flashing to spark the black night, and that each contest between the brothers would end in a tie. Impossible, of course, unless on that side things were different. Despite her embrace of Christianity, her mother was in that place too. Being Lakota, she would have waited all these years for her men, both of whom she loved and who both loved her.

When dark began to fall, Raylene pulled out matches and lit the little pile of gray-green sage and leaves, which flared as the match flame caught. The fire was small, but it would do. She took up one twig of sage that she had set aside and pushed its tip into the fire. As it began to smoke, she held it above the grave and made circles, then to the rhythm of a Crow song learned in childhood, scooped smoke upward. *Something red my father wears now where his life was. Oh, young men whose wound stripes are on your sleeves, walk you reverently pronouncing my father's name. Oh, my father, the old men remember you! I hear them saying there goes a warrior's son.* Fitting, she thought, for a father killed in the sort of dispute that propelled whole nations into war — tradition, patrimony, honor.

As the fire died, she said a silent prayer for Thomas's safe journey to the spirit world and promised she would do the same for Annie. Her stomach gave a growl, but she was fine. She had fasted all day, taking only water as Ray and Thomas had described warriors doing in preparation for meeting an opponent in battle. Today she felt strong, her mind clean. This was no guarantee of success, but she was glad for having followed the teaching of her fathers.

She waited, her mind at peace, her thoughts clear, until the little fire burned itself out, sending a coiling stream of smoke skyward. *Goodbye, Father. Uncle. Brother. I carry you with me.* With those words, a river of peace started in the center of her and flowed upward and outward, taking with it her confusion and anger at his betrayal. Feelings she had carried this last month.

Mrs. Gunther opened the door to Murphy's insistent knocking. "Oh, hello." She looked past Murphy. "I thought you'd be with Raylene."

"I came to ask if she's here."

"She said she had business to attend regarding Annie.

Aren't you supposed to be helping her?"

"She, ah, often does things her own way. You might have noticed."

Mrs. G led him into the house. "We've had supper already," she said, "but there's a bit of lamb pie left if you're hungry. Just a slice."

"I don't think I could eat right now, but thank you," said Murphy, fedora in hand.

"Coffee then? Or tea?"

"Tea, please." Murphy followed her into the cheerful kitchen, fragrant with aromas of buttery pie crust and savory lamb, and something that reminded him of his aunts' cooking — rosemary, perhaps. Whenever he was with his aunts at family meals, they talked of domestic things and compared recipes. Having no interest in kitchen skills, he would simply listen until his father interjected observations about Missouri's governor Park and "that damn Pendergast, making all the Irish look like crooks," or the state of his accounting business. This last might have been another of his efforts to remind Murphy about what he'd left behind for detective work.

Now he accepted a mug of tea from Mrs. G and took a sip. Anxious as he felt inside to find Raylene and protect her from making a deadly mistake with bootleggers, he knew not to push too hard too fast with someone from whom he needed information. Alienating a potential informant usually produced the opposite of cooperation. "Mrs. Gunther," he ventured, "you do take care of your boarders. Lamb pie? That would be a delicacy in my house."

Mrs. G was oiling bread pans at the counter, a large bowl covered with a tea towel resting on the nearby stovetop. From his place at the table, Murphy could feel the oven's glow of heat.

Mrs. G said, "I like to think of my boarders as nieces, most of them are like that to me. Annie was, Raylene less so, though of course I barely know her." She glanced at Murphy. "I hope she feels okay. She's been keeping strange hours but I can usually get her to eat something."

Here was Murphy's chance. "Has that changed?"

Mrs. Gunther, bless her, fed Murphy some details. "No breakfast today, or supper. She keeps checking my city directory and making notes. Today she's been gone since early. I don't like to harp on the girls, of course. The young ladies. But sometimes they need a little guidance about eating properly. *Motherly advice* is how I think of it."

Murphy assumed that most of Mrs. G's boarders had probably seen a bit of life, else they would be in marriages or in their parents' homes where motherly advice abounded. But he said, "They are lucky to have someone concerned about their welfare." He sipped his tea. "Does Raylene not tell you where she's going during the day so as to, you know, help you plan meals?"

Mrs. G lifted the tea towel and glanced under it before putting it back in place. "I know about her mission, you could call it, regarding Annie." She fastened her gaze on Murphy. "Isn't it strange that you have not found that gravesite? I mean you and she together. That's a shame, but there's got to be an answer. She seems to spend a lot of time on it, wouldn't you say?"

"She is determined." What he was thinking was, *If you only knew what she's been doing.*

"While that dough rises, I'll fetch the item Raylene left for you."

Murphy perked up, though the item, whatever it was, would probably not point to where he could find Raylene this evening. *This evening.* Evenings were when she cased the cemetery and held her own version of stakeouts. He had thought her finished with collecting evidence, but maybe he had thrown a wrench in her plans. His warnings about lack of police cooperation might have pushed her to collect more evidence. The cemetery, though, was a poor place to sit alone in the dark because the crooks, whoever they were, might detect her meddling. They'd be protective about their coffin switching and their bootleg bourbon. Mrs. G returned with a beat-up black valise that had seen better days. "Here," she said. "I was to hold this for you."

If things went wrong, he thought. Raylene's words to him. They had gone wrong, alright, in the last two hours. He slid the valise toward him, noting that its lock had been cut around. He worked the top open to peer inside. "It's empty," he said.

"It was Annie's and this is how Raylene left it. I wouldn't nick someone else's goods. Isn't that what you'd call it?"

"Of course you wouldn't. I just thought — oh, it's fine." He needed to slow his thoughts. With most cases, he maintained a dispassion that kept him levelheaded. With Raylene these days, he found his thoughts distracted and sometimes disorganized. He was pondering what he knew about her preoccupations versus what she might have discovered and what she might need to next accomplish, when footsteps sounded on the hallway stairs. In came Vivienne dressed in slacks and a sweater.

"*Bonsoir*," she said upon noticing Murphy at the kitchen table. "You are here again."

Murphy stood and nodding slightly said, "I am interrupting your evening." He glanced at Mrs. G. "I can be on my way."

Vivienne waved a hand. "I don't mind looking at you while you wait for Raylene." She glanced at Mrs. G. "We don't get many men here."

Murphy shrugged and retook his seat. "I came to find Raylene but I'm told she is out with no set return."

"Ah yes, on a mission," said Vivienne. She filled a mug with steaming water from the kettle on the stove and brought it to the table where a saucer held tea bags.

Murphy's pulse began to knock. "Did she tell *you* her mission?"

"*Mais oui*, a little." She said this as *leetle*. "She is looking for boot leggings."

"She told you that?"

"Well ... she did not tell, she asked."

Murphy assumed a nonchalant expression. "She asked you for boot leggings, uh, bootleggers?"

Vivienne sat up straighter. "Not for the makers, for the boss. There is just now but one for all the city."

Jackpot!

Mrs. G had turned from her work at the counter, hands plastered with flour, bread pans left idle. She seemed near to calling a halt to the conversation so Murphy sped it along.

"What's his name, this boss?"

"Mister Gargotta. Don't ever call him Charles. Call him *Mister*. He is downtown. In the night. Very generous with ..." Here she rubbed fingers and thumb together and Murphy got the message. The man was rich and spread it around.

He asked, "Any idea where that man spends his evenings?"

Mrs. G cut in. "Now wait. That's enough talk about mob bosses. This household doesn't traffic in such information."

Murphy held up his hands and nodded as Vivienne sat silent. He sure needed that information, but he wasn't about to make an enemy of Raylene's landlady. In work like his, the burning of bridges left only ashes. He said, "We will say no more." He lifted his tea mug as if saluting Mrs. G, and smiled benignly at Vivienne.

Mrs. G studied the two at her kitchen table before turning back to punching and dividing bread dough and patting it into loaf shapes, a slight floury mist rising up around her hands. Murphy thought fast, lifting his own hands to ask a silent question of Vivienne.

After a moment's thought, Vivienne rose and stretched in place. Draining her tea, she spoke to Murphy. "So nice to see you again. Good evening and use care." She stepped toward the sink beside Mrs. G, saying, "I think I will be done for the evening. I plan to see *six* in the morning." She threw a glance at Murphy. "Mr. Murphy —"

"Call me John, please."

"You're a busy man. You probably see *six*." She raised a hand in farewell and disappeared through the door to the hallway.

Vivienne's words threw Murphy a curve. Since when would a young Frenchwoman he'd only met twice speak of a time for waking? Someone might say they rise "early," but not the exact — hold on. She was speaking in code.

Vivienne was gone, so Murphy glanced exaggeratedly at the wristwatch he had worn today in place of his pocket watch. "Look at the time," he said to Mrs. Murphy. "You have been so kind to let me visit, but I'll be running along."

Mrs. G closed the oven door on her two pans of dough and checked the stove's timer. She turned to Murphy.

He lifted the valise he had pushed to one side, saying, "Thank you for being the go-between. I'm not sure what to make of this valise, but thanks."

"I'll see you to the door," said Mrs. G, wiping her hands on a striped tea towel.

Murphy carried his fedora as he said goodnight. While tossing the valise into the trunk of his auto, he pondered the code that Vivienne was trying to convey. Six ... six. What did that number mean? Raylene's troubles were heating up. She was looking for the biggest fish in the bootlegging pool, a situation where a partner could be critical. If only he could find her in time to assist.

Thirteen

Raylene stepped into the nightclub and paused to let her eyes adjust to the low light. She had debated whether dressing up in Annie's clothes would help her gain entrance, but decided to come as she was from the cemetery. Luckily, no bouncer stopped her, or maybe there was no such person on duty just now.

Jazzy music permeated the air, but it wasn't coming from the stage at the far end, where a sloped-shouldered worker in threadbare clothing steered a dust mop in circles. The odor of cigarette smoke hung in the air. She knew that if the club had been in business long enough, nothing short of a tornado would get the smell out.

Approaching the unoccupied end of the bar, Raylene waited to catch the bartender's eye. City bartenders had ways to put customers in their place. They might studiously polish glasses or dust bottles to let you know you had no pull in the place. If you weren't a regular you might wait a long time to purchase a drink. Not all bartenders practiced this sort of silent belligerence, just those who thought themselves better than their customers. In her opinion, insecure types needed to keep customers waiting, as if slinging drinks was a higher calling than many others.

When the bartender, stuffed like a sausage into his black vest, decided to wait on her, he strolled down to her end of the bar and ran his gaze up and down the parts of her that he could see. "What'll it be?" he said, his expression showing he didn't like what he saw.

Raylene spoke as if she said regularly, "I'm here to meet with Mr. Gargotta. Have you seen him tonight?"

"You? *You* got a meeting with the man?"

"I was told to find him here."

"You were, huh, by who?"

Raylene glanced at the drinkers who were paying them no mind and said, "If you want to explain later how you decided who he meets with, be my guest." She shrugged as if such a slight were of no import to her.

The bartender studied her a moment, a frown on his fat face. At last, he said, "He ain't here yet. You can sit and wait until he comes in." After a pause, he added, "In which case you should buy a drink."

Raylene figured she didn't need a battle with the bartender. She was saving her battle for Gargotta. "I'll have Jameson," she said, beckoning Murphy to mind.

The bartender made a face. "I look like a leprechaun to you? Try again."

Raylene studied the bottles lined up along the back of the bar.

The bartender broke in. "I got some good house whiskey." He pointed at four greenish-tinted bottles side-by-side with a label whose design was dice with 6 spots showing against a round yellow circle. That yellow circle again.

Raylene held up a hand to stop him. "Old Crow and water, tall," she said. She could nurse the drink or let it melt.

The bartender set Raylene's highball next to a shallow bowl of peanuts and took her two bits.

She sat at the bar for three quarters of an hour, listening to the grumblings and bragging of the men and women bellied up to the bar. Occasionally one of them would glance her way but she stuck with the passive look she had pasted to her face, perfected during the times she had lingered in Thomas's saloon to watch people come and go. Here and there, a raised voice would reach her intact with a tidbit about some hot dame at Red's or The Santa Fe or a quote from the newspaper that incited someone's ire.

A few more customers drifted in. This was no high-end place, but plenty of people needed their drinks however they could get them. When the door swung open again, it admitted a man with a tray loaded with four plates heaped high with food. She caught a whiff of beef steaks and buttery potatoes. Her stomach took notice, shooting her a hunger pang.

The delivery man wore one of those wraparound aprons seen in restaurants. He crossed the width of the room, skirting tables, and rapped twice on a closed door in the south wall. When the door opened, he went through. A minute later he came back out, stuffing cash into his apron and his tray empty.

Raylene turned to look at the bartender, who seemed to studiously avoid her gaze. When at last he threw a quick glance at her, she stared at him until he blinked and turned away. That's when she got up from her spot and crossed to the same door in the wall and rapped on it twice.

Over on Sixth St., Murphy was cruising for nightclubs. Vivienne's clue had set him searching as soon as he had heard Mrs. G's front door close behind him. Dashing for his auto, he had tried to imagine how many restaurants and clubs around town sported names with the number six or had addresses with a six in them. He knew Vivienne worked on the city's Missouri side, but had been in no position to question her further her while Mrs. G looked on, so now here he was on Sixth, driving slowly to catch any business that might be a restaurant or club, the most logical establishments where customers like Gargotta would splash some cash. He almost wished he had been more of a man about town since Catherine's departure. He might know more of these places from personal experience.

He conjured Vivienne rubbing her fingers together. Would a moneyed big-time booze boss like Gargotta frequent diners or dives? He thought not. More likely, a man of crime might salt his reputation by being seen around town for an hour here and an hour there, making small talk with patrons and workers, constantly on the move until reaching a familiar location where owners or employees provided him cover. Before tonight, Murphy had paid little attention to news about Gargotta and his ilk, whose enterprises played out far from Murphy's life and work. Sure, he had read newspaper accounts in recent years about some hit or other against someone beyond Gargotta's inner circle who encroached on the big man's operation. Or the disappearance of a witness against him, that sort of thing. Now he cared very much about Gargotta.

Sixth Street extended from the Intercity Viaduct, one of many connections between the east and west sides of the Kansas River, which hung like a shoelace untied from the Missouri River. Businesses stood shoulder-to-shoulder here, interrupted by north-south avenues that broke Sixth into segments. Roughly a mile to the east, the street appeared again as a thoroughfare.

On this stretch of Sixth, Murphy stopped at four addresses, two of which were saloons. The city had a boatload of hole-in-the-wall places barely big enough for a bar crammed with stools and frequented by folks from nearby businesses. In neither of the saloons did he spot Raylene or anyone that looked like a crime boss. The drinking customers had an underfed look whereas he didn't figure Gargotta for someone who missed many meals. The restaurants proved a failure as well, one having been converted to a soup kitchen that had already served the evening meal. All its tables were full of down-and-out types, or if empty, were being wiped clean by a ragged-looking fellow who probably earned his supper that way.

The other restaurant, the Pig Poke, offered Louisiana cooking, jambalaya and other spicy fare, where the lady waiting tables replied in the negative about recognizing Gargotta's name. Murphy left and stood outside on the sidewalk, his alarm growing at the thought that he might not locate Raylene before something happened to her for speaking truth to power, even criminal power.

The east end of Sixth seemed too far from the glitz of downtown for Gargotta to bother with. It stood to reason that someone who liked attention and who curried the favor of business owners through overt largesse buttressed by a menacing reputation, would not seclude himself in an out of the way place unless he needed privacy or was lying low. He would stick to the clubs where he was well known and where he could receive the admiring glances of those who served him and drank with him and bought the booze he peddled. That meant downtown and the surrounding streets where so many of the jazz clubs and drinking joints kept the doors open far into the night. Because he'd been trying to avoid Mrs. G's disapproval, he had not asked Vivienne for her new place of employment, which he figured for a nightclub on par with that dinner joint where he'd first glimpsed her.

Murphy jumped into his coupe and headed for Main St., taking the next corner at speed. *Please,* he thought. *Please show me a six.*

As she waited at the door in the wall, Raylene thought about the disadvantage of being one against two or more. She wouldn't mind having Murphy supporting her claim against a gangster who would not like to be told off by a woman, an Indian no less. But she would not jeopardize Murphy's future for the long shot she was about to take. This was his city, not hers, where his career likely turned on knowing who to handle gently and who to threaten. She reckoned that having Gargotta as an enemy meant you had to watch your back, so she was the right person to have such an enemy. She did not live here and had no intention of sticking around once she resolved the matter of Annie's death and located her grave. She would return to her life of horses and cowboys. If Gargotta didn't take her down.

The hulk who answered her knock wore a three-piece suit in worsted wool, nicely cut for someone she figured for a bodyguard. He took up enough of the doorway to be a blockade though she detected the warmth of the room seeping outward around him. She said, "I am here to speak with Mr. Gargotta."

The man looked her up and down, taking in her work pants and western boots, and the denim shirt that showed from beneath her coat. He said, "Mr. G's eating his supper. Come back tomorrow."

"Tomorrow he will likely dine somewhere else. I would speak with him tonight."

The man puffed himself up. "Aw, Jesus, are you thick or somethin'? Mr. G ain't seein' nothin' but his supper, and you ain't his supper, so scram."

She couldn't very well push past a man who likely weighed more than twice what she did, and calling names could cost her the fight before she faced her actual opponent. She said, "At some point, supper will be over, or the night will be over, so I will wait right here."

The bodyguard turned red beneath his Mediterranean tan.

"Well, you got some kinda —"

A shout came from within the room. "Tito! What's the trouble?"

"The trouble," said the bodyguard, "is that there's a cowboy Indian chick here who wants to see you and I ain't lettin' her interrupt your re-past."

"What's she want?" came the invisible man's question.

"I don't — Hey you, whaddaya want?" the bodyguard asked Raylene.

"I want to know why he claims to be distributing ordinary booze when he's actually selling poison."

The bodyguard drew himself up with a frown. "You watch your — that ain't —"

The disembodied voice broke in again. "What is it?"

The bodyguard held up a hand to Raylene and closed the door in her face. She could make out voices through the flimsy wood, but not the exact words. In half a minute, the door opened again and the bodyguard moved aside, saying, "Let these ladies out before you step in."

Two women wearing evening attire and carrying coats with fur collars came mincing out. One said to Raylene, "Thanks a lot. I didn't even finish my supper." Supper came out *suppa*.

The bodyguard watched the women sashay away while Raylene stood looking at a square-shaped man pulled up to a round table set with two dark bottles and three plates of food. On one of the other two tables rested a single plate of food. His resemblance to newspaper photos she'd seen of him was remarkable. He probably posed for photographs when reporters came round looking for his reaction to some mob arrest announced by police. The suit he wore now was framed by the wide lapels preferred in prosperous years. Clearly, booze was still a money-making trade.

Gargotta sat, composed, dabbing his mouth with a napkin

until the bodyguard invited Raylene in with one hooked-finger.

Kansas City's nightclub signs glowed against the darkening sky as Murphy checked four more clubs with the number six in their addresses and against his better judgement, a diner called Six Bits. And then he came to a club in the fourteen hundred block. Though a section of its neon tubing was blacked out, he could still make out Pair-a-dise with two neon dice showing six spots. A long shot. A busy-looking supper place next door had lights ablaze and he'd already passed an open parking spot back on the corner, so he circled round two more blocks, encountering another one-way street while watching for more likely looking prospects. Seeing none, he drove an extra block and turned left, replaying Vivienne's verbal signal regarding the number six.

A strict interpretation would be a joint named something with a six, but since Vivienne was French, there was no telling her interpretation. She might have meant an address, in which case almost every block held a six on offer. Or she had meant for him to traverse the entirety of Sixth St., which he had not done. If this godawful random searching did not pan out, he would have to rethink his approach.

Driving in the left lane of the one-way, he spotted a club with a sign reading Club 666. *At last!* He yanked his coupe into a parking slot without taking the time to back in. Its rear stuck out a little, which he didn't like to hazard, but he had no time to waste for such conventions as perfect parallel parking. He jumped out of his auto and dashed to the front door, yanking it open.

Piano music hit him as he came face-to-face with a steely-looking bouncer. Candlelight and soft overhead fixtures cast a warm glow throughout the club, which held maybe a dozen or so customers at tables and five others at the bar. Not bad for a Monday night.

"Help you, sir?" said the bouncer, giving him the once-over.

Murphy noted the sign behind the big guy that read "Neckties required for gentlemen," and felt a pinch of satisfaction that he was dressed in suit and tie. His usual. He had left his overcoat in his unlocked coupe, but he wasn't about to go back for it. He had planned an opening gambit and now said, "I am meeting a friend who is meeting with Mr. Gargotta."

Now the bouncer studied him, likely noting the windblown look he'd acquired in the last two hectic hours. He had freshened up a little at the boarding house, but that was before all the driving about and jumping in and out of his auto and dashing into and out of restaurants and bars. The start to his evening had been somewhat more frenzied than his usual — a bowl of Ruby's soup followed by evening radio programs and a few pages of whichever novel he was reading. To the bouncer he offered a well-practiced calm-but-expectant expression.

"If your *friend* made arrangements with Mr. Gargotta, your *friend* would know that no meetings take place here on a Monday and never have."

Though the bouncer's reply brought disappointment, Murphy could not have been happier at striking so near his target. He said, "My mistake. Perhaps you can you give me the Monday meeting location."

The bouncer shook his head slightly. "If you don't know and *your friend* doesn't know, it's not my job to tell you."

Now Murphy did something he occasionally had cause for when he worked a case. He reached for his inside suit coat pocket for his billfold.

"Easy now," said the bouncer, watching Murphy's movements.

Murphy eased his suit coat open to let the bouncer watch his billfold come out. "Is there something I could do to help your recall, or your willingness?" he asked.

"Not a thing."

Murphy's hopes sagged a little. Maybe this guy was playing hard to get. "Come on, everyone could use a little cake, every job a little sweetening. If I have it on me, it's yours."

"You don't have enough to buy me off."

"Are you sure? This job can't be that lucrative."

"It's never only the money. You must know that."

This took Murphy aback because the benefits to his railroad job had felt nonexistent lately, unless he counted his tryst with Raylene last night, which far surpassed any evening he'd known in the last few years. "So, it's no, huh?" he said.

The bouncer shook his head. Murphy slid his billfold back into his suit coat just as two dolled-up women strode in, interrupting their jabbering to greet the bouncer, calling him Frankie before waltzing on through. The bouncer watched them for a few seconds before turning back to Murphy. "There's music tonight if you go for those jam sessions, musicians working up their numbers."

"I'll pass," said Murphy. "I'm going to find that meeting."

"If you say so," said the bouncer.

Murphy left and strode back to his car. Pulling the driver's door open, he could see right away that his overcoat was gone from the passenger seat. He scanned the street, but could spot no thief jogging away with it. He shook his head and climbed in and when the engine caught, gave it an irritated rev before pulling away from the curb. He had a meeting to find.

As Raylene stepped into the private dining room occupied by Charles Gargotta, she glanced around to note whether others besides the gatekeeper were present. The second and third tables in the room were unoccupied, though set with white tablecloths and low candle centerpieces. She wondered if Gargotta was the primary customer for this special service or if others in town used the place.

Gargotta motioned to his bodyguard, who held up a hand in front of Raylene. "Off with your coat," he said.

"I would rather keep it."

"I'm gonna check it for weapons. You better not be packin'."

Raylene waited a beat before relinquishing her coat. The man had given the same caution as Murphy had regarding the police station. Criminals and cops all worried about the same things — someone getting the drop on them — which was, she supposed, because they went around doing that very thing to others.

The goon felt her coat all over, testing its pockets and giving it a shake. When her truck key gave a jingle, he pulled it out and held it up to the light. The ignition key was affixed by a small ring to a hammered silver feather. Uncle Raymond's handiwork. She felt emboldened by the sight of it. Raymond had been unafraid to take on dangerous work or to hold her and Annie close when they'd gotten in a scrape at school. He had lived with honor and for honor had killed. He had even died honorably. Thinking of him now steeled her heart.

"You drive?" asked the goon.

"Don't you?" said Raylene.

She thought she heard a chuckle from Gargotta's direction and threw a glance his way.

The goon slid her truck key back into her coat pocket and pulled out the grainy grey photo prints of her hand holding the booze bottle from the coffin she'd drilled open, the coffin looking like a dark blob in the background. After a brief look, he put them back and turned to catch the boss's eye. Gargotta nodded and the goon turned back to Raylene. "Up with your hands."

"Pardon me?"

"Get 'em up. I'm gonna frisk ya or you're outta here."

Raylene lifted her arms. She suspected that the goon, who appeared rather steamy, wore his suit coat in the warm room so as not to display the holster and handgun he must surely be wearing. In fact, she detected a slight bulge under his left arm. As the goon ran his hands over her shoulders and arms and skimmed them down her back, she wondered idly which tailor in town took the measurements of a man who frisked other people for weapons.

The goon's hands traced her hips and thighs before he moved around to the front of her. With a grin, he bent in half to brush the backs of his hands across her pants pockets and down to her ankles. As he stood, running his hands up the inside of her legs, she studied the top of his slicked back hair. When his eyes met her eyes, his hands had strayed too far. She dropped her arms as she leaned in and with the toe of her boot, kicked between his legs with enough force to push his *cojones* into his brain.

He flung his hands upward as if to keep his balance, one meaty ham catching Raylene across her left cheek and eye socket as he howled, "Jesus Christ son of a bitch!" Eyes watering, he cradled the body parts that would soon be swollen.

"Keep your hands off my crotch," hissed Raylene as she dashed to a place behind the closest empty table. She brought a hand to her cheek which was beginning to swell along with one eye.

"Holy Mother of God! She sent my nuts through the roof!"

"Tito, your language," said Gargotta.

"Boss, my privates are crying!"

"Well, let 'em cry without cursing the Lord's name or his son or his mother, ya got that?"

The goon let go of himself with one hand, which he waved in the air. "It ain't natural not to curse."

"It *isn't* natural," said Gargotta.

"See? You know it. Just gimme a minute with her."

Gargotta said, "I told you before — women don't take kindly to the way you frisk."

The goon had two hands free now. "But —"

There came a knock on the door and all eyes looked that direction. "You expecting anybody, boss?" said the goon.

"No one. Not even whoever *she* is," said Gargotta, waving a hand at Raylene. "I was trying to eat my supper. Now the girls are gone and my supper's gone cold."

The goon unbuttoned his suit coat and reached for the door as it burst inward, smashing into his nose. Stunned, the big man grabbed this new point of pain as blood began dripping through his fingers. Murphy stood in the doorway, looking surprised that the door had given so easily. This gave the goon time to grab him, pull him inside, and sock him hard with one bloody fist.

Murphy went down on one knee as he lifted a hand to his jaw. He shook his head as if trying to stop bells from ringing. As the goon lifted Murphy for another punch, Raylene pulled her boot knife and leaped upon his back, pressed the point to his neck. "Let go and hold your hands out," she spoke into his ear. "Move and I'll see to it that you bleed out before help can reach you."

Released, Murphy wobbled to his feet as he backed away. "I was only trying to get in."

"The fuck, you say," said the goon. Blood from his nose had

dripped onto the front of his beautiful suit. "I was opening the damn door when you broke in."

"Keep those hands out," warned Raylene, sliding her outside hand under the goon's suit coat to extract from its shoulder holster a snub-nosed .38. She motioned with it to Murphy as the goon twitched his shoulders a little.

Murphy closed the door and stepped wide to retrieve the gun from Raylene. After checking to see that it was loaded, he closed the cylinder and pointed it at the goon. Through his own bloody nose, he said, "Come on down."

Raylene rappelled outward and dropped to the floor, knife in hand. "Mr. Gargotta," she said to the man who was now standing behind his table but had otherwise not moved. "Call off your man. The door injury was not on purpose."

"He didn't wait for me to answer," said the goon, "and I ain't gonna forget it." He had moved to the table with the lone dinner plate where he took up a napkin and dabbed at his nose and suit coat.

"He was only coming to my aid," said Raylene.

"I'm the one needs aid. What you did to me, I might never have kids now."

"If you do, will you teach them to molest women?"

Gargotta broke in. "Quit your yammering, both of ya!" To Raylene he said, "I didn't invite you but I heard you slander my name. You better tell me who are you and who he is." He waved in Murphy's direction.

Raylene said, "My name is Raylene and that is ... Father James."

When Murphy looked stunned, she said, "Sorry Father, I thought I'd better tell them." She gestured. "Father, this is Mr. Gargotta, and the one who answered the door is his right-hand man."

"You're a priest?" asked the goon. He motioned to his own

neck, which held smeared blood. "You're not wearing one of them collar things."

"He came from the rez to help me find my sister," said Raylene.

"Which rez is that?" asked Gargotta.

"The Crow reservation in southeast Montana."

"Is that what you are?" said Gargotta.

"I am half-Crow. You might know that though Catholics have been in Indian country a long time, Indians don't become priests. Priests always come from elsewhere."

Gargotta looked to be wavering between belief and suspicion. "How come he can handle a gun?"

"If you are ever on a reservation," said Raylene, "you'd better know how to handle long guns and revolvers. He also locates missing people and such, and that's how we found my dead sister in Kansas City and the coroner's report pointing to poisoned alcohol. Isn't that right, Father?"

Murphy didn't carry a law badge or a gun, which had a tendency to make people nervous. But a gun could be useful in circumstances such as these. He felt a little safer in the current circumstances with a gun in his hand, and said, "Yes, well."

"People die of alcohol poisoning kind of regular," said Gargotta. "There's lots of drunks around."

"I don't mean alcohol poisoning, but poisoned alcohol," said Raylene, "which is commonly made deadly by using wood alcohol or industrial alcohol."

"So *you* say," said Gargotta, "but it's not like regular alcohol is all that hard to cook." His goon had finished messing with the front of his suit and was watching the two intruders warily.

"Distilling takes time," said Raylene, "but industrial and wood alcohols are used in train yards and manufacturing.

They are everywhere, and they provide a shortcut. Buy it in town and skip the work."

"Who needs a shortcut?" said Gargotta.

"Time is money. If you can make it cheaper and no one is wiser, you get to keep a piece of the profits you're not entitled to. I don't expect you'd want them taking liberties with your profits. Tainted alcohol doesn't kill everyone, just random people now and then."

The goon broke in, "Boss, what if he's not a priest? He's not wearing the right getup. Maybe he works for Pussy's people and they're trying to finger you for something they can make a vendetta out of."

Gargotta narrowed his eyes at Murphy, whose nose had bled on the front of his suit and whose left cheek was swollen and purple. "Nah, Pussy and me have what you call a understanding, but you make a good point." To Murphy he said, "If you're a Father, tell me something Catholic."

Murphy blinked a couple of times and swiveled his gaze between the goon and Gargotta. Holding the gun on them, he said, "Do either of you speak Latin? No? Alright then. *Per Christum Dominum nostrum,* Through Christ our Lord." He crossed himself and straightened a little as if he were at a pulpit. "This last weekend was the celebration for All Saints Day. On the reservation, we add elements for memorializing the tribe's elders, but I'll reiterate for you, in case you missed local services." He summoned his best impression of the priest at St. Christopher Parish and a bit of schoolboy Latin from his Catechism. "Oh God, omnipotent and eternal, grant that we might venerate all the saints in one festival. We beg you to grant us, on behalf of many intercessors, the full abundance of your mercies. We ask that Archangel Michael defend us in our fight, that we will not perish in the terrible judgement." Murphy held the gun out before him and made a cross with it in the air

"Okay, okay. Enough about judgements," said Gargotta.

Murphy was on a roll with his broken Latin. If this helped Raylene in making her point with Gargotta, he would preach till midnight. He said, "Those teachings talk about God's judgement, not ours. We did not come here to judge you." Here, he looked from Gargotta to Raylene and back again. "That is our Lord's prerogative. If you are Catholic, you know your divine positive law, the commandments, sent down by God. Number five, for instance. Thou shalt not kill.

"The Hebrew version forbade murder but in English we would forbid 'killing.' In divine law there's a distinction when killing is in self-defense, which could be forgiven, but killing innocent people is not self-defense, it's considered murder. *E pluribus unum*. Is that familiar to you?"

Gargotta nodded but looked as if he couldn't quite place it.

Murphy continued stalling for time while trying to sound official. "It means 'From many, one.' Its meanings are applicable to much of life. From many people, one city. We see that here in Kansas City, people of different occupations, different languages, different customs. Or, from many people, one leader." Here, he pointed toward Gargotta with the pistol, who straightened a little, "You, I take it, are a leader in your, uh ... industry, while others lead other organizations. The phrase also applies to drinkers of alcohol. From many drinkers, one dies, or a few die. And those who die are innocents, especially when alcohol has been poisoned." Here Murphy paused. "Do you get my drift, gentlemen?"

Gargotta scratched his chin as Murphy waited. Perhaps they'd call him on his fakery.

Raylene watched in silence. Murphy, she thought, had woven quite a spell with his Latin. She and the other children of the Pine Ridge had learned lessons in English from nuns, which was required, and memorized a few bits of Latin as responses to prayers the priest intoned during Mass, but Murphy must have soaked up Latin for years. She made a show of crossing herself and saying, "Thank you, Father." Tito lifted a hand to his sternum as if unconsciously.

In response, Murphy crossed himself and said, "*Tricanus libertanus.*"

Gargotta rubbed his jaw and at last said, "Okay, Father, I get your point. I don't exactly like being preached at, but I'm not in the business of killing innocent people."

Murphy stepped over to the table closest to Raylene, who slid her boot knife back into its sheath. She said, "We don't think you're intentionally trying to kill booze-drinking people. That would ruin your business eventually, because if they knew about it, no reasonable people would drink your products. But my sister died of tainted booze and that means someone is messing with the booze you are distributing."

"I didn't give anyone instructions for using poison," said Gargotta.

Raylene said, "Someone else runs the stills, yes?" She kept her distance and squinted at the bottles on the table before Gargotta. "You are not even drinking any of the so-called house whiskey from this bar. I have an old friend who went blind from bootleg sold in this town and other people have died."

Gargotta reclaimed his seat at the table. "You still haven't told me how you figure it's *my* booze that's the problem. And I'm not saying it is."

Raylene said, "For one thing, you have a lock on this market, so it's your hooch that my sister drank while in a saloon called Down the Block. The men delivering booze to that place bring the same kind of distillery bottles with fake labels printed with a yellow circle. It looks to me like each saloon gets labels printed for them like they're a special issue. Am I right so far?" When Gargotta didn't counter, she continued. "And the men who deliver are associated with Conboie Undertaking —"

Gargotta broke in, "How'd ya figure?"

"Because I've been inside their business and they act like they are hiding something. Plus, they have a truck that's sufficient for moving dozens of cases at a time — that would be the sort of transport that you'd want. And there's someone who calls saloons to tell them how much bootleg they need to buy while using the name Bert Lam. Bert Lam is too similar to be a coincidence when Lambert is Conboie's right hand man."

"What a stupe," said Gargotta, a frown on his face.

Raylene kept her focus. "In looking for my sister's grave at Union Cemetery, I observed men burying a pine coffin in a spot they marked with a phony name, which made me curious." She motioned at Murphy. "Together, we dug up that coffin of bottles and cut it open and I have one of the bottles in my truck." She pulled the photos of the foggy evidence from her pocket and dropped them on the table. "These show my hand and one of the buried bottles, the same green color as the ones behind this club's bar that are pasted with a yellow circle label. These photographs are poor, so of course they're not perfect proof."

The room was silent. Murphy's eyes tracked all the room's players. Raylene was watching Gargotta. The goon still had blood crusted in his nostrils and seemed slightly deflated, but Murphy knew that at a signal from his boss, the goon would launch another attack.

It was time to quit the place, so Raylene delivered her final lines. "The sexton at Union Cemetery hammers something wooden after dark, cheap coffins maybe, for duping people who buy fancy ones, or cheap coffins for burying bottles of hooch siphoned from your distribution network. Your people, of course would detect missing bottles, so that would be a reason to substitute others blended on the cheap with poisoned goods. Then they could sell the quality stuff in another town where you don't have reach and would never be the wiser. Except now you are wiser. And then there's a separate matter. While in Union Cemetery, I observed two men burying a pine coffin in a grave marked for a man whose family was not in attendance. I know the family had arranged for a top-line casket, the expensive kind, but clearly it had been switched for a cheap box. The undertaker profited." She took a breath. "I also recall reading that your nephew died."

"Hey now. Leave my sister's boy out of this. He didn't cook any hooch for anyone."

"That is not my claim, but he died in Kansas City and was buried on a stormy day while you were ... detained in Chicago."

"Yeah, them Chicago boys are getting downright un-reasonable. I beat it though." Gargotta smiled as if pleased at the memory.

"The graveside service was held a week after the burial. The newspapers reported the appearance of a Chicago priest."

"What's it to you?"

"I am thinking that the Conboie crew would not have recognized your nephew's surname, which wasn't the same as yours, so they might have swindled whoever bought the casket. Which I'm thinking might have been you."

Gargotta stood again and pointed at Raylene. "You're making me mad now. You can't know that, so don't say what you don't know."

"I'm saying that if he were my kin, I'd want to know if I got cheated out of a fancy, expensive casket by the same crew that's been stealing my hooch and substituting cheaper, poisonous alcohol." She turned to Murphy. "Father, any last words?"

"Remember the fifth commandment," said Murphy, unloading the gun's bullets and dropping them into his overcoat pocket. "We would all like to be spared terrible judgements, but of course they come, eventually. *Novus ordo seclorum. Vilis.*" He nodded to Raylene and they turned almost as one for the door, Murphy setting the empty gun on a table before they went out into the smoke-filled club with the piped-in music. When the door closed behind them, Gargotta was staring into the distance as if calculating his options.

The Pair-a-dise bartender glanced up as they crossed toward the front door, taking in Raylene's black eye and swollen jaw, and Murphy's bloodied nose and suit. He might have missed Murphy's cheek marked by a purple fist shape. As if nothing were out of the ordinary, the man picked up his bar towel and went back to wiping glasses.

Outside, Murphy walked Raylene to her truck as other pedestrians gave them a wide berth.

She said, "Impersonating a priest is probably a sin."

"I noticed *your* numerous lies," countered Murphy.

"Your church lessons were convincing," said Raylene.

"You did good to unearth the part about the nephew."

"Thank goodness newspapers thrive on details and gossip."

They arrived at Raylene's truck beyond the corner of Fifteenth. She asked, "What was your last bit.of Latin?"

"New order of the ages," said Murphy. "It's on the paper dollar."

"And *vilis*?"

"An insult we boys used in school." He paused. "Is that it then, with Gargotta?"

Raylene glanced across Main Street to the Five and Dime that was closed for the night. She said, "Sometimes, if you know your opponent, words can be your weapon. I thought it might work because crooks do not worry about honest people, they worry about other crooks."

"And worry might lead to action?"

"I can hope."

Without an overcoat, Murphy was finally chilled. His face throbbed in a way that interrupted the amorous thoughts he had carried around all day. In spite of her black eye, which must hurt like hell, Raylene had remained clearheaded and brave. He was thinking that she looked like someone he ought to kiss again, except a set of boisterous pedestrians brushed past them, laughing and joking, breaking his mood. He said, "May I see that knife you carry in your boot?"

"Mm, no. I don't display it in public, but thanks for asking." She gave him a wry smile.

"Very clever. Changing the subject, I need to report to work tomorrow."

"I would like to speak with your boss. Perhaps we could meet there."

Murphy no longer worried that Raylene would jeopardize his job by confronting Campbell about her sister. It now might be instructive to observe Campbell trying to evade Raylene's questions. "I used to go in early," he said, "but the gallows officially open at 8:00 tomorrow, and you are invited."

"I'll be there at eight." She glanced up at the sky. "Snow is coming."

Murphy checked the sky, which looked clear. Streetlights obliterated any view of stars, but there was the moon, low above the buildings. As Raylene climbed into her truck, he stood watching, hands in his pockets. Tomorrow morning seemed like a long way off.

Fourteen

Murphy attended to his morning routine with care, gently lathering before shaving his black-and-blue jaw with his safety razor. He was trying to decide if his nose looked bent, or perhaps extra bent, but before long gave up and finished dressing before writing a letter to his wife in his best hand. Revelations, confessions, honesty.

Rather than change his routine, he drove to his usual diner for some decent chow before witnessing Campbell receiving the second degree from Raylene. His boss was formidable, but Murphy had seen Raylene in action, not only last night, but up in South Dakota. She would not shrink before his boss's belligerence or bluster.

The waitress who brought him a menu, the redheaded one with the tight curls, glanced at his swollen face and poured him some coffee. Before noting his usual order and turning to go, she said, "I hope it was worth it."

Murphy smiled wryly. "It was."

After eating and with a second cup of coffee at hand, Murphy sat distractedly reviewing Campbell's likely approach to firing him. The man was fairly predictable for this sort of circumstance. He would ask questions he knew the answer to, first being certain that Murphy had not appeared with the missing necklace in hand. Any question about the jewelry would be closed-ended, not open-ended like an investigator used. Of course, Murphy was not the subject of an investigation. He'd been ordered to find the missing jewelry.

A part of him churned inside at the thought of being fired within earshot of the rest of the staff. He wasn't the most senior. The two most senior detectives who had not yet returned from investigating workers on strike in Denver would be tougher to replace. But he had been loyal and had closed as many cases as those senior men, proving himself indispensable when it came to interviewing U.P. employees about possible theft or fraud. He was patient and thorough and he could make a case for why he ought to remain on the job, but these were hard times, and workers served at the pleasure of employers, not the other way around.

There was this too: Campbell wouldn't respect a worker who made too much of a defense. An employee either succeeded at assignments or they failed. Luckily, Murphy's success rate had been good, at least on behalf of the railroad. Unfortunately, he had failed Campbell personally and Campbell had, unfairly of course, threatened to blame him for busting his marriage.

With an extra minute or two to spare, he reviewed yet again last night's face-off with Gargotta and the bodyguard. As he had washed the blood off his face last night, his adrenaline level had plummeted and he had barely climbed under the covers before falling fast into dreams of fistfights and shootouts and chases at high speed, the latter two being occasions he had never had and wouldn't mind avoiding forever.

His pretend-sermonizing and sleight-of-Latin phrasing had been a perfect example of seat-of-your pants problem-solving, if he did say so. Not that he had pronounced everything perfectly, but that wasn't the point. The point was in besting the opponent, and he had done just that. Raylene had been one step ahead with the Father James caper. Always thinking ahead, that woman. It only made him admire her more and think warmly about other private talents of hers that those goons would never see. Rising, he pulled out his billfold and left extra cash for the redheaded waitress, thinking to himself, *It's been nice knowing you.* Over by the windows, the head of freight sales was taking breakfast with two local business types. This diner was a convenient meal stop for U.P. workers, some of whom might be found there almost any morning or lunch hour. He would have to find a different eatery.

After parking in the east lot of U.P.'s freight headquarters, Murphy lingered a moment. It might not do to appear early for the guillotine. He had truly liked his job, even the uglier aspects that sometimes cropped up when dealing with people as opposed to ... say, cattle. Beasts were surely less dishonest and less conniving. Less envious, less covetous, less of all those sins. But *people* — he smiled inwardly at the thought — people could be stoical on the outside but sur-prisingly sensual on the inside. They could even save your ass. Raylene, for instance. A part of him wanted to convince her that his marriage was an obstacle they could overcome. That he could overcome.

He had let himself minimize the irreversible nature of Catholic marriages, but regardless of his random church attendance, he had been a Catholic all his days and had married in the Catholic Church, till death did they part. They had consummated their marriage. Few things in life were so black-and-white.

He exited his vehicle and locked it. No use losing a blood-specked suit bound for the cleaners. As he started toward U.P.'s main freight entrance, he spotted Raylene's feline walk in the distance. He found himself cataloging details about her as if she were his sweetheart or about to become his sweetheart. She wore her riding clothes and a sheepskin-collared denim jacket buttoned against the chill and had tucked her gleaming hair behind her ears. His fantasy about her warmed him.

He raised a hand and she picked up her pace. Stopping before him she said, "Good morning." He could tell she was studying the damage to his face the way he was studying the bruise on her cheekbone and her black eye.

"Good morning," he said. "And yes, my jaw hurts like hell, though your face looks plenty tender."

Raylene thought it was nice to share something with someone, even cosmetic damage rendered by a goon. She had spent a good chunk of the last month on a solitary journey to locate Raymond and punish him, followed by her Kansas City search for Annie's grave, which in spite of needing help to accomplish was in truth her private pursuit. She had given her word to the memory of Annie as no one else had. Murphy had been a welcome partner at the cemetery and in the back rooms of the police station, where she didn't doubt that he had bribed a few individuals. He had also been a fine lover, by turns tender and hungry, and nearly insatiable. Because he knew so much about her search for Annie, he was the closest thing she had known to a true partner, but they were in different places in their lives. Also, from different worlds.

Back to the moment at hand, she said, "Discomfort sharpens my resolve. Maybe that's an Indian thing."

Murphy wasn't sure how to take that, so he said, "Did Mrs. G swoon at the sight of you?"

"Does Mrs. G ever swoon? I lied to her about it, and she let me. You might want to keep your distance so she can't interrogate you."

He said, "I'm a tough one to crack."

"Until you face *her*. I told her you saved me from a mob

scene downtown. Drunken revelers."

"A boost to my credentials. Does Mrs. G know how well you lie?"

"My uncle used to say, 'Look them in the eye when you lie.' I'm here to say that works on landladies."

"You were terrific last night," said Murphy. "Not righteous exactly, but passionate about your mission, and I almost ruined your plan. Plus, you stopped that goon from killing me." Her type of terrific made his heart pound.

Raylene glanced at the scudding clouds overhead. "Once you were there, I was glad. You made us into two against two." After a breath, she said, "Do you have that valise?"

"The empty one? It's behind the seat in my coupe."

"My sister stored papers in it related to our family but it has a secret you must not have discovered."

The valise associated with the Moon girls had been reportedly taken from Mrs. G's house by an Indian man claiming to be Annie's father. Murphy himself had found it empty, but he knew not to question other people's claims when time was better spent proceeding toward clarification. He retraced his steps to his vehicle and extracted the valise.

When he rejoined Raylene, she showed him that it was empty before she shook it. The first time, he heard nothing, but with her second effort, he heard a *clunk*, which was odd.

She turned the open top of it toward him to show its empty interior, then gave it another shake. Again, that *clunk*.

"Holy cow," he said. "A hidden compartment?"

Raylene grinned. "There's a near-invisible false bottom. Whatever is in there has a bit of weight and is wrapped with something that's come loose. I haven't tried to get it free because I figured it wasn't mine to start with. It might be nothing valuable, one of my uncle's silver-making tools, but I doubt it. My uncle hid it there or Annie did. Let's act as if it's important and valuable, and use it on your boss."

"With pleasure," he said, gesturing that she should lead the way.

The path to the freight office's front door led near enough to a mail box that Murphy detoured three or four steps to post the letter he'd been carrying. Then he caught up again with Raylene and opened the entry door for her. Suddenly, he was eager to meet with Campbell.

November 2, 1936

Dear Catherine,

It's that time again for a bit of news from Kansas City. The nurses have told me that letters from me appear to you as if from a stranger. I don't mind. I write to help me make sense of my work and I feel better when I let you know that I am still here, still thinking about you. Maybe I am in denial about how little our past matters to your current challenges. I even wonder if you recognize your father's letters. I hope so.

It was very nearly three years ago now that you went away to Colorado. There is something about saying "went away" that reduces the sting. I can think about you going off to pursue your dreams of performing in the theater or campaigning for temperance, or joining your father's staff in his Senate office, though you never spoke about any such things. What were your dreams? Was there anything beyond hearth and home? If so, you would not have been alone among women, but as likely to be disappointed in today's meager opportunities for success.

I am beginning to favor women finding a path in business or governance or even industry — Can you believe you are hearing that from me?

My week has been eventful in a good way, and though it did not implode last night when it could have, I feel more fireworks coming. When I write next, and I'm confessing now that I might write less often in future weeks, I will provide more details. That news plus five-cents will buy you a cup of coffee.

Yours,
John

Murphy led Raylene through the freight operations building and into the section holding Campbell's office, his staff, and the offices for detectives. As they trundled past secretaries and clerks, he doled out benign smiles while trying to look as if this was business as usual.

"Hey, you're back," said one of the younger clerks who probably thought Murphy had been on vacation. When he saw Murphy's battered face, he blanched and glanced at Raylene. She was purpled too.

Nearing the threshold to Campbell's office, he paused to listen to sounds of an irritated one-sided phone conversation drifting outward. To the secretary who sat closest, he mouthed, "Something bugging him?"

"Everything," she whispered. "Are you okay? Better watch out."

"I'm okay," mouthed Murphy.

When he glanced at Raylene, she said, "Let's do it, Father."

Smothering a smile, Murphy advanced to the boss's doorway, rapped on the frame to announce himself and stepped in as Campbell looked up from slamming the phone back into its cradle. Papers in disarray sat before him on his desk.

When Campbell registered Murphy, he spoke around a much chewed, unlit cigar. "You're late. And what the hell happened to your face?"

Murphy glanced at his watch. "It's 8:02. Never mind my face. I'm here."

"Yesterday, you would have been late. Today you're *too goddamn late.*"

Murphy noted the cane leaning against Campbell's desk. Gout always made Campbell prickly. He said, "We agreed on paid leave for five work days, which brings us to number six — today." He removed the old overcoat he'd salvaged from the back of his coat closet and folded it over the closest chair.

"I don't care that you can count days. My goddamn wife found out about the jewelry that's still missing, which you haven't found. I slept on the goddamn slipper couch last night and left this morning before she was up. I hate it when I don't get to shave, but that's not the worst of it. I might not be a married man by the time — wait — who's this?" Raylene was standing alongside Murphy.

"Pherson Campbell," said Murphy, "meet Raylene Little Moon. Annie Moon's sister."

Campbell blinked at Raylene. "You're beat up too. What the hell's going on around here?" When neither offered an explanation, he continued. "I'm sorry about your sister. I am, but if you'll excuse us, I have business with Murphy."

Raylene thought that her physical appearance and Murphy's might play to their benefit. She said, "Actually, you have business with me." She had already scanned the office's furnishings and now stepped close to the back of the second sturdy chair facing Campbell's desk. "Annie's valise," she said, lifting it to set it on the chair's seat. "I understand you're looking for jewelry that was at one time in Annie's possession. I'd like to know more about it."

Campbell turned a shade redder. "I don't have to answer your questions. Your sister was an adult who made certain choices. She wasn't the only one making choices, but everyone involved was an adult."

"I'm not concerned with labels. I came to pay my respects at her grave but the undertaker's people won't provide information and I haven't been able to find it."

Campbell brought both hands up. "Are you accusing me of hiding your sister's body?"

Raylene settled in for a verbal contest. "You might have a reason to, but neither of us" — her gesture included Murphy

— "confronted you about it. Too much hung in the balance, but that has changed."

Campbell brightened a little. "Are you his source for leads about the jewelry? There are still two pieces at large, somewhere. We thought you might have them."

"We thought?" She looked at Murphy. "Mr. Murphy, was it your theory that I somehow obtained jewelry from a sister who was buried before I even reached town?"

Murphy brought a hand to his chin. "We didn't know at first that you *weren't* in Kansas City when your sister died. And we didn't know the identity of the Indian man who called upon Annie's landlady for that valise." Murphy had donned his invisible cloak of interviewer. For the second time in twenty-four hours, he was pretending to some other line of work. Last night, a priest, today a prosecutor, or a pretend lawyer. He said, "So tell me, Miss Little Moon, did you ever set eyes on the jewelry your sister Annie had in her possession, jewelry belonging to Mrs. Campbell?"

"I did not."

"I followed you all the way to South Dakota to find out for sure, to attempt to talk you into handing over the jewelry. Are you telling me you knew nothing of it at that time?"

"I only knew that you wouldn't quit pestering me about it, even when I was trying to send you away from the reservation."

"I was injured by then," said Murphy.

"Your broken arm seems to have mended."

"Yes, thank you." He was trying to keep from smiling at the fun of this charade. "So, if you didn't know where the jewelry was, or even about this particular jewelry, did you know that your sister had received jewelry as *gifts*?"

"I did not," said Raylene, glancing at Murphy's boss, whose attention swung between her and Murphy with each question and response.

"And when did you come to know about pieces of jewelry that Annie had purportedly received?"

"When you kept asking about them. When you followed me north. When we looked for and found those hidden pearl earrings in her first bedroom." Raylene looked at Campbell.

"Did you know whose earrings those were?"

"They looked pretty fancy for an Indian girl doing saloon work. I don't know that my sister would have been all that interested in them. She would have enjoyed receiving a gift, but I can't feature her wearing anything fancy on a regular basis." Raylene now looked at Campbell, so engrossed with the proceedings that he had abandoned his cigar. She asked him, "Do you think she had the wardrobe for any of that jewelry?"

Campbell blinked before he shrugged and said, "I don't know women's fashion."

Raylene again: "Would you say Annie dressed similar to your wife? You do know how your wife dresses."

Campbell licked his lips and seemed to be formulating an answer. "I can't say."

Raylene turned her query on Murphy. "Mr. Murphy, were you familiar with Annie's taste in clothing?"

Murphy shook his head.

"How about her taste in men, romantically speaking?"

Murphy glanced at Campbell, then away. "Her taste ... uh ... No, I'm not privy to her taste."

"So, you were doing your job, working a case on behalf of someone who presumably knew what was going on and had the authority to send you on a chase for jewelry that could have been anywhere."

"I did find the green stone earrings at a pawn shop. An Indian man had pawned them."

"And then the trail went cold?"

"I didn't find any of the pieces in South Dakota, if that's what you mean."

Raylene took a step to one side and gestured at Campbell.

"Mr. Campbell, do you know my sister's taste in men?"

Murphy stood transfixed. Campbell, a man used to giving instructions and barking orders when needed, seemed to be at a loss. He lifted a hand off the desk and motioned with it while blinking at some distant calculation. At last, he said, "I'm not sure."

"Would you say she was interested in you?"

"Yes ... yes, I'd say that."

A secretary came to the doorway with papers in her hand. When she cleared her throat, Campbell barked at her to go away. As she backed out, the noise level in the outer office dropped a notch before she snicked the door shut.

"I believe I knew my sister better than most people," Raylene continued when the secretary was gone, "and I don't believe she was involved with you at all, or only peripherally. I have seen some of the men who caught her attention. None of them looked like you or talked like you. Not one of them was your age."

"Well, now, you don't have to —"

"There's more. Annie left an abortionist's shop with a man who was young and fit and drove an automobile that wasn't the same as the one you drive. I checked. And the photo in which Annie is wearing the so-called missing necklace shows just a slice of someone's coat sleeve from presumably a person with a hand on her waist or back, the way a man would pose with a woman. But the angle of the sleeve is such that its owner is considerably taller than Annie while you look to be only an inch or two taller. In that photo, she was with someone taller than you.

"And finally, I heard that you received those pearl earrings as if you hadn't known they were missing." Here, Raylene glanced at Murphy, who nodded.

"Mr. Campbell, I'm not convinced you gave Annie the jewelry you claim is missing. Someone else did and you are covering for that person. And don't say it was your wife because we all know there was no reason for her to do so."

Campbell sat puffing as if the office air had become thick and foul. His eyes darted around as if tracing steps already taken or anticipating steps yet to come. Raylene and Murphy remained standing, letting Campbell find his voice without their help.

At last Campbell pulled out a handkerchief and coughed into it and nodded to himself. Then he said, "Agatha's sister's son. That's my wife — her nephew. He was staying with us after his mother died. He met Annie somehow and fell for her. His thievery would have been another blow to my wife, so I tried to get the pieces back." He blew out a breath as if he'd run a footrace.

Murphy looked hot under the collar. "You let me think you had given them to a lover. You lied to me."

"I didn't say she was my lover," said Campbell.

"But you gave that impression."

"I was trying to protect ... people."

"Jesus," said Murphy. "I got my arm broken for those damn jewels, and my glasses broken and my car nearly stolen. My wallet, my suitcase of clothes, and you couldn't even come clean about what was going on."

"You were getting paid. You were on the payroll. What difference does the reasoning behind it make? It was your job to find them."

"No," said Murphy. "It was *your* job to find them, and I did your job for you."

"Well, you didn't quite finish the job, did you?" snarled Campbell.

"All but one," broke in Raylene.

"No, no, no. There's still a ring *and* a necklace."

Having crossed to the chair, Raylene lifted the valise, which gaped on one side where early in October she had cut around the locked clasp to read her sister's journal and miscellaneous papers.

"What's with that?" said Campbell.

"I think it contains something with weight, perhaps the necklace."

Campbell studied Raylene with suspicion. "That thing?"

"I thought I'd trade you for it."

"Trade me? You're talking about my wife's necklace."

Raylene glanced at Murphy. "In my world, gifts given aren't reclaimed as if they've been stolen. As far as I'm concerned, whatever's in the compartment at the bottom of this valise was Annie's. It belonged to her so now it's mine."

"It's not yours!"

"It is right now. But I'll exchange it for the name on my sister's grave. I would like the name of the cemetery too, but to save you from having to pretend ignorance, I'll settle for a second item — the last name of your family member who had some sort of relations with my sister."

Murphy watched wide-eyed as his boss struggled with some internal conundrum. Would he admit that his nephew had been involved with a Moon, or might have gotten Annie pregnant?

Campbell finally said, "Let me see it."

Raylene handed him the valise.

Campbell gave it a shake and peered into its empty interior. Then he gripped the opening and pulled outward, grunting and grimacing. The leather did not budge.

"Cowhide," said Raylene, as Campbell picked up a letter opener and slashed at the sides and bottom of the bag, leaving only marks and dents. "I want that name."

"It's going to take a saw or an ax or something," said Campbell.

At that, Raylene slid her hand under her jacket and brought out her hunting knife. She held it up so it gleamed in the light, then with the blade hooked the valise's handle and brought the whole thing to her side of the desk. "You want what's in this or you don't," she said. "The name you give me had better be the truth because I will be looking for it on a grave."

Campbell paused just a moment before he snapped his mouth shut. Then he spelled, "L-A-U-R-I-E. My wife's nephew."

Raylene had observed his body language. He wanted what was in the valise and he knew that she knew it. She laid the valise on its side and gripped the outer portion and brought her knife to a spot a fraction above the stiff bottom and sliced a gash through the leather, opening a gap through which she pried an object wrapped in a soiled strip of cloth. A bit of gold showed where the cloth had come loose.

Campbell reached for the object but Raylene blocked him by spearing her knife through the blotter on his desk. He withdrew his outstretched hand as she untied the strip of cotton, which appeared now to be the tail from a shirt marked by brown spots that looked like dried blood. She laid the necklace — gold with green stones — on Campbell's blotter and retrieved her knife, returning it to its sheath.

Campbell's eyes grew wide as he brought the necklace close and turned it in his hands to examine its links and stones and finally, the closure that was ornamented with fine scrollwork. He said, "By God, that's it." Another moment passed before he came out from under the weight of his astonishment and turned to Murphy. "You told me you had a lead," he said. "I had lost hope, but by damn you found it." Closing his eyes, he blew out a breath and appeared to regain his equilibrium. He opened a desk drawer and gently set the necklace inside before closing it.

Looking again at Murphy, Campbell said, "So. There's a lot of work that didn't get done while you were away. We're concluded here, I think, so you can see Miss Little Moon out and when you get back, we'll sort out which cases need your immediate attention."

Murphy looked from Campbell to Raylene and back, his thoughts sliding this way and that. He felt himself sinking a bit at the recognition that he was being welcomed back into Campbell's employ. A part of him felt relief, another part, dread. He slid his overcoat from the chair before him and signaled Raylene with his eyes. She left the mangled valise on Campbell's desk and preceded Murphy to the door, turning back to speak to Campbell as she reached for the knob. "You're welcome," she said. The two went out past the secretaries and clerks, who snapped back to their work.

The breeze had freshened and the sun beamed in patches through clouds overhead. On the sidewalk, Raylene stood stone-still. People walking by might take her for someone stunned, but Murphy knew that she was likely planning how to use the information Campbell had supplied. When she turned to him, he spoke before she could ask him his plans regarding Union Pacific. "That was almost amusing, in a strange way. I never would have guessed."

"Did you notice that he couldn't even look at me once he had the necklace?"

"I noticed, but I don't care about him. You and I aren't done. Let's find Annie Laurie."

Fifteen

Had Campbell been truthful? Something told Raylene that he had revealed the least amount of information that would get her and Murphy out of his hair. She asked Murphy, "What do you know about your boss's nephew?"

"I never met him, but Campbell mentioned him once in relation to a position with Union Pacific. He called him Brandan. I'm assuming he's the same one."

"Do you suppose a sexton could be bought off to bury someone without documents? Unless they ask for a birth certificate or a driver's license, how would they know who they're burying? Annie would not have had any documents."

"I guess the coroner's office figures it out and provides paperwork. I haven't arranged anyone's burial myself, but I'd bet that's the protocol. If Brandan and Annie married, Brandan could have arranged her burial."

Raylene closed her eyes to let the sun pulse through her thoughts with a fiery orange. "I didn't find any record, but say you're right. A wedding certificate might suffice. Our father would have buried her as Annie Moon or as a Yellow Moon. But if she wasn't in the ground yet, hadn't been buried before Thomas was killed, he couldn't have seen it through." Behind her eyelids, the orange lights dulled from a passing cloud before flashing orange again.

"Which means," said Murphy, "that someone other than your father arranged her burial.

"But was Brandan Laurie even in town when Annie died?

If he wasn't, someone would have had to have some pull with the coroner's people to bury a person without official paperwork. And, the police were investigating." She shook her head. "Any of those officials might take a bribe."

"Or be persuaded by a well-placed businessman asserting family privilege."

"I would put money on bribery being involved. We already had jewelry being offered in payment for an abortion. If Campbell's nephew stole jewelry to offer for Annie's abortion, he could have been the baby's father."

"Or a good friend. Would Campbell apply pressure involving a burial? Does he seem that type?"

Raylene nodded.

"At this point I have to agree. So then, if Campbell helped with Annie's burial, which cemetery would she be in?"

"Are they Catholic?"

"Campbell and his wife are, but that doesn't mean the nephew is."

"No. But that Church is rich, which means it likes money however it can get it, so maybe money bought Annie a plot with the Catholics."

"I'll drive us around to the Catholic cemeteries," said Murphy.

Raylene shook her head and laid a hand on Murphy's arm, the one broken by the Pine Ridge men. She said, "Yours is an attractive offer, but I would rather take my truck because if we find Annie, I need to sit with her and say things the way my people do. You have been the right partner for so much of what has happened this last week, but I am the only one who can send Annie to meet her ancestors." After a moment, she said, "Aren't you expected in your office?"

Murphy looked around as if the traffic going by could provide an answer. He would not protest Raylene's need to drive herself because doing so would sound small and he would not be small with her. But he hated to let her out of his sight. When she was satisfied with her farewell to Annie, she might leave town without a backward glance. A real possibility. He said, "I gave my word that I would help you find Annie. I 'll meet you wherever you say."

The two drove their respective vehicles around the city's quadrants, asking at each Catholic cemetery for an Annie Laurie buried sometime between September 19 and the 26th. After striking out at the last one, Raylene and Murphy stood outside the cemetery's gate.

"Snookered by the notion of Catholicism," said Murphy. "I suppose there are a couple of old cemeteries on the grounds of Catholic churches, but at this point they would likely be for Kansas City leaders whose young generations still worship there. Or maybe for parish priests. We've got a number of secular cemeteries left and the day isn't done. We could make one or two." When Raylene didn't answer, he added, "Yes? No?"

"Let's start with Elmwood," said Raylene.

"Okay. Is there something special about it?"

The sexton there gave me rose hip berries."

"Gave you what?"

"Those pods that form after roses bloom. They are used as good medicine, plus, the caretaker was friendly."

"I'll follow you there," said Murphy. He started away then turned back. "Raylene," he said before heading to his coupe. "We'll find her."

The caretaker at Elmwood had left a note on his cottage door indicating he would be back at 4:00, so Raylene and Murphy walked the closest grassy swells planted with monuments and markers. Walking like this, quietly checking names of the deceased, Raylene felt a subtle thread tugging at her. *Annie.* At least she thought so because who else would reach out to her from this place? She hadn't felt the thread on her first visit, but perhaps she had not been concentrating. This thread felt weaker than she would have expected, altered perhaps by Annie's pregnancy, or by poisoned booze, or even by being buried with a stranger's name. Still, it could only be Annie.

Murphy kept an eye on his watch so they could return to the cottage in time to catch the sexton, who turned out to be Edward Baker, arriving in a box truck bearing two barrels of horse manure and one rather scraggly rose bush. Exiting his truck, he paused to study Raylene's black eye and bruises and Murphy's purpled jaw. "Should I ask after your wellbeing? I don't like to pry, but I do recall your previous visit here." He proceeded to cart one of the barrels to the leaf-strewn garden.

Raylene answered, "In spite of my bruises, I am well. This is John Murphy. He's helping me look for my sister. I have a different name to check against your records — Annie Laurie."

The caretaker said, "Had the wrong name, did you?"

"Others seem to be involved with her burial, perhaps paying to bury her secretly."

The caretaker straightened. "I do not take bribes, so put your mind at ease." He dusted his hands on his trousers and led them round to the front, which he unlocked before flipping on two lamps inside the parlor. "If you don't mind, I'll wash up first. Keeps the books clean."

He disappeared through an adjacent door and came out two or three minutes later, rubbing his hands together. "Tell me those dates again."

Raylene spoke the dates and stood back a little, her heart beating double-time. Standing beside her, Murphy cast his gaze to various objects before returning it to the man examining a large leather-bound ledger.

"Two burials this weekend and three last week," said the caretaker, hooking eyeglasses over his ears and flipping back through pages. "Annie, you said. I'll check back to September first."

"The key will be Laurie."

The sexton glanced at them both. "Irish?"

Murphy chimed in. "I'd say Scottish, originally" He'd been silent thus far, the quintessential quiet detective, listening and observing. He hooked his hands behind his back.

After a minute or two, the sexton murmured, "Ah, yes. We seem to have a Laurie that closely matches your request."

"It's not exact?" said Raylene, stepping closer.

"The timeframe is right — September 23 — but the name is Annora 'Annie' Laurie."

"Annora?" said Murphy. He looked at Raylene. "Is that your sister?"

Raylene shook her head. "She's not Annora. She's Annie."

The sexton said, "There are quotations around the Annie, as for a diminutive."

"Annie is her *given* name," said Raylene.

"I'll look up the plot and you can check the marker, which would have been placed early in October. Right about the time my wife died ... those weeks were a bit of a blur." The sexton fished a slip of scrap paper from a small neat pile and wrote out the details. On a separate tracing of the cemetery layout, he penciled an arrow on the section and assigned plot. "Take the front path to the right as you leave. It swings east and you'll find the section in the southeast corner. Some of those plots are shaded by old maples that have been there for many decades." He handed the papers to Raylene, who looked at them and showed them to Murphy.

"We can hope," said Murphy.

"Wait," said Raylene. Speaking to the caretaker, she asked, "Can you tell from your records which undertaker brought the body?"

The sexton nodded. "Not from this ledger, but we sign for the body and we keep a form that specifies. Didn't used to be that way in the old days. They used to just mark everything in the ledger." He turned to a filing cabinet in the corner beyond him. "The 'remands' as we call them, the deceased being remanded into our care ... they're filed here. I'll check for Laurie."

With the bottom drawer open, the sexton flipped past multiple dividers before stopping. His head bobbed slightly as he read. "Here it is," he said, straightening. "In this city, the authorities utilize two primary undertaking businesses, dividing the spoils, you could call it." He peered at two forms he had plucked from the drawer. "Annora Laurie was brought here by Kansas City Undertaking. They might have assisted with interment." He glanced again at one of the forms. "And they ordered the marker. It's usually a package. Says here the marker was placed two weeks later on Oct 9th. That's sixteen days after burial."

"Does anything on those forms jog your memory as to a person or people observing that burial? Do you recall anything?" asked Raylene.

The sexton crinkled his eyes in concentration. "I'm drawing a blank," he said at last. "Lots of burials have family and friends at the graveside. Ministers or rabbis. Once the grave is filled, we leave them to linger if they want. Some do and at that point, there's no hurry. I don't recall in this instance. That's not much help and I'm sorry for it."

Raylene was still trying to make sense of the Annora thing. Perhaps Annie wasn't here in this place with the civil, almost sweet, caretaker with his roses and their pods. Perhaps the

Laurie surname and the burial date were just a coincidence, and her Annie was not this Annora Laurie. She sensed, though, that this was Annie, *her* Annie, and thought that at least the burial had been overseen by a gentle man, not any of those criminal Conboie people. She motioned to Murphy and they left the cottage, taking the path to the right.

The two walked in silence. There was birdsong, the rustling of leaves, even a blast from a train in the distance, but Raylene heard none of it as she focused instead on two things — the pull toward Annie, and her questions about the sort of man Annie had coupled with. As far as she knew, Annie's taste in men ran to outdoor types, sometimes troublemakers, those who in another time might have resembled her and Annie's father and uncle, men toughened by life and ready for a fight. Nothing like Campbell. Nothing like Murphy, for that matter. Even if Campbell's nephew was perfect for her sister, he had buried Annie with a wrong name. Or, someone had, and Raylene didn't like it one bit.

When they reached the section indicated by the diagram, Raylene stopped and pointed. "It will be in the outer row."

"Shall I help you look?" asked Murphy. He let her start in the direction of the trees as he broke left to check markers. When he glanced over, she had stopped before a stone marker set into the ground. He walked over to stand beside her.

Lettering etched into the stone read:

ANNORA "ANNIE" LAURIE
WIFE SISTER FRIEND
1908 – 1936

"It appears she was a wife," said Murphy.

"They must have married in the months, six, maybe seven, since I last visited, back before calving season." She looked up.

"So, there was time. The missing jewelry was recent too, yes?"

"Exactly."

"Given that she was only trying to quit a pregnancy two months ago, that must have been when she knew. Once you know something like that, you have to decide."

"Did she not write to you about her marriage?"

"She was a scribbler of thoughts, never letters." Raylene blew out a breath. "I still do not understand the Annora name, and whoever this Laurie is, he robbed her of her own name."

"Lots of women, maybe most, take their husband's name." Murphy was thinking about his own wife, who had been Catherine Clark before she became Catherine Murphy.

"That might be so, but I doubt Annie chose to change her name and leave her identity behind." Raylene wondered, though, if she was wrong about this. "This name thing suggests more questions for me to ask your boss."

Murphy checked his watch. "We can hit the office but it's almost quitting time. We might not catch him."

"I can imagine that your presence during more questioning might backfire for you. I can be the bothersome Indian who won't let him off easy. Pressing him won't cost me my job."

Murphy had to acknowledge that Raylene was right, as usual. She could rattle Campbell's cage and not need to face the man on any other day. He was starting to wish that he needn't face Cambell again himself.

The U.P. freight offices were in the north of the city, easy to reach from Elmwood. Still, by the time Raylene returned to her truck and drove there and found a delivery zone to park in, the time was 5:10. She retraced her morning route, striding right past two clerks and a secretary, but when she reached Campbell's office, she found it empty.

Backtracking, Raylene said to the secretary, "I am looking

for Mr. Campbell."

The secretary was one of three who had been in the outer office earlier in the day. Taking in Raylene's black eye and bruised jaw, she said, "You were here with Mr. Murphy, do I have that right?"

"I was."

"I'm sorry but Mr. Campbell has left for the day."

"I suppose he's helping host the Library League fund-raising party?"

The secretary's eyes registered that Raylene had called it correctly.

Raylene motioned to a folded newspaper sitting to one side on the secretary's desk. "There's a nice write-up in today's paper about the League and Mrs. Campbell's presidency."

"That's right."

"I suppose Mr. Campbell will return tomorrow."

"Possibly. Would you like me to check his schedule?"

"No thank you. I'll just drop in," said Raylene, signing off with a nod. Of course, she wasn't specifying where she would drop in.

Pherson Campbell's home address was listed in the city directory. The name Campbell was common but there was only one Pherson listed and Raylene had days prior made a note of the corresponding address on her city map. Now she drove to the Campbells' home in the neighborhood of Hylde Park and found the surrounding curbs filled with parked cars. Having located an open spot on an adjacent street, she made her way to the Campbell's home.

The impression of distant music reached her through the leaded windows flanking the double front doors. She rang the bell and waited in the glow of etched light globes. After some time, a waiter carrying a tray of canapes answered the door.

"I would like to speak with Mr. Campbell," said Raylene.

"I'm guessing you're not a guest." He seemed to be studying her dungarees.

"No. I have other business with him."

The waiter squinted at her. "Sorry but he's engaged with guests."

"I am sure his guests are important, but I would have a word with him."

The waiter relented. "Wait here and I'll ask, but I can't guarantee."

"I understand."

The waiter closed the door, leaving Raylene on the wide brick step. Dark had fallen and with it, the temperature. She buttoned her coat up to her neck as she waited.

At last, the waiter returned, this time without the tray. "Mr. Campbell says anyone needing him can phone his office tomorrow."

"That won't do," said Raylene. "I'm sure he can spare five minutes."

"He was quite firm, believe me." The waiter looked as if he would rather be passing canapes than speaking to an Indian.

Raylene, in no mood to debate the waiter regarding her intentions, said, "Please tell Mr. Campbell that if he does not appear within two minutes to speak with Annie's sister, Annie's sister will crash his wife's party in order to get his attention."

The waiter pursed his lips and stepped back inside, closing the door as Raylene began her countdown.

"One ten, one eleven, one twelve." Raylene was almost to one hundred thirteen when the Campbells' front door opened and Mr. Campbell stepped out to join her in the glow of his porch's light globes.

"Miss Moon," he said.

"Little Moon," said Raylene.

"I was told you are threatening my wife's soiree."

"She is likely to have the answers I need, those you have withheld. I could speak with her if you'd rather."

Campbell narrowed his eyes. "You can deal with me. What is it now?"

"I'm wondering where your nephew is."

"He's not here."

"Not at your house?"

"Not in this city."

"Well, you may know this. My sister was buried with the name Annora. Is that *your* doing?"

"Why would I get involved with your sister's name?"

"I wondered that myself on the way here from the cemetery. Do you want to tell me why?"

Campbell shook his head. "I have nothing to tell."

"I'm going to guess that you had more involvement than you admit. In the first place, your nephew, who I assume is white, became involved with my sister, an Indian. *Lakota*, for your information. And I can imagine the dismay some families might feel at their child mixing with another race."

"You have that wrong."

"Did you know that the marker on my sister's grave labels her a wife?"

"Is that right."

"That's what it says, which means that if authorities were doing their job, there must have been a marriage license provided."

Campbell was looking everywhere but at Raylene, so she brought his gaze back to hers with, "Or, perhaps Annie was buried fraudulently by someone in your family and the authorities need to investigate."

"By God, no!" His attention was fully with her now, so she

went silent, studying his face as a parade of emotions passed over it.

At last, he said, "Alright. I provided money to supplement what my nephew said he needed to help finance an abortion. That sort of thing isn't cheap, not like a regular doctor's visit or a new suit or something. I'll have you know I did that even though it goes against our beliefs, the Missus and mine." He waved a hand in the air. "But Brandan was adamant and he had just lost his mother and said he was going to help Annie take care of things. He would do right by her. So, I let it him handle it. I figured it was handled. I guess some time went by, but next thing ... he was saying that Annie was dead. Not from an abortion, Thank God." He blew out a breath. "He said that she had no one else here so he would see to her burial." He shrugged. "I couldn't have told you that he even liked women. Wouldn't have guessed he knew what to do with a woman. He was, uh ... different ... and kept to himself." Campbell let out a breath as if a weight had been lifted.

Raylene gauged Campbell's demeanor. Most of what he said smacked of truth. "I would like to speak with your nephew."

"To speak with Brandan, you would have to ring his boarding house in Chicago and hope that he would take your call or call you back."

Raylene looked toward the street. Bats were flying loops in the air above the street lights. "What does he do there?"

"After his theft of the jewelry was uncovered, he left town and turned up later in Chicago. He had a decent work history at U.P., so apparently, they gave him work as a floater, doing time in ticketing, food services, moving to whichever part of the operations calls for additional hands." He lifted one shoulder. "He could be anywhere in the U.P. system."

"There was time for him to have married Annie before she

died."

"If they married, I wasn't invited, and the government lets you do pretty much anything if you buy a permit."

The conversation had reached a dead end. Campbell didn't have to budge from his story, and Raylene couldn't make him. She could, however, seek corroboration of his story if the marriage license bureau had caught up on its filing before she left town.

He broke into her thoughts. "I'll be going back to my guests."

She held his gaze a moment longer. "If I find you have been false, you will see me again."

Campbell rolled his eyes and turned for the door.

Raylene descended the house's front steps and went along the sidewalk beneath the dance of bats in the sky.

Murphy figured that Raylene would attempt to confront Campbell at his U.P. office. Why wait until morning when she could corner him before closing time? She had not said she would return to Elmwood Cemetery, but he lingered anyway, at first walking around as dark overtook the quiet landscape. Finally, he gave up and backtracked past the caretaker's cottage, closed up tight for the night with a glow behind its front curtains. Climbing into his coupe, he sat awhile, imagining the best and the worst for Raylene's questions of Campbell. Would the man provide answers? Perhaps not, but being now in possession of the missing necklace, he had little left to lose by speaking with her.

When enough time had passed that he doubted Raylene would return, he drove home and called Mrs. G's boarding house to ask after Raylene, who in fact, had returned home and eaten a late supper.

"Just checking on you," he said when she came on the line.

"Is everything okay?"

"Things are not okay if you count Brandan Laurie marrying Annie and having her name changed when she was buried. If they were married, I have little recourse."

"Recourse about what?"

"About that grave marker. It has no Moon on it. Even if she married a Laurie, she remains a Moon."

"How about explaining that to the nephew? I don't think you need me with you, but I'd be happy to make it two against one."

"He has left for Chicago to work for the railroad. There's no way to check on him from a distance and I will not be asking your boss for that favor."

Murphy thought a moment. "My advice is to order another marker. There's no need for any of Campbell's family to know it. Don't take offense, but I've heard no indication they'll be visiting her grave. You might convince Mr. Baker to make the swap, but he'll have to believe you're related."

"The thought had crossed my mind. I also want to look again for a marriage license containing Annie's name and perhaps a record of a civil ceremony."

That sinking feeling returned to Murphy, signaling that Raylene was nearly done with her business in Kansas City. He tried to keep his emotions out of his voice. During detective work, he easily mastered his feelings. But his dealings with Raylene no longer contained the distance there had once been between them of detective and subject. Even worse, he had no claim on her, especially no claim on her emotions or her body, which he wished to get to know better. That buckshot pattern on her surprisingly-muscled forearm. Her lean frame and the dark hair covering the cleft between her legs. No claim on her body, no claim on her heart. His heart, fractured by Catherine's illness and departure, wanted to reach for

Raylene's but he could not deny the obstacles between them. He said, "So, you'll be busy for much of tomorrow."

"That is likely, given I don't have a specific date to ask the registrar to confirm. Then there's the records office, where the filing is behind schedule, and I should settle my bill at the stable."

Murphy wanted to ask, *Will you come to me before you go?* He had already shattered his wedding vows by making love to her, yet instead of feeling painted by sin's brush, he had felt the logjam open inside of him enough to admit a trickle of possibility. He had no one else to tell this to — not the fellows from work he sometimes met for a beer, not his fishing buddy from church, an agreeable sort but not a person who would receive a story of adultery well. He needn't even tell God because God supposedly knew that he was breaking free on the inside while stranded within the constraints of society. He said, "You are probably itching to get out of town."

There was a pause on the other end. Then, "Among other things, I need to close the bank account I opened here and properly thank Mrs. G., and I need to visit Annie's grave. But yes, I am ready to return to my life."

Murphy swallowed hard. He had to ask. "Will I see you before you return to your life?"

"If that's an invitation to your home, then I'll say yes. Sometime after dark tomorrow, after I'm through at the cemetery. I would like that."

All the tension built up from the day's confrontation with Campbell, his search with Raylene through cemeteries, and finally, Raylene's disappointment-bordering-on-anger at Annie's grave marker fell from Murphy's shoulders. He let out the breath he'd been holding. "That's ... what I hoped. I would like that too. Will you come for supper? I can try to cook us something."

Raylene smiled to herself. She doubted that Murphy was any more a cook than most men. It was a rare man who tried to do more than boil water or brown a steak. One exception was Raul, who cooked for the H-bar-H ranch. She had not pined for Raul since arriving in the city and that had probably been for the best. "Let's not worry about food or an exact time," she said. "But if you will be home throughout the evening, I will join you."

Thoughts racing, Murphy nodded. Now he hated to quit the conversation, but he needed to plan what to say or do that would help Raylene see him the way he wanted her to. He had courted his wife in the usual way of men, with flowers and perfume. A picnic in the park, a box of heart-shaped candies. Now, though, he needed to impress Raylene without suggesting he possessed any right to do so.

Sixteen

By early morning, Murphy was dressed and shaved and combed for the day, one hip pressed against his kitchen counter as he sipped his coffee. The phone rang in its nook in the hallway and he went to answer it.

"Murphy! Are you coming in today? I can forgive yesterday's absence. I'm sure you had your reasons, but I've got cases here that need attention and at the moment you're my senior man."

Murphy paused as Campbell's reference to forgiveness landed like a sharp object in the palm of his thoughts about the heated session they'd had yesterday. He said, "I won't be in. I'm going to take another day to sort things out."

"Sort things? Jesus. Is it something to do with that sister of Annie's?"

"Her name is Raylene. I heard she spoke with you last night at your house."

"Uh, yes, we spoke. She accused me of endorsing her sister's marriage to Brandan. I doubt they married. Could be bunk. And then there was the matter of a grave marker being wrong."

"I guess Brandan would know for sure. Or you or your missus."

"What? Well, sometimes we have to take people's word for things. How else does business get done? Mostly through words and a handshake. I'll say this — Annie's association with my wife's nephew was ill-timed. He was in no shape ...

well, he was needy, you know? With his mom recently deceased and ... people do funny things when they're heartbroken." Campbell cleared his throat. "Alright. One more day, and we'll put it down as personal time off. But we need you back on the job. Business waits for no one."

Murphy had listened to the tone of Campbell's ramblings and thought the man sounded like he was covering for some poor decision or personal failure. "I'll see you tomorrow," he said.

"Tomorrow."

In the quiet of his kitchen, Murphy understood that in addition to visiting Saint Christopher Parish church and his father-in-law, he would pen a letter to his wife and add a necessary errand to the shopping he planned.

Late afternoon found Murphy sitting in his coupe on Fifteenth, the street bordering Elmwood Cemetery along the southeast section where he figured Annie's grave was situated.

He knew that Raylene did not desire company, would not tolerate company while she visited that grave for her own farewell. All manner of people had settled in Kansas City because it was at the crossroads of routes headed in every direction.

He knew Jewish people, who were like almost anyone else except when it came to religion. They sat *shiva* to mourn their dead, so he imagined Raylene sitting a type of *shiva* for her sister, only without the relatives gathered round and without the table laden with casseroles and brisket to feed the mourners.

He himself had not seen many relatives buried, though he had attended Catholic and Protestant funeral services down through the years. As a child he had never thought to memorize a prayer for mourning someone dead, but now he recited a silent version of those he had heard that might bid

Annie to find rest in the arms of the Lord who had raised her from dust, and that called angels and saints to welcome her.

When he saw a dark figure at a distance through the trees with what looked like an armload of blankets, he knew it was Raylene. Toward the end of their one intimate evening, she had answered his questions about how she traveled and described a few details about her horse and her ranch life.

Now he watched for an hour as she moved about to snap blankets open before sitting then folding forward almost in half, after which he could just make out a bit of movement. His view was largely blocked by the trunks of old maples shedding their leaves as if weeping tears of gold for the dead and the living, but he imagined her grieving, which she would permit only in private. As dark fell and she became a moving shadow, the bright glow of a small fire erupted. He nodded to himself. She was safe, and fine without him.

He started his coupe, and headed home to prepare for what he hoped would be Raylene keeping her word about joining him.

In the cemetery, Raylene had spread two of Raymond's blankets across Annie's mounded grave and from her saddle bag extracted two hand chisels and a sturdy hammer that ordinarily rode in a box in her truck. These she set to work with, modifying the stone marking Annie's grave. Kneeling on blankets, she took her time, breaking now and then to stretch, and within an hour, when the sky had turned a deep purple, she straightened for the final time to stretch her shoulders and arms. There. Good enough.

After repositioning the blankets, she gathered a few leaves and twigs from under nearby trees. With the matches she always carried, she set a small fire burning atop the spot she sensed that Annie's heart lay. Beside her, she had the notebook Annie had used to scribble entries about outings she had taken around Kansas City interspersed with sections detailing deliveries of alcohol and kegs of beer. There were notes about which saloon customers were regulars on certain days and then ... those entries about "myup baby," which Raylene had decided did not mean a sweetheart, but a pregnancy.

The baby reference was not the entry that had splayed open Raylene's world the way the entry about Father and Thomas had, as if Father and Thomas were two different men instead of one and the same. Of course, Thomas and Raymond had been an identical pair of men of somewhat different temperament, though both had been Father to Annie and her. On the inside she had been spitting mad at Thomas for having let Annie drink rotgut whiskey sold by profiteering mobsters. But eventually she came to understand the independence Annie had found in a big city where she could be anonymous when it suited her. She had chosen who to spend time with. Hadn't Raylene herself made choices regarding Raul at the ranch and, more recently, John Murphy?

She began feeding the notebook pages into the fire, where they caught quickly. Entries about shoes needing repair or which film was playing at the cinema, and which customer had sweet-talked Annie into going for a walk after work. All the pages, up in flames. Next, she added the torn piece of shirt from the Campbell necklace, the one stained with the blood of Raymond or Thomas. As smoke curled into the air above, she sang a childhood song devised long ago by Annie about the west wind telling tales of faraway places, speaking in the tongue of grasses and the language of birds. Many of the words came back to her, but even if they had not, the song still lived inside memories carried deep within her.

Then she recited a memory she had of being very small and

held aloft in Thomas's strong hands, the hands that had gentled ponies, bagged a clutch of prairie chickens, and clasped her mother close through nights on the reservation.

In her memory she was looking out across a sun-warmed earth to trees near the river, then down again at Annie with the sun glinting off her hair. The eye in Raylene's heart saw all her *thióspaye* in orbit around one another, destined forever to travel outward and circle back, leaving, returning. For that reason, even when separated they were never alone. She spoke low to the rising smoke because it was visible above the grave. "I don't know what happened with you and Brandan Laurie, whether you were friends or lovers, or something in between. I did not locate a marriage record, though it could be somewhere in that mess of a records office. If what you had was not love, he might have been trying to help you out of a difficult spot. I would have helped you raise your baby, I would have. But time ran out. I would turn back the clock to change what happened, but there is no way to do that. I know."

She took out the cornhusk *khéya* doll from their childhood and laid it on the embers. Its spirit could join Annie's on the other side. But as it began to smoke, she felt, or perhaps heard, a silent keening and snatched the doll back, tamping out its heat against the dewy grass. "Okay," she said. "I'll carry it with me. It will be no burden. Khéya and you will always be with me and I will always be with you."

As the fire relented, a coyote, which some people called the nightwatchman and others, the creator, began yipping from somewhere north of where she sat. The cover of Annie's notebook had burned down to its spine, leaving a small metal coil, circular and ever-winding. Raylene reached up and pulled a few strands of hair from her head and dropped them onto the last tiny embers. Then she gathered up her blankets and tools and left behind the world contained by the bodies resting in the soil.

Passing the caretaker's cottage, she mentally thanked Mr. Baker for his kind ways. Then she climbed aboard her truck and pointed it south toward Chestnut Avenue and John Murphy's house, where she parked directly in front. Let the neighbors think what they would.

Murphy's home, though smaller than his boss's, was considerably more substantial than any her family had ever occupied. A solid house owned by a solid man, simply located in the wrong place. Were it somehow transported to the prairie and surrounded by a piece of land for horses and chickens and a garden, she might then feel a little hunger for its sturdiness and the cut of its multiple rooms, sufficient space for multiple generations. When a person needed the wind in their face, they need only step outside and saddle up.

Raylene expected to work on ranches for a good long time. She was young yet. But some future day, it might be nice to have a small homestead with a sweet-water well and a corral for training horses to a saddle or plow or for cattle work. Morgans, maybe, or mustangs. One or the other. She had heard about a family in Montana that raised paint horses. Any future seemed possible, and to that end, she worked and saved as much of her wages as she could. With luck, in twenty years or more, she might buy a little piece of land with good grass. Then she'd be set.

When she finished her fanciful thinking, she left her hat in the truck and walked the front path to the front door and rang the bell. Murphy appeared almost instantly to let her in.

Arriving inside his house for only the second time ever, she stood silently until he reached for her and took her into his arms. She smelled of smoke and night wind and they held each other until at last he drew back.

She said, "I hope that Laurie person, whoever he is, did not have a Catholic priest pray over my sister. No offense to you. I don't want their prayers because the teacher-nuns always targeted her for speaking with boys or not doing her schoolwork. Or for using dandelion flowers to rub yellow on her cheeks. Everything we did was wrong." She looked out at the middle distance as if seeing back in time. "I always suspected the Pine Ridge priest, who was director of the school, of using sex to punish girls who broke rules. I watched him watching the girls who were nearest to being women. Scrawny me, I was never the target. But I couldn't get her to speak of it."

"Well, I said a prayer for her."

"Then it's good that you are not actually a priest."

"I guess so." He took a breath. "Is tonight our goodbye?"

Raylene nodded.

"Then let's not speak."

He took her hand and this time he led her to the living room where he had spread a new sheepskin blanket on the rug. There were two pillows with fresh pillow cases and a bottle of Jameson and two tumblers. He turned one lamp off before dimming the second one. Then he pulled her to him and kissed her the way he wanted her to remember him.

That evening just before midnight, Murphy stood on the sidewalk as Raylene pulled away in her truck. She had declined to accept the sheepskin blanket but carried a gift box from him that she would open later.

Though they had both dozed for a time atop the pallet he'd made for them on the floor, true sleep was beyond reach because his skin still sparked from her touch and his mouth still held the taste of her. He felt alive as only a single, smitten, unmarried man should feel. But though he was smitten, he was not single or unmarried, so he paced between his living room and kitchen, kitchen and hall, and back again. He had not said bedtime prayers since childhood but his behavior this past week called for a prayer, either a celebration, or an act of contrition. Something. This led to him mentally composing a letter to Catherine that he would never write and never send.

Dear Catherine, it's me again, the man you used to know as husband.

I have a confession to make which is that I have not been behaving like your husband. That's something it seems fair for you to know, but even if I somehow conveyed it to you, I know you could not now register the truth of it. There was a time when you would have heard this truth and been angry, and justifiably hurt. And perhaps seek to leave our marriage.

One thought brings me comfort — that I can claim to have never strayed in thought or deed when we were together. It's not that I never admired some other woman's smile or walk or wit. What man alive does not glance around in appreciation? But I loved you and was faithful and even knowing that forever is a long time, intended to remain faithful forever. I meant my vows.

Now, though, when I cannot even recall the fragrance of your skin, I find I am wanting to know the skin of another woman. Life's ironies are all around us, but they mostly elicit a grin or a shake of the head. Somehow this one seems fitting for a married man — the woman I now long for does not long for me. I would know if she did. She has come to me willingly, briefly, and I am like a young man instead of thirty-three, a college boy panting on the inside for more while mightily resisting any public display of desire. She's like an apparition, appearing, becoming solid and real before suddenly she is gone.

I spoke to your father today. I did not tell him what I say now to you — you completed me, the young me. But you did not much change me and since you went away, I have been in limbo, taking up space. The ghost changed me. She is gone now too, but I am not the same.

He was admirably even-tempered, your father, though I could see the disappointment in his eyes, and he said as much. But he also said, "I was wondering when you would bring this up." He is a man, too, and understands that I must continue pursuing a full life, which includes other types of intimacy, perhaps once more even love.

Another confession: I do not know how to quit our marriage because my word has always been my bond. Does that make me weak, or strong? I thanked your father for listening while I did all the talking. He could have cursed me but somehow resisted (His Protestant temperament, I suppose). I promised him I'd keep working to finance your care. He agreed to continue his financial help. I am grateful for that and told him so and of course he might change his mind someday.

I suppose I am grateful too, that you don't comprehend what I'm explaining, that I will not write again. I will telephone the nurses to check on your care and they will no doubt remind me, gently as always, that you do not seem to recognize my name. I am sorry that is the case, not for my sake, but yours. So ... this is goodbye. I myself heard that recently and didn't much like it.

Blinking, Murphy realized his eyes were wet and he was standing before his living room window looking out at the curb where Raylene's truck had sat for a few hours. Exhausted at last, he pulled the sheepskin blanket from the floor and wrapped himself in it and fell asleep against the couch.

Seventeen

In the morning, Murphy dressed in his best suit and cooked some cut oats and doctored them with butter and maple syrup, which he ate as he read the paper, one small article being of particular interest. He left the house before Ruby could arrive to find him looking sleep-deprived, with contusions and his shiner still obvious. She had not seen him since the night of Gargotta, and he would not traumatize her. You never knew what a young woman would find objectionable enough to quit a job over. He didn't want to lose her too.

At the office, he accepted four incident reports from Campbell but avoided small talk by saying he would get right to them. Beckoning the junior detective into his office, he set to reading the reports aloud and explaining how to set up each case. They discussed in detail which complainants to seek first, by phone or in person, and what types of corroborating facts to gather, such as physical evidence, interviews of passengers and rail employees. Even photographs, if any existed. The junior man took copious notes and seemed eager to take on the cases they agreed needed immediate attention. Off he went, notes in hand and overcoat upon his back.

At one point Campbell looked in on his way past Murphy's doorway. On the phone for a different case, Murphy registered his boss but did not acknowledge him. In the back of Murphy's mind was the thought that he must stay the course and resume being a valued employee of the great U.P., showing up every damn day for assignments handed out by Pherson Campbell. He must put all his energies into financing his wife's care. As he'd long known, a steady job was nothing to sneeze at.

However, sitting in his office beyond the main room of secretaries and clerks, he felt hollow. He had spent the previous week in the company of a woman who had taken risks to seek justice for her sister, a process which, though he had not asked her about it specifically, he imagined had likely brought her some inner peace. She had acted with purpose and honor and as a result probably slept well, while here he was back under Campbell's thumb wishing he was somewhere else. Anywhere else.

He checked his watch. It was too early to leave for lunch — in fact, he could feel the rumble of the 10:15 from St. Louis arriving in the freight yard — but he began counting the minutes until he could make an unobtrusive exit. To calm the churn inside him, he took up pen and paper and constructed a balance sheet related to the last week or so, this one focused not only on facts but also emotions, respect, honesty and lies, threats to safety, threats to independence, and a slew of financial needs and risks. *A fool's accounting* that would dishearten his accountant father.

Good thing he was not his father, only himself, with a dozen entries on the credit side facing a dozen on the debit side. Not a one contained actual dollar signs, much less numerals, only impressions and disappointments and satisfactions and desires, the stuff of one man's life. He studied the columns until he could not sit there one minute longer.

It was 11:00. He tore the page from its pad and folded it into his suit pocket. After neatening his desk and donning his overcoat, he took his fedora and went to stand before Georgia's desk. She was on the phone but tilted her head to signal that she would be with him in a minute. He took a sharpened pencil from her desktop and wrote "Early lunch" on one of her phone message slips then went out into the cool November day.

First, he filled his coupe's tank with gasoline. Knowing Ruby would have finished tidying his house and making him a pot of soup, he drove home to pack an overnight bag that he might not use. Also, the Local News section of the morning paper. Back in his automobile, he headed for Elmwood Cemetery.

He found the gates of Elmwood open and drove through the wide entry, swinging right along the paved drive that took him very near to the section holding Annie's grave. He needed to see the ashes from Raylene's fire and to stand before the final resting place of someone dear, perhaps dearest, to someone dear to him.

He found the grave, unchanged from a distance, and realized with a start that most of the cemetery's trees now stood bare of leaves, their naked shapes raising empty arms toward the sky. Annie's mound held a few blackened twigs, and the remnants of ashes that had blown here and there in the night wind.

He glanced at the marker, which still read WIFE SISTER FRIEND, but now the name on the top line was altered. Obliterating the word ANNORA was a crude circle carved just round enough to resemble a moon shape containing bumps and shadows. The outer legs of the "A" letters protruded a bit on each side, looking for all the world like the tips of wings tucked behind. Murphy smiled to himself. *Of course. The moon comes first and every-thing else follows.*

First the Moon. Exactly how he now felt.

His watch read 12:10 when he arrived back at the office.

"Do you expect Mr. Campbell to return after lunch?" he asked Georgia.

She shook her head. "He meets at 1:00 with the licensing board over that expansion to the maintenance yard. He hates to go but they expect a manager to make an appearance. Anything I can do for you?"

"Tear me a piece of that steno paper, will you? I'll write him a note."

She handed over a blank page and he used the pen from his shirt pocket to print "I quit" on it, signing it with a flourish. "Just put it in his IN box, okay?"

Georgia looked at the note then at him. "You know not to joke."

He nodded. "That I do." Glancing around, he added, "Wish everyone well for me."

"You just got back but now you're leaving?"

"I'm going to find someone I've been looking for."

"What does that mean?"

"I'm going into the private investigation business and there's already someone I need to find." He tipped his hat and turned for the door. Raylene had about a four-hour start on him, though hitching up her horse van and loading her horse would have taken time. And acquiring supplies, if she hadn't done so yesterday. She would have left from the Kansas side of the river, first from Mrs. G's and then from the stables, which she had once described to him. Pulling a van with a thousand-pound horse on board ought to make for slow going. If he ran his coupe hard, he might catch her before she put up somewhere for the night.

The Intercity Viaduct, which carried traffic under the Kansas River, would allow him to speed through town on that side, passing other autos and wagons while watching for any patrol car that might move to intercept him. Then again, the northern route out of Kansas City over the Hannibal Bridge might be more expedient if he wanted to reach the upper third of Missouri before crossing west into Kansas. He brought his thoughts up short to ask himself what Raylene would do. Was she for expediency and perhaps extra traffic on roads that paralleled the Missouri River? Or would she take a direct but slower route across Kansas and Nebraska?

His money was on her taking a slower route with less traffic through country familiar to her. If visiting her sister and father had occasionally drawn her to Kansas City from the Pine Ridge or those parts, the most direct would be on the smaller roads of Nebraska and Kansas, not unlike how he sometimes drove on U.P. business in rural parts of those states. Last month, for instance, when he met with Sheriff Howe in Onaga about the hobo found dead by the tracks, one of the few unresolved cases to his name. After losing the homemade knife related to that case, it had shown up when Raylene's brandished her boot knife at Gargotta's goon. In spite of her denials, he still believed they were one and the same.

His decision was made — he would take the viaduct and cruise west for roughly thirty miles along the meandering Kansas River and the U.P. westbound tracks until he reached the cutoff to Route 73, which would take him to Grantville, then Topeka, then to 75 north. He took his vehicle up to speed and held it there.

Raylene steered her truck through the rolling Kansas countryside. No need for speed. She was headed home and would arrive there with Kota intact. The truck's dual rear axles made it heavy, more so with the horse van attached. Rushing might only result in an overheated engine or some other unwelcome event.

The morning had been busy and she had gotten away late, what with Mrs. G insisting on serving her a large breakfast while plying her with questions and advice, more condolences regarding Annie and Thomas, good wishes for smooth traveling, and an actual hug. A sleepy-eyed Vivienne had appeared, resplendent in a silk dressing gown. They had exchanged plans, Vivienne's for California, which remained her dream, and Raylene for the H-bar-H, just west of the Pine Ridge near the border with Wyoming, where they might take her back.

Out at the street, Raylene repacked the bed of her truck with supplies she had secured for her journey home and tucked her water canteens alongside the paper-wrapped sandwiches Mrs. G had provided. Then at Brugmann's, Heinz was training a ruby-colored yearling to a rope halter, so of course she watched him for a time before interrupting to compare notes on how the youngster was doing and who in local circles had advanced an offer for it once it was trained to a saddle. Eventually, she had loaded Kota and headed for home.

The Pine Ridge had been her childhood home, though of course home would have been wherever her mother had settled with Annie, Thomas, and sometimes Raymond. These days, her home was the H-bar-H.

She considered the road before her. With Billy Horse no longer living near Omaha, she had no reason to aim for that city, but she did imagine him with his people, and perhaps the coyote pup, if he had kept it. In spite of meals and naps by the fire and Billy's companionship, the pup might someday leave Billy for the prairie in order to search for its own kind. That's how things worked. Two very different creatures might mix, but eventually, there could come a parting.

The Kansas countryside ahead would provide small towns

in which to buy fuel or extra foodstuffs. The same in Nebraska. Because good grass might be hard to come by in the drier parts of the states, she carried a half-bale of hay that Heinz Brugmann had sold her, along with some oats. A good man, Heinz, a different kind of man than Murphy, who sat softly in her mind now. She had never expected to meet a city man who would stick in her thoughts the way he had, especially not one who had started out as her adversary. He had trailed her to the Pine Ridge in pursuit of what she might provide him — information, the missing jewelry — neither of which had then been within her grasp. At the time she had considered him an irritation, but later he turned out to be a help as well as an able lover. A nice surprise.

The further north she drove, the more obvious the drought. The previous week's rain must have followed a southerly course, bypassing some of these grass- and ranchlands. Such was nature, a force toward which people adjusted their expectations and pursuits. At least when it came to farming and ranching: those types needed nature's cooperation; nature did not need theirs.

With every mile she put between herself and the big city, any city — Topeka included — she felt her lungs open and her tension ease. No more sooty clouds of steam hanging like laundry above the rail tracks ringing the city, no more whistles of trains and honks of automobiles, no traffic jams or clots of pedestrians on every sidewalk. Open country held breathing room and taught a person to slow just a bit to note the bend of grass in the afternoon wind, the trill of a songbird serenading the sun, the rustle of leaves drifting like snow from the trees. Snow was coming, she could feel it. It would not come today, but the further north she traveled, the closer she drew toward winter.

Just above Holton, where she purchased fuel, the so-called

"improved" road she'd been on turned to gravel. Signs indicated more improvements ahead at Route 9 through Falls City, just over the Nebraska border. From there she could choose a more rambling, westerly direction or head north for a time. At the rate she was headed, she would do well to reach Fairview by nightfall, but truly, with the supplies she had on board, she could sleep overnight almost anywhere in her truck.

A tiny, meandering stream appeared on her left, the grasses nearest to it greener than the acreage beyond. Judging by the sun, she'd been on the road for roughly three hours, which seemed as good a time as any to let the truck cool. Reducing her speed, she watched for a turnout or an adequate shoulder for stopping and eventually found a spot she thought would suffice where a dirt road crossed the gravel road she was on. Fences along this stretch of fields were in poor repair, which meant no one's cattle would be grazing them. With no houses in sight, this was a spot for letting Kota stretch his legs.

Kota wore a braided headstall and bridle with no bit. After walking him down the van's ramp, and to the stream, she looped the reins over his withers and turned him loose with a slap on the rump. The stream was little more than a trickle so he moved to stand with his front hooves in it as he slurped noisily. When he turned to munch the closest green shoots, she went back to the truck to fetch her saddlebags and the picnic meal Mrs. G had made for her.

There had been no meat left after last night's chicken and dumpling supper, so the sandwiches Mrs. G had wrapped neatly in paper contained butter and pickles. The bonus was an extra slice of sour cream coffee cake. A thermos bottle had been left behind years prior by a previous boarder, and Mrs. G had insisted Raylene carry it full of coffee "to keep you going."

Mrs. G had been as easy to live beside as almost any woman could be, if judged by the few weeks Raylene had boarded there. Raylene was used to the company of cowhands, people of few words, but she didn't have to wonder what Mrs. G was thinking because most of her thoughts came out directly. The tenor of Mrs. G's questions and conversation and cautionary asides telegraphed the good heart behind them. If not for those, a judgement about her character could be based on the type of boarders the woman took in: immigrants and Indians. While Raylene did not plan to return to Kansas City again, she wished many prosperous years ahead for Mrs. Gunther.

Before too long, Kota, like an oversized dog, had dropped to his side in a narrow patch of green and was rubbing his face back and forth as if to absorb the joy of that which had fed him. Raylene had seen him do this before and believed it was a gesture of gratitude for that which gave life. Grass was the embodiment of sun and rain and earth in one perfect form and creatures that grazed it carried a bit of the sacred within them, horses being the finest example.

When Kota heaved himself to his feet and shook, Raylene rose from her sitting spot upstream and tucked her empty food wrappers into her saddlebags. At her whistle, Kota swung his spotted form in her direction. Knowing he would follow, she set off for the truck.

By the time she swung the van's rear doors open and affixed the ramp, Kota had arrived to put his nose in the dip between her shoulders. She could tell he was ready for more horse-like conduct than riding in a van or resting beside a stream. His time at the Brugmanns' stable had been a respite from days of being stuck in the van on their way to Kansas City. She had exercised him only twice between her tasks around the city, but his cutting skills and cow sense would still be sharp when they reached the H-bar-H. The only question was whether he and she would find work there again.

Before moving along, she unstrung the tarp covering her truck bed and began to restack some of the supplies that had shifted. The only breakable item was an oil lantern left her by Ray. She had packed it carefully but there was no use in letting things knock about.

There came the rumble of a rig traveling along the road. She looked up as an empty hay truck slowed before stopping thirty yards beyond. Following her practice when alone in the backcountry and faced with a stranger, she unbuttoned her coat and unsnapped the sheath holding the knife at her waist.

A fair-haired man wearing overalls rolled out of the hay truck and crunched his way toward her along the gravel. "You need help?" he called.

She waved him off with one hand, calling, "No thanks," as she crossed behind the van to keep the truck bed between herself and him. "I'm just securing my gear."

The stranger kept coming. "Sure now? I always stop for people on the roadside."

She could see his eyes flitting from her to the goods in the truck bed as he ambled forward. Now he was two strides from her truck. She could make out the stains on his clothing and how his eyes narrowed as he glanced down the road in thought.

When he looked up again, she made a show of unsheathing her knife, the one Ray had killed Thomas with, and picked up the closest length of her tie-down rope to shave its frayed threads, which slid off like butter. His gaze followed the motion of the knife and she flicked her eyes from the rope to him. Eventually, he seemed to make up his mind.

"Okay then," he said. "Looks like you're alright." He nodded to himself as at an opportunity missed and turned back to the road.

She watched him reach his rig and climb up into it. In a moment it was back in motion, kicking up a cloud of dust that drifted east. When the rig was out of sight, she dropped her guard and put away her knife. She finished repacking her supplies and refastening the tarp, using up ten minutes or so, a sufficient buffer. She could retake the road.

Murphy roared through the countryside, passing vehicles when it was safe and slowing at one point for a harvesting combine rumbling along at just beyond a snail's pace, its driver bouncing in place up top. As he reached the junction with Route 9 where the pavement gave out and gravel began, he arrived behind an open-ended flat-bed truck with slatted sides hauling what looked like salvaged lumber piled in the back. He was carefully checking the oncoming lane when the flat-bed bucked up and over something in the roadway, its heap of lumber sliding like matchsticks off the truck's bed and onto the road where they bounced like beans into Murphy's path.

But for an oncoming school bus, Murphy could have scooted left. Instead, he thumped over two boards in quick succession and felt his front left tire blow. Braking, he muscled the wheel to the right, running over an additional board and a slice of plywood as he steered onto the narrow shoulder, bringing his coupe to a stop as close as possible to the ditch without tipping into it. He blew out a breath and opened his door to a quiet roadway studded with lumber. Glad now that he had changed from work shoes into outdoor boots, he set to work pulling out his tire wrench and spare, listening for traffic approaching from his right while squatting next to the northbound lane.

Each time a vehicle approached he rose to face it as it slowed to dodge lumber. The school bus had somehow missed getting caught in all the debris.

By the time he had his tire off, the lumber truck was back on the southbound shoulder as its driver fetched lumber from both lanes, thrusting the pieces back onto the heap in the truck's bed. When the driver noticed Murphy changing a tire in his good suit, he called out, "Our lumber do that?"

"It did," said Murphy, lifting his spare tire into place and seating it onto the wheel bolts.

"Need a hand?" asked the man, lifting another slab of two-by-four.

"Guess I've got it now."

"Bum bad luck. I'm sure sorry. Told the boss we couldn't carry that much, but he said otherwise." The man dragged another hazard from Murphy's lane.

"Bosses," said Murphy.

"You got that right." The man headed back toward his truck, which a second worker had pulled forward another ten yards.

Murphy spun the nuts back onto his wheel and proceeded to tighten them. After lifting the punctured tire onto the spare carrier and bolting it down, he pulled out his handkerchief to wipe some of the road dust off his suit and tire grime from his hands. A lost cause. Then he climbed in and rolled his coupe carefully onto the road before putting his boot to the accelerator.

"Since it's not rodeo season, do you suppose I could camp on the old grounds?" Raylene asked the clerk in a country store where she had stopped to buy bottles of lemonade.

The woman behind the counter paused in counting out change and looked toward the ceiling. "It's gone to pieces. Used to be the rodeo came every year but not no more. Maybe when folks come back from ... wherever they went. Can't say I blame 'em. I been thinkin' bout that myself." She handed Raylene two nickels and three pennies.

"No one would mind if I did?"

"You won't be in nobody's way. There's still a hand pump on the far side to bring water. Last I knew. Sheriff stops to check on you, tell him I told you to go ahead."

Raylene thanked the woman and went back to her truck and drove it another half mile up the highway.

Dark was falling and Murphy was beginning to despair of having no exact knowledge as to whether he was on the right road to catch up to Raylene. He decided to stop at a Sinclair station due to close up in 20 minutes. He didn't yet need fuel but business folks sometimes responded better to questions being asked by paying customers and he wasn't sure how long he'd drive after dark.

When the attendant had topped off his tank and washed his windows, Murphy asked, "Have you seen a green Ford with dual rear wheels come through pulling a white horse van? Lakota woman in her twenties driving it?"

The man blinked at him. "Lakota — You mean Indian?"

Murphy suppressed a frown. "Technically Lakota. If you've seen her, I'd sure like to know." He handed the man a dollar.

"Well, I guess I did. Small woman wearing ranch gear gassed up here maybe an hour ago. We get a lot of people passing through."

"I don't suppose she said where she was headed next."

"Her cash was good so I don't suppose I asked her." The man handed Murphy his change and put his hands on his hips. "What's the matter, she steal that rig? Or the horse?"

Murphy raised his eyebrows at the man. "Did she look like a thief?"

"I didn't say that."

"Well, she's not," said Murphy before the man could rile him. He had no time for anger because he still had hopes of catching Raylene before she turned at one of three or four roads leading west. He pocketed his change and turned for his vehicle. In moments, he was driving again.

The rodeo grounds looked to have seen better days, even in the last slant of dusk. Weathered boards demarked a corral that had served as an arena. There were two chutes to one side with missing boards which had probably ended up in someone's campfire or for repairs to a chicken coop.

Raylene drove onto the dirt and gravel parking area, which she figured ought to lead all the way around to a staging area for livestock. After she had driven three-quarters of the perimeter, she pulled to a stop with her rig pointing back toward the roadway. She climbed down from her truck and stretched. She had already downed one of the lemonades and would drink the other with the second of the sandwiches from Mrs. G. There was just enough daylight left for a bit of a walk around the property with Kota.

The staging area offered no grass for grazing, so when she brought Kota back to her rig, she measured out a portion of oats and a handful of hay and left him eating from a pail as she made a tiny campfire, just a few foraged sticks and one chunk of cord wood, a bit out of the wind thanks to the front of her truck. She had no need for a campfire meal, though she might be glad tomorrow to warm the last of her thermos coffee over reconstituted coals.

Leaning against the grill of her truck, she could make out sounds that arose as full-on darkness fell, the wing-squeak of a night hawk, a dog barking in someone's far off yard. The sound of vehicles out on the road rose as they approached and fell away as they passed. She was mulling the type of argument that might convince the boss of the H-bar-H to rehire her when a vehicle on the road slowed so much as to almost stop. Automatically, she unbuttoned her coat.

The vehicle, its headlamps just cones of light, turned in very near to where she originally had, which put it beyond some of the intact fence slats of the arena corral. After a minute, the vehicle's engine shut off and its door opened and closed. A figure got out and crossed into the beam of the headlamps, heading in her direction. Given its silhouette and footfall, she figured it for a man.

She straightened in order to be prepared for a stranger and pictured in her mind's eye where Kota was with his pails of food and water, his reins looped over the van's rear bumper. She rested a hand on her knife.

The silhouette drawing closer seemed familiar, but of course she was hungry and still a little thirsty from a long day on the road, plus her thoughts had been far away and so might be less sharp than was ideal. Rules of the road said *Be watchful, be ready*, but she wasn't at all ready for the voice that reached her across the last of the dirt and dead weeds and the campfire's blue and yellow flames.

"It *is* you," said Murphy. "I saw the white of the van. If there hadn't been a fire I might not have stopped, but something told me to."

Raylene breathed relief. "I didn't expect ..."

Now that he was here, he couldn't quit explaining. "I stopped on a hunch, which turned out to be valid." When Raylene didn't speak, he said, "How was your drive so far?"

"It was ... a lot like they often are."

"You made good time. You're probably used to the drive."

"I've come this way before."

Now there was silence between them, Raylene wondering why Murphy had driven at least half a day to catch her camping beside broken rodeo stock pens. "Is it Mrs. G? Did something happen?"

"No. It's not Mrs. G. Just me. I saw Annie's marker today with the moon carved into it. I knew it was your tribute and I wanted you to know that I knew." He lifted his hands and let them drop.

She nodded slightly, watching him. Even taking into account the flickering firelight, his overcoat looked somewhat worse for wear, his hair rumpled and she would swear there were smudges on his face. "Did you fight someone again?"

He ran a hand through his hair. "Oh. I guess I could blame my flat tire, but that doesn't matter." He reached into his overcoat and brought out a folded section of the morning newspaper. "There's an article in today's paper." She took the proffered paper as he continued. "It mentions city authorities authorizing a dig in Union Cemetery. They're going to unearth some graves for evidence of fraud or criminal activity. They don't mention what sort of fraud and nothing about Gargotta, but he must have gone to the chief and sold him on the idea. Even Gargotta wouldn't dig up a public cemetery."

"They might have seen our handiwork."

Murphy chuckled. "If they haven't, they will."

She turned the paper toward the fire's light, but without holding it near the erratic flames, almost directly in them, there was no reading the story at that moment. She had made her entreaty to Gargotta then left larger powers to nudge him further. Any reported effort by authorities may or may not result in a lesser flow of poisoned booze into the city's saloons and nightclubs, but it was better than nothing. Murphy's gesture warmed her. He had driven all this way to let her know that perhaps her efforts had not been in vain. "It was good of you to come all this way with the news. Otherwise, I might never have heard."

"That's only part of it." His eyes met hers. "It felt like our goodbye wasn't enough. There's so much happening and I know it wasn't sudden but it felt like it and I had to come and say goodbye again. Either that, or ask you to come back with me. To start over again tomorrow. With me. In the city."

Raylene considered the face containing eyes she had gazed into from the closest vantage a person ever could. He was a man of commerce who came from city people, while she was a product of the prairie who'd been raised on a reservation. It seemed that whoever they were and what-ever they had, people always wanted something else. She had sometimes felt that way herself though she tried to be satisfied with what she was skilled at and fond of, with that which sated her when she was hungry in mind or body, and the song of a rain shower and the spots rippling on Kota as he ran. The stories of ancestors and the deep memories that no one could take away or alter. Rituals for the spirit, tasks for the hands. Each day arriving after the last was done. She asked herself again if all of that could be enough, and found that it was.

She said, "I thank you for everything we did together in your city. Your help made the difference. And ... our bodies spoke to each other in ways that not all do. I will remember that."

Murphy saw the firelight flickering on her face and hands, leaving half of her in shadow, and hearing the words *your city* knew that his hope that she would return to him was futile. He paused a moment before saying. "I kissed you before you left, but I'd like to kiss you before I go."

Raylene would have recalled the memory of Murphy's mouth on hers for some time to come, but she said, "That would be nice."

So, he moved around to her side of the fire and studied her face for a moment as if to commit it to memory before taking her into his arms. She met his kiss with her whole being and he held her for extra moments before relinquishing her. He nodded at the thoughts tumbling round in his head and the unsaid things that now he would never say. "I'm changing my work arrangement but I'll still be around." He shrugged. "You know, in case."

She put one hand gently on his coat sleeve. "Whatever you choose, you'll do well. I'll be up north."

November's cold had fallen down around them. Murphy, whose kiss had not changed his mind or Raylene's, buttoned his overcoat and turned for his car. Raylene watched his silhouette, black against the night, until he reached his vehicle and started it up and turned it back the way he had come. She went to the rear of the van and loaded Kota and closed him in to keep him safe before she finished her lemonade and sandwich. Her woolies made a pillow upon her bed of blankets in the truck's cab. Before retiring for the night, she kicked some dirt onto the fire, which had burned down to coals like orange eyes.

In her truck, she opened the gift box Murphy had sent with her and found inside it a beaver fur scarf which she wrapped around her neck, tucking the ends into the front of her barn coat.

This day, which had held a lot of leaving, would follow the November moon over the horizon. She now knew where all the bones of her people lay, so tomorrow she would travel the last miles to her place among cattle and ranch hands and the songs of South Dakota's winds. When tomorrow delivered her home, her heart would be at peace.

~ ~ ~

Acknowledgements

A book can be likened to an island, with an enormous mountain lying just below the water line. This book is no different.

My mountain includes Mary Crow Dog's searing autobiography *Lakota Woman*; also *Hard Times--An oral History of the Great Depression,* by Studs Terkel; *The Children Sing in the West,* by Mary Austin; and *American Indian Myths and Legends,* selected and edited by Richard Erdoes and Alfonso Oriz; *Woodcraft,* by Bernard S. Mason; *The Sioux of the Rosebud--A History in Pictures,* with photographs by John A. Anderson and text by Henry W. Hamilton and Jean Tyree Hamilton; *Old Man Coyote,* by Frank B. Linderman; *Renewing the World--Plains Indian Religion and Morality,* by Howard L. Harrod; *The American Heritage Book of Indians* from the American Heritage Publishing Co.; *The Schooling of the Western Horse,* by John Richard Young; *West of Everything,* by Jane Thompkins; *Bury My Heart at Wounded Knee--An Indian History of the American West,* by Dee Brown; and *Wisdomkeepers— Meetings with Native American Spiritual Elders* by Steve Wall and Harvey Arden.

A deep bow and tip of my hat to fellow authors Lisa Mortara and Bill Kuechler (rest in peace) for their unerring support and helpful criticism; beta-readers Deb Lowrey, who also provided K.C. research assistance, the amazing and ever-generous Angela Sell, Jennifer Driver Mannix, and Grace Caudill; journalist and publisher Cathy Nelson provided connections; and special thanks, as mentioned earlier, to cultural consultants Danialle Rose and Thomas Ghost Dog.

Research assistance was provided by the Union Cemetery

Historical Society, and staff of the Kansas City Library;
Though this story is set in 1936, I've primarily used the
spelling of Lakota language as provided in the modern digital
New Lakota Dictionary (NLD), Ulrich, J. (ed), New Lakota
Dictionary App., Lakota Language Consortium, Kyle, SD.

To my one and only—Jim Riley—Thank you.

Author's Note to Readers

Some readers will wonder how a non-Native American chooses to write a story populated with Lakota characters. Here's how.

Authors write the most believable characters they can and steer them into challenging circumstances, pushing them from one end and pulling them from the other in order to take readers on some sort of adventure or journey. That's what I've attempted with Raylene and the Yellow Moon cast.

I desired the right heroine for this particular story, and Raylene is right. She's intuitive, strong, and honorable. She overcomes obstacles put in her way. I have attempted to respectfully portray her within Lakota culture, ranching culture, and as a woman in a largely male-dominated white world. Any deficiencies in this regard land on my doorstep and no-one else's.

You have likely figured out that although I've constructed an important male character, I'm not a man nor am I of Irish descent. I never worked for a railroad or worked as a railroad detective. I've never been a ranch hand, or lived in Kansas City or the Dakotas at any time, especially not during the 1930s. This is the magic of fiction. In order to construct an immersive world for readers, I have for years researched the details inserted into Yellow Moon Rising and Yellow Moon Justice. The rest is imagination.

Of course, an author hopes for readers. If you've made it this far, you must be a reader, and I thank you for that.

Best always,
JoJo Riley

www.ingramcontent.com/pod-product-compliance
Lightning Source LLC
Chambersburg PA
CBHW031607240626
47153CB00002B/664